"You have ne

You have been sheltered."

Ana's eyes widened as she slowly got to her feet. "Sheltered? You have no idea about the circumstances of my life, Mr. Tyler."

Lucas watched her step closer. Her floral perfume wrapped around him. Gardenias, perhaps, with a hint of jasmine. The scent called to his bloodstream and he suddenly felt hot as he slipped a finger beneath his cravat and tugged.

He drew a breath but she kept moving forward. Now her body heat joined her perfume to twist its way around him. Lucas could no longer deny that the burning in his blood was desire. And if she came much closer, Anastasia wouldn't be able to deny it either.

She took another step and her body brushed his. Powerful urges drummed through him. To pull her closer. To kiss her. To stake some kind of claim.

"Don't tell me I have been sheltered," she whispered. "Because you do not know me at all."

Jenna Petersen

Desire Never Dies

AVON BOOKS
An Imprint of HarperCollinsPublishers

This is a work of fiction. Names, characters, places, and incidents are products of the author's imagination or are used fictitiously and are not to be construed as real. Any resemblance to actual events, locales, organizations, or persons, living or dead, is entirely coincidental.

AVON BOOKS
An Imprint of HarperCollins*Publishers*
10 East 53rd Street
New York, New York 10022-5299

Copyright © 2007 by Jesse Petersen
ISBN: 978-0-06-113808-9
ISBN-10: 0-06-113808-8
www.avonromance.com

First Avon Books paperback printing: January 2007

Avon Trademark Reg. U.S. Pat. Off. and in Other Countries, Marca Registrada, Hecho en U.S.A.
HarperCollins® is a registered trademark of HarperCollins Publishers.

Printed in the U.S.A.

10 9 8 7 6 5 4 3 2 1

*All books are for Michael,
but especially this one.
Thank you for the past ten years
of loving me and laughing with me
and being my very best friend.
My unwavering belief in happily ever after
is all thanks to you.*

Prologue

London, 1808

"Your plan is progressing well, my lady." Charles Isley paced the perimeter of his companion's sitting room. Outside, he heard the strains of music from the crowded ballroom, but was confident that the two of them would not be interrupted. Her ladyship had positioned two footmen outside the parlor as guards. No one would even know he had been there.

No wonder she was forming a group of female spies.

"Very good, Charles." The lady did not turn from the window, but Charlie heard the smile in her voice. "I'm very pleased to hear it."

"You have chosen one lady to approach for your scheme and she has said yes," he continued. "But you said you wished for more than one spy to work for you, for the ladies to work together. Who else did you have in mind?"

Her ladyship did not hesitate. "I have thought very long about that and have chosen a name that was not on your list."

He cocked his head with curiosity. She had asked he compile a list of potential spies weeks ago, and he had assumed all the women she picked for her clandestine group would be selected from it. After all, he had researched the women meticulously.

"I admit, you've taken me aback," he said, sipping the drink he'd been offered upon his arrival. "Who is the lady?"

"Have you ever met Lady Whittig?"

Charlie searched his memory. "Perhaps. The name seems familiar." He started as a picture of a shy woman, timid and in deep mourning, came to mind. "Wait, do you mean *Anastasia* Whittig?"

His companion turned to face him with a little smile. "Yes, the very one."

"She is—is—" He searched for a word that would not offend.

Her ladyship shrugged as if she understood the cause for his hesitation. "Yes, Anastasia is very reserved. But she possesses an uncommon intelligence."

Charlie didn't doubt that, but there were other issues. "She loved her husband deeply. He died six months ago, yet she has hardly been seen in public since."

A shadow passed over his companion's face, and he could see she was thinking of her own husband, gone for just a year. Just as beloved. Just as missed.

"I can tell you from personal experience that sometimes a vocation is what we need most when our grief overwhelms us," she said softly.

"Yes, my lady. But what can she do to aid our group?"

Her ladyship's melancholy fled, replaced by a wide smile. "I once saw her read a page from a new book. She could not have ever read it before. Within moments, she was able to recite the passage word for word, without once referencing the original."

Charlie's eyebrows raised. "That *could* be useful."

"I think, if properly trained, she would be a master with codes. And I also believe Anastasia Whittig has much more to her than we even guess now."

Charlie made a few brief notes before he gave the lady a bow. "I will make contact with her immediately and report to you in a few days as to her answer."

He turned to the door, but her ladyship's voice halted him. "Charles." When he turned back, she continued, "Be gentle with her."

With a smile, he bowed again. "I will endeavor to treat her with the utmost care, my lady. I would not lose a potential spy if I can prevent it in any way. Good evening."

Her ladyship turned toward the window again. "Good evening, Charles. And good luck."

Chapter 1

London, 1813

The crash jolted Anastasia Whittig out of her concentration. She blinked, pushing her spectacles up the bridge of her nose as she looked at the ceiling with pursed lips. What in the world were the servants doing up there, teaching each other to dance? She hated interruptions, especially when she was so dratted close to finding the key to this latest invention.

Glaring at the stairs that lead from her secret workroom to the main floor above, she returned her attention to her efforts.

The second crash made her jump. It was followed by more pounding feet and, to Ana's surprise, the door above her stairway flew open. Normally, the servants knew better than to invade her private area, so for them to open her door, without even knocking, was an indication that something serious was afoot.

A maid came down two steps. Her cap was crooked and her eyes wide and wild. Ana cocked her head.

"What in the world is it, Mary? I'm in the middle of—"

The girl panted, fear painted across her face in pale colors. "Lady Allington, my lady, she—she—"

The bottle of kerosene in Ana's hand slipped free, hitting the floor with a crash that she hardly heard above the sudden rush of blood roaring in her ears. Lady Allington was her best friend, Emily Redgrave, mistress of the house they shared. She was also a spy.

Just like Anastasia.

Emily had been out that night on a case. There would only be one reason for Mary's terror, for her intrusion. Something had gone terribly wrong.

"Where is she?" Ana cried as she ran for the stairs. She stumbled as she grasped the banister to pull herself up. Panic rose in her chest, choking her, making it hard to breathe as she followed the girl through the kitchen.

"She came in through the back, Lady Whittig," the girl panted. "And we carried her to the parlor."

"*Carried* her?" Ana repeated in shock. "Oh my God."

Mary burst through the parlor closest to the back

of the house. Ana shoved past her to see a circle of sobbing, trembling servants surrounding the settee. Elbowing her way through the crowd, she stopped in horror at what she beheld.

Emily lay on the couch, eyes shut. Her skin was pale, her brow sweaty, and even the stir of the noisy staff didn't wake her as she rested in unnatural slumber. Another maid knelt over her, pressing a dishrag against her side. Ana could already see blood seeping through the cloth.

She dropped down beside her friend. "Let me see, Hester."

The girl darted a glance in her direction and then pulled the cloth away. Ana recoiled. Emily's torn gown revealed a large wound. The fabric was soaked in blood and edged with the remnants of gunpowder.

She had been shot.

Grabbing the towel from Hester's shaking hands, Ana returned it to its place and pressed to ebb the flow of Emily's blood.

Nausea washed over her, fear froze her, but Ana shook it off. Now was not the time to get the vapors. The servants looked to her for what steps to take next. The next few decisions she made could save her friend's life . . . or ensure it bled out on the settee in the parlor.

She measured her tone carefully. The household was already hysterical enough, there was no need to make the situation any worse. She turned to one of the men in the group. "Robert, ride as fast as you can to Dr. Adam

Wexler's. You know the way. Tell him we need him. If he is with company, do *not* tell him anything else. Once you are alone with him, inform him Lady Emily was shot."

Her driver nodded. "Yes, my lady, I'll be back as quickly as I can."

She turned to Benson, their butler. He was pale, his eyes fixed on Emily. He might be a stodgy fellow who disapproved of female spies, but he was loyal to a fault. All their servants had to be in order to keep their secret safe.

"Benson, listen to me," she said softly, drawing his attention. "Fetch Henderson and tell him to get Charles Isley. Make sure he tells Charlie nothing except that it is an emergency. Have him come to the back and be sure no one sees his entrance so late at night or it will arouse suspicion."

Benson bowed as he moved for the door. "Yes, my lady."

"The rest of you, prepare Lady Allington's room for her convalescence." She choked, hoping her injured friend would survive to have one. But it gave the servants something to do besides stare as Emily bled. Keeping them busy was a kindness. One she couldn't grant herself. "Make her room as comfortable as you can. And please," she added for the benefit of those who weren't already aware of her secret life, "do not speak of this. Your indiscretion could endanger her ladyship even more."

The servants nodded and began to leave, whispering in fear as they departed. Ana could only pray for their silence as she returned her attention to Emily.

"Emily," she whispered, pushing a tangled lock of sweaty blonde hair away from her friend's eyes as she fought back tears. Her mind spun, taking her to places she didn't want to remember. Taking her to her own husband's bedside over five years ago. He had also died from a bullet, a hunting accident on their country estate. He'd been hurt so badly, nothing could save him.

She shook her head. *No.* She would not lose someone she loved again. She would *not* lose Emily. She pressed the cloth against Emily's wound harder and her friend let out a little cry. Ana leaned close.

"I'm here. You're safe now." She bit back a sob. Emily wouldn't want to hear her crying. "You are home."

Emily groaned as her eyes opened, a shocking bright blue even when clouded with pain. "Alone?" she coughed.

"Yes, the servants have all gone. You'll be fine, dearest. Adam is coming." Emily drew a ragged breath, fighting for words, but Ana shook her head. "Save your strength. Don't try to talk now."

Ana winced as she realized her statement was more for her own benefit than Emily's. She simply didn't want to hear her best friend's words of good-bye. Couldn't accept that this was truly happening.

Emily gave a pained growl of frustration. "Trap, Ana. It was . . . a . . . trap."

"Ana."

Charles Isley's voice cut through Ana's haze as she paced the room. Hesitating in her steps, she looked at the man who was their superior.

"Please sit down." He motioned to a chair near him by the fire. "You'll run yourself ragged if you pace the parlor all night."

She shook her head and went back to walking the perimeter of the room. "I cannot sit, Charlie," she whispered. "I can't pour tea or chat amiably or pretend like my best friend wasn't brutally attacked tonight. I do not have the strength to be anything but what I am. Upset and frightened."

Charlie sighed as he ran a hand through his thinning hair. His normally ruddy, round cheeks were pale, and she saw the strain in his expression. He was trying to remain strong for her. Just as she was for him.

But they both knew the seriousness of the situation. How close they had come to losing Emily. How easily they could lose her still.

"Have you sent word to Meredith?" Ana asked, searching for words to fill the horrible silence.

Meredith Sinclair . . . Archer, she corrected herself, was the third in their band of female spies. She had married a year before, becoming the Marchioness of Carmichael, but she still worked on cases.

Charlie nodded. "I penned a note as soon as Adam came to report on Emily's condition. Our fastest runners are heading to Carmichael now."

"It will take at least a day for the missive to arrive and two more for them to make their way to London," Ana mused, clenching her fists at her sides as she walked. She could only imagine Meredith's reaction when she heard the news, and it hurt her to imagine her friend experiencing the pain and fear that already gripped her heart. Especially when she'd been so happy since her marriage.

Ana paused at the window to look outside. The gardens always gave her a sense of peace, serenity. Even though it was dark, she could picture the flowers she herself tended; see the trimmed bushes in her mind's eye. Yet they couldn't push away the images of Emily bleeding.

She looked down and saw the splashes of red on her black gown. With a shiver, she returned her attention to the darkness outside. Behind her, Charlie rose from his seat and took a few steps toward her.

His voice was gentle as he said, "Emily *will* survive to see Meredith again, Anastasia. You heard what Adam said when he came to give us a report."

Ana gave an unladylike snort more attune to Emily's personality than her own. Yes, Adam had come downstairs and told them Emily would likely survive the night. And since he was one of the best field doctors who had ever served His Majesty's Army and now served His Majesty's spies, Ana believed him.

But if Charlie thought she was so naïve that she hadn't seen the flash of worry in the doctor's eyes, or the way he clenched his bloody hands behind his back as he spoke, then the man underestimated her.

She had seen that look from doctors before. Her husband's physicians had also avoided her eyes. Emily might survive the night . . . but she was not out of danger.

"Please don't treat me like a child, Charlie," she said softy as she turned and snagged his stare. "I have seen death before, as have you. We don't know if Emily will make it another day or not. Neither does Adam."

Charlie drew back, clearly surprised at her calm appraisal of the situation. In truth, so was she. While Meredith and Emily were swashbuckling crusaders, full of life and laughter even as they battled the worst traitors and criminals in the country, Ana was quiet. She rarely argued a point. Confrontation was not her strong suit.

She wrinkled her brow. Her quiet disposition wasn't always a good attribute in a spy, but her other talents made up for it. Her skills with code-making and breaking had been put to the test and passed many times over the years. And her inventions were legend, even amongst the ranks of the male spies who wondered if the rumors of the "Lady Spies" and their mysterious female spy master, Lady M, were true.

Charlie reached out to touch her arm. "After so many

years of living here in Emily's home, watching her work in the field, decoding her notes, do you have any doubt that she is the strongest woman in England?"

Tears pricked Ana's eyes and she gave Charlie a watery smile. "There is no question. Lady M herself could not be stronger."

Charlie nodded. "Then believe that her strength will bring her through. She will use all her training to come out of this injury alive. She will fight. That is the best chance she has."

Ana sighed as she patted Charlie's hand. She walked to the fire and stared at the flames with unseeing eyes. "You're right about her strength. She's the best spy amongst the three of us, certainly. But that begs the question." She looked at her superior over her shoulder. "How did this happen?"

Charlie's mouth drew down. Aside from a brief recounting, they had been avoiding this subject. But they couldn't pretend it away any longer.

"She said 'trap,' didn't she?" he murmured.

Ana winced as she recalled Emily's unfocused stare, her choked voice. "Yes. That was all she could manage before she lost consciousness a second time." Folding her arms, Ana whispered, "Something went terribly wrong tonight. The field is a dangerous place, too dangerous."

Charlie drew in a breath to say something, probably argue as he always did when she lamented the dangers of their work, but before he could get out a word, the parlor door came open and a stranger strode inside. Ana spun on the intruder, but he didn't even look in her direction as he headed for Charlie with a purposeful gait.

He was a tall, broad-shouldered man with dark hair that swept across his forehead and teased the top of his ears. His focused eyes were the color of slate. He carried himself like he belonged in her parlor, though he hadn't been invited or even waited to be escorted by her harried staff. She tilted her head. He seemed vaguely familiar, but she couldn't place him as he stopped in front of Charlie and gave a brief salute.

"She was shot?" he said without preamble.

Ana reeled. This man knew about Emily?

Charlie nodded once. "Yes."

"Who is this?" Ana asked, pushing away from the fireplace as she made her way toward the man.

The stranger stiffened, spinning on her and pinning her in place with a piercing glance. His wariness was evident in the way he held himself, the way his eyes swept over her. Analyzing. Judging in an instant. She felt the very odd sensation that she had been stripped bare, laid out for this man to examine until he knew her every secret. Until he knew her very soul.

Charlie motioned to him. "Ana, this is Lucas Tyler. He was to be Emily's partner in her investigation. He was the man she was on her way to meet when she was attacked tonight."

She heard nothing more as hot blood rushed to her

ears. All the emotions she had fought to manage since she saw Emily bleeding bubbled and spiraled out of control. She stumbled toward the man, unable to keep herself from balling her hands into trembling fists.

"*You!*" she cried, pushing into Tyler's personal space without any thought for the propriety of such an action. Her anger was too powerful to deny. "This is *your* fault! Emily may be dying because of *you!*"

Chapter 2

Lucas looked from Charles Isley to the woman. He didn't know who this bloodstained beauty was, coming at him with trembling fists and brown eyes shining with tears and accusations. And he certainly didn't know what she was prattling on about. He was just as shocked about the attack on Emily Redgrave as anyone. But clearly this stranger knew *something* about Emily's position as spy, or Isley wouldn't have revealed so much information in front of her.

He ignored the woman since he could think of nothing to say to her indictment and asked Isley, "Is she dead?"

At that, his accuser stumbled back, her heated words dying on her lips as a tear trailed down her cheek. Just one. Silent, but it cut through Lucas like a straight blade, and at once he regretted his callous question. He didn't know what kind of relationship Emily had with this woman, but clearly the lady cared for his would-be partner. He shouldn't have been so blunt.

He was grateful when Isley stepped forward, his gaze flitting to the woman before he refocused on Lucas. "No. She was badly injured, but she lives. The doctor seems hopeful at her chances for survival, though there is no certainty."

Lucas let out a long breath of relief. He had met with Emily several times in the past few weeks to compare notes and prepare for their case. They had butted heads at each and every turn. She was a stubborn, headstrong woman, determined to do whatever she wanted, his suggestions be damned. But he certainly wished her ladyship no harm and had come here with a heavy heart when he heard of the attack on her.

"That's very good, Isley. I'm pleased to hear she has survived and has a chance. But surely you must see that this proves what I've been saying to you all along."

Isley's expression shifted, the frustration and anger lighting in his eyes as they always did when this subject was broached. "Don't start on that, Tyler. Not now!"

Lucas folded his arms. "Now is the perfect time. Women should not be working in the field. It's too dangerous, as tonight has shown. Clearly, Emily made a wrong move and—"

The woman he had all but forgotten let out a gasp of outrage, and once again she flew at him. A blast of floral scent preceded her, and her eyes sparkled with life and anger. Despite himself, despite the situation, Lucas was surprised by a sudden and very powerful explosion of lust. His body heat notched up and blood rushed to the most inconvenient places, even though she was railing at him.

What the hell?

"Emily is an excellent spy," the young woman all but growled. "Tonight she was trapped, ambushed. That had nothing to do with her sex."

Lucas stared at the woman. Did she tremble like that when she was kissed, as well? "Who are you?"

She stopped her tirade and seemed to notice that she was mere inches away from him, up on her tiptoes and right in his face. Not many men had dared to do that in his lifetime. And the women who had gotten so close were generally coming in for a kiss, not a fight. With a blush darkening her creamy skin, she backed away.

"I am Lady Anastasia Whittig," she said, her voice

softer, calmer. Her chin inched up with pride and out-rage. "*I* am one of the spies you believe incapable of performing her duty."

Lucas felt the corner of his lips curl up in an unstoppable smile at the way she held herself. A spitfire. He'd never been able to resist a spitfire and this one was a beauty, indeed. It had been a long time since he really saw a woman when he looked at her. Normally he gave them their pleasure, relieved his own needs, and never thought of them again. He just didn't have the time nor inclination to involve himself past a night's tumble.

But he saw Anastasia Whittig. In fact, he drank her in.

Big brown eyes that reflected every bit of emotion bubbling inside her. He had no doubt they would reflect desire just as brightly as they showed anger. Chestnut hair in a lopsided bun. Even her black mourning gown couldn't cover up the lush curves of her body. It didn't take much to imagine what she would look like without the gown confining her.

He shook off the thought. What was he thinking? This was *not* the moment to get caught up in lust for a woman. And especially not one of these Lady Spies, the quasi-mythical group that he honestly hadn't believed existed until a month ago when he was ordered to work side by side with one of them.

"It really doesn't matter anymore what I believe about this group's abilities," he said, tearing his gaze away from Anastasia with difficulty. "If Emily is so badly hurt that her very life is in the balance, she cannot break codes, let alone continue with our other plans. I'll have to go back to working on my own."

He stifled a smile. Though he would not have asked for it under these circumstances, alone was what he wanted anyway. He didn't want some woman under his feet, needing to be rescued at every unexpected turn of their case. Besides, this situation was personal. He wanted to investigate it by himself. And now it seemed he would be able to just that.

Isley folded his arms and his eyes narrowed. "You need the talents these women possess."

"I—" Lucas began, but Isley cut him off.

"Your organization has made no headway with this case for nearly a year. During the time you've bumbled around, more and more agents are being exposed and attacked."

Anastasia broke her glare away from Lucas and looked at Charlie. The difference in her expression was night and day. Where her stare simmered with repressed anger when she looked at Lucas, she was nothing but light and sweetness when it came to Isley. Both the irate passion and the trusting innocence were equally appealing.

"Is that what Emily was investigating?" she asked.

Isley nodded. "There have been an increasing number of attacks on agents both at home and abroad recently," he explained. "We believe someone has uncovered their identities and is either selling them to the highest bidder or carrying out assassinations and attacks himself for profit. Emily and Mr. Tyler here were working together to find out who is exposing our agents and how they are being attacked."

Anastasia nodded. "Do you believe Emily's identity was revealed? Is that why she was assaulted tonight?"

Lucas's head came up. He had never considered that a Lady Spy might be unmasked. Would anyone take their organization so seriously? But it made sense. Emily wouldn't have gone through a bad neighborhood to reach their rendezvous point, and Isley had made no mention of a robbery or other motivation for her shooting. The attempt on her life could very well be related to her secret activities.

If someone had discovered Emily's involvement in the world of spies, that meant they were getting closer to exposing *him*. And if that happened, Lucas would be removed from this case and any others until the assassin had been ferreted out and the extent of his exposure was known. The War Department wouldn't let him work cases if they felt he was in danger of being caught because of identity leaks.

He *couldn't* be removed from this case. It was too important. Too personal. He had to solve it and solve it quickly.

Isley shot Lucas a glance. "It's hard to say if Emily was discovered. The use of women as spies is one of the deepest secrets in the War Department. But either way, Mr. Tyler needs our help. He's been *ordered* to take our help."

Lucas flinched. Yes, that was true. "Very well, Isley, but just what are you suggesting?" He folded his arms. "We've established Lady Allington won't be going into the field any time soon. What would you have me do?"

Isley gave a little smile that Lucas didn't trust at all. A cold chill ran up his spine. Whatever the man was about to say, he wasn't going to like it.

"No, Emily can no longer work with you," Isley conceded. "Even if she weren't hurt, we can't take the risk that her identity has been exposed. But there is one person who can help you." He turned to Anastasia Whittig. "Ana."

Ana actually felt the blood draining from her cheeks as both men turned to her. Despite her bravado in proclaiming herself a spy when Lucas Tyler questioned the ability of female agents, she *wasn't*. In fact, in spite of her training, she was terrified of the prospect!

Lucas looked her up and down with the same sharp, all-seeing stare he had turned on her a few moments earlier. And like before she felt judged.

He shook his head with a dismissive air. "*Her?* In the field?"

Ana's hackles rose, pushing aside her fears. What right did this pompous, arrogant man have to declare what she was and was not capable of? He who did not even know her beyond a few piercing glances and less than five exchanges of conversation?

She folded her own arms in mimicry of his tense posture.

"Actually, Mr. Tyler, *I* am the expert with code-breaking in our organization, not Emily, so if you're looking for assistance in that arena, I'm the better choice. And if it means finding the person who attacked my friend and bringing him to justice, then I am more than happy to work in the field." She couldn't believe the words that were falling from her lips. Nor, apparently, could she stop them. "In fact, I insist upon it."

Her rational mind screamed at her to stop talking. That she didn't want to take to the field. That she wasn't ready. But it was too late. The words had already escaped. Charlie was staring at her with a proud beam on his face. And Lucas Tyler was smirking in a way that made her want to load a pistol and charge into battle, if only to bring his superior attitude down a notch or two.

Irritating man.

He turned away from her pointed glare. "Look

Isley, I never wanted to work with a woman in the first place, but at least it was clear Lady Allington knew what she was doing." His gaze swung back to Ana. She shifted beneath it and the angry heat it inspired in her chest. "Have *you* even been in the field?"

Ana let her tense arms slowly ease to her sides. She shifted, dodging his seeking eyes. She hated how just a look from this man made her so nervous and unsure of herself. "I—I have worked on cases."

His eyebrow arched. "In the field, my lady."

Ana pursed her lips. She couldn't avoid such a direct inquiry. "Only once. I assisted our other associate, Meredith Archer, in closing a case last year."

He barked out a laugh of triumph. "And that is all?"

She nodded with reluctance. "But," she continued, "I have done research, broken codes, developed devices . . ."

Lucas raised his hands and let them drop at his sides as he turned back to Charlie. "You see, she's sequestered herself away doing research. She's hardly faced any real danger. Her uncertainty could be deadly to us both."

She gasped in outrage. "You twist my words! I never said I was uncertain." Actually, she was very uncertain, but she wasn't going to admit that to this man of all men.

He continued, dismissing her statement as if she hadn't even spoken. "Her hesitation could put me in danger, and I certainly can't guarantee her protection."

Anastasia fisted her hands. Her whole body shook with outrage. "I never asked for your protection, Mr. Tyler! I can take care of myself."

He spun back on her. "How?"

That stopped her. She wrinkled her brow. "How?"

He shook his head. "You cannot even answer the question."

"Yes, I can," she insisted. What was it about this man that brought out the worst in her? "I can shoot."

He looked incredulous, but in that, at least, she was sure. She wasn't the deadeye Meredith was, but she could fire a gun and hit her mark when required.

"And I have trained in physical defense," she continued.

On that score she was less certain, but she remembered her training well enough. Emily insisted they practice down in Ana's workroom once a week to keep their skills honed. She had even put Emily to the floor a few times, something she was very proud of when she was honest with herself.

Lucas opened his mouth to retort, but Charlie stepped forward, moving between them as he raised a palm toward either side. "All right, enough. This fighting won't change the situation."

Ana frowned. Lucas rolled his eyes.

Charlie looked at Lucas. "You have your orders and your orders were clear. You are to work with one of my operatives and you shall. You will continue to pursue this case with Ana as your partner. That is the end of the discussion."

Lucas expelled a harsh breath that left little doubt to his feelings on the subject, but he hardly spared Ana even a glance.

"It seems as though I've been given little choice." He finally looked her way and his eyes held hers for a long moment. Perhaps a little too long. "You," he said softly. "Get yourself ready. You may think that being able to shoot a pistol or throw a punch will be enough, but when you're in the field with me, I shall expect you to keep up."

Ana drew in a breath. Was this really happening? Was she really going to do this? "Fine."

"Read over Emily's notes." He turned on his heel and headed for the door. "I will be back for you in a few days. Isley, keep me appraised of Lady Allington's condition."

And then he was gone, leaving Ana as confused and turned around as she had been when he entered the parlor. But this time, her heart fluttered. Throbbed strangely in a way that made no sense.

She turned to see Charlie eyeing her closely and forgot her misgivings about Lucas Tyler for a moment. She had too many about her future to dwell on him.

"I'm not ready," she whispered, the full weight of what was going to happen hitting her at once. "I'm not meant for the field. I never was."

Charlie's expression softened. "That isn't true. You've hidden away in your basement keeping yourself company with your inventions and codes for far too long. If you weren't meant for the field, Lady M and I never would have chosen to train you."

She cocked her head. The mysterious Lady M, their spymaster. She wasn't even sure the woman existed. Sometimes she wondered if the lady wasn't some figment of Charlie's imagination, made up to let the "Lady Spies" feel closer to a woman who was supposedly their benefactress in both their investigations and the charity guild that hid their true purposes.

"Do you really think I'm capable of this?" she asked. "Capable of filling Emily's position? Working with this man who obviously thinks very little of me? Uncovering the secret of who is betraying the spies when so many others couldn't?"

Charlie nodded slowly. "I do, Ana. And don't be afraid. Lucas Tyler may seem gruff, but he is one of the best spies in the country. He shall be with you, every step of the way. Now I'm going to go speak to Adam about Emily's condition."

As Charlie patted her hand and left the room, Ana looked around her. Lucas Tyler would be with her every step of the way. Now that it had been said out loud, she realized something.

She was more afraid of that than anything else.

Chapter 3

❦

"**I** cannot tell you how happy I am that you've arrived." Ana embraced Meredith, squeezing her as tightly as she could as they stood in the foyer three days later. After the past seventy-two hours, she needed to know her other best friend was safe and whole.

Meredith pulled back and looked into her eyes. Ana saw Meredith's worries and the redness that betrayed the tears she had shed. No doubt her sharp friend saw the same evidence on her own face.

"I am glad, too. Tell me straight away, how is Emily? We received your messages along the road and when we arrived here in London, but I need to hear it from your lips."

Ana squeezed Meredith's wrist in reassurance. "She is getting stronger. Adam seems more hopeful with each visit."

The relief was plain on her friend's face and in the way she swayed slightly. It was as if Meredith had been holding herself rigid in preparation for the worst news. Now that it hadn't come, she could relax.

"I only wish Tristan and I could have arrived sooner."

Ana motioned to the stairs and they began to go up together, arm in arm. "Nonsense, Merry," she said with a shake of her head. "I'm only sorry your visit to Carmichael was interrupted. How is Tristan?"

Now that she knew Emily was improving, Meredith smiled. "He is better than well. He is . . . perfection. And I have news. Tristan has begun training to become an agent, himself. We hope to work together on a few cases before we settle in and start our family."

Ana halted on the steps, staring at Meredith with wide eyes. "That—That is wonderful, Meredith!" she gasped. "I can hardly believe it. But you two work so well together, of course it makes perfect sense now that you've said it. I'm sure he will be a talented spy."

Meredith beamed. "I am so very happy, Ana."

Ana nodded as they continued up the stairway, but she couldn't ignore the sharp, unpleasant tightening in her chest at Meredith's words and smile. She didn't begrudge her friend her happiness. Meredith and Tristan had fought for it, earned it. But Ana knew what her feelings were, even though she hated them. Jealousy.

She remembered being "so very happy." She'd spent her entire childhood enamored with her late husband, Gilbert. When he finally noticed her, despite her spectacles, despite her painfully shy ways, it had been like every fantasy come true, and she had clung to his love like a lifeline, knowing she would never have anything like it again.

But her love and the life she'd known had been snatched from her. In the past few days since Emily's attack that fact had been brought home to her time and again, whether when she looked at Emily's gaunt face or dreamt of Gilbert and the life they once shared.

But then, with troubling frequency, she had also begun to dream of someone else. Lucas Tyler's image, with his smirks and all-seeing stares, troubled her after she blew out her candle at night. She told herself over and over that it was just because she had been so busy readying herself for their case, of course he would be on her mind.

"How much must I prepare myself?"

Meredith's voice cut through Ana's haze and she realized that they had come to a stop before Emily's chamber door.

"I'm sorry?"

Meredith tilted her head, her blue eyes suddenly focusing on Ana's face. "You must be tired, Ana. I'm sorry I wasn't here to assist you."

Ana shrugged, pushing away her troubling thoughts. "Please don't trouble yourself with that." She hesitated. There was no way to cover the truth. "Emily is very pale. And she is often in pain, though she tries to hide it."

Meredith's lips pursed. "Typical of our dearest friend."

Ana nodded. "She takes the laudanum with great reluctance, and it makes her very sleepy, so she may only be able to converse with us a short while."

"I merely want to see her." Ana winced as Meredith's eyes filled with tears. "To touch her and know she's whole and still alive in the world. When I feared she wasn't, I didn't know what to do. It was like a part of me was torn away."

Ana nodded as she grasped Meredith's hand. She understood completely. "I am glad you've come. So glad to see you."

Meredith smiled before she pushed the door open and they entered the chamber together.

Ana stayed at the doorway as Meredith stepped forward until she reached Emily's bed. Whatever words the two women exchanged were quiet, out of her hearing, and then Emily's pale hand lifted and the two women touched.

"Is Anastasia here, as well?" Emily croaked.

Ana stepped forward with the false smile she had been wearing for her friend's benefit over the past few days. She had a sneaking suspicion Emily saw right through it. The fact that she didn't point it out was proof enough of the seriousness of her injuries.

"I'm here, Emily. I only wanted to give you a moment with Meredith before I interfered."

Her friend's eyes sharpened. "Bah. We are a team, aren't we?"

"Always," Meredith reassured her.

"Then tell Ana she cannot shut me out from our business," Emily ordered as she dropped her hand back on the bed in exhaustion. "She won't talk to me about the case I was assigned before I was shot."

Meredith looked at Ana. She shrugged in return.

"Dearest, I'm sure it's best if you rest and not trouble yourself—"

Emily groaned in frustration as she tried to sit up and failed. "How can I rest when I know the attack ruined weeks of work? And that smug Lucas Tyler is probably so pleased that he will get to work on this case alone again."

Ana sighed. She had kept the details from Emily, but now that Meredith was there, she wondered if she should just tell them the truth. Certainly she needed their guidance. Reading over Emily's notes about the attacks on other spies and the building urgency to find the culprit only made her more and more nervous about the impending case. And more and more anxious about Lucas Tyler's return.

"Tyler won't be working on the case alone," she said softly as she came to the chair at the foot of Emily's bed where she had all but lived in during the past few days.

Meredith glanced at her sharply and Emily's eyes grew wide even though she didn't try to lift her head a second time.

"What do you mean?" Emily asked.

Ana swallowed hard. "I—I will take your place, Emily. I'm going to be working with him to determine who is uncovering and betraying the spies."

Meredith nearly flipped over her chair as she came to her feet, and Emily began to cough. The room became a flurry of activity as Ana dove for Emily's laudanum, and Merry grabbed for a cup of lukewarm tea at the bedside. When the pain medication and the tea had been administered and Emily's coughing had subsided, the two women stared at Ana.

"Ana, you're taking the field?" Meredith whispered, dark blue eyes wide.

Ana's heart sank. From their shocked expressions, she could see neither of her friends thought she was ready for such a dangerous prospect. They doubted her abilities and that made any bravado she had built wilt like a flower on a burning hot day. She dipped her head in disappointment.

She couldn't do this.

"Well, I never thought I'd say this," Emily said. "But thank God I was shot."

Ana's chin snapped up as she caught Emily's eye. Her friend was actually smiling for the first time since Ana found her bleeding in the parlor.

"I—I don't understand," Ana stammered.

"Emily and I have longed for you to finally spread your wings and join us in the field," Meredith said, her pretty face filled with joy and excitement. "And while I don't echo Emily's statement of gratitude for her injuries, I do share her enthusiasm that you've finally come to the decision to work on a case outside of your research and evidence analysis."

Ana's mouth dropped open. "You—You think I am capable?"

Emily's brow wrinkled. "Of course. Anyone who knows you would!"

Ana drew in a breath and the emotions she'd been holding back bubbled from her lips. "Tyler said I was a danger to him and to myself. He tried to tell Charlie that he wouldn't work with me."

Emily's eyes narrowed. "Of course he would, the pompous ass."

"Who *is* this Tyler?" Meredith asked, her eyes darting between her friends.

Emily continued to stare at Ana with an interested gleam in her bright blue eyes. "The spy I was to work with on my case. The War Department idiots couldn't uncover anything even after a year's investigation and Charlie convinced them that one of us could help."

"What kind of man is he?" Meredith asked.

Emily barked out a laugh that made her wince in pain. "He's a typical society rake. Arrogant. Self-congratulatory. Handsome and he knows it far too well." She rolled her eyes. "It's the dimples. He thinks they're a weapon."

Ana ducked her head. Yes, the man was handsome. No one could deny that.

Meredith put a finger to her lips as though she were pondering those facts. "But is he a capable spy?"

Emily didn't hesitate, despite her earlier censure. "He is."

Ana cleared her throat. "Charlie says he's one of the best in the country."

Meredith's eyebrows arched slightly, but then she merely said, "Hmmm."

"Can—Can you advise me?" Ana asked, hoping to steer away from the strangely uncomfortable topic of Lucas Tyler.

Emily smiled. "I think you'll recognize your natural abilities very quickly. But I do have some advice. Be careful of Tyler. He will do all he can to cut you out of the investigation. He'll stop at nothing to solve this case and will use every weapon in his arsenal to make sure things are done his way. This is personal to him, though I don't know why."

Ana nodded slowly, allowing that comment to sink in. Tyler had already made it painfully clear how little he thought of her. She would just have to do everything in her power to prove him wrong and make sure he didn't shut her out of this case.

She shivered. Her first real foray into the world of spies and she would have to be utterly perfect. With a man like Lucas Tyler watching her every move, she couldn't afford not to be.

Lucas watched as Anastasia leaned over a pile of paperwork, nodding as Charlie gave her a few instructions. He should have been attending more closely to their conversation, adding to her education or clarifying the finer points of the case he had been building for the better part of a year. Instead, he found himself merely staring, watching as her brown eyes moved back and forth when she read. The way her slender hand moved up to massage her neck when she left her head tilted down too long.

He cleared his throat and shifted in his seat. So he found her attractive. There were many women he found attractive. He could resist her. There were, after all, a great deal more important things at stake than the charming way Anastasia Whittig swirled a lock of brown hair around her fingertip.

"Do you understand, Lady Whittig?" he asked, slouching back in the chair like he hadn't a care in the world.

Slowly, she lifted her face to look at him, and her eyes narrowed behind her ridiculously endearing reading spectacles.

"Yes, thank you for your concern." Her voice dripped with condescending sarcasm. "I think I understand the basic concept of investigation, Mr. Tyler."

Lucas should have been annoyed. After all, she had so little experience in the field, yet she patently refused to ask him questions or even look at him. Instead, he felt a strong urge to *laugh* at her spunk.

Isley shoved away from the desk where he had been showing Anastasia the marks on the map where different spies had been ambushed, including the latest attack on Emily as a possible continuation of the betrayal. He rolled his eyes as he looked at the two of them.

"Well," he said as he started toward the door. "Since you two are getting along so famously, I think I'll go check in on Emily and say hello to Meredith."

Anastasia did not break her glare with Lucas and she didn't retort. Just to goad her, Lucas did the same, holding her stare with a steady one of his own. After a moment, she gave up in exasperation. She looked back down at the map as she removed her spectacles and set them on the table.

"You believe me to be stupid," she said softly.

Lucas straightened up in surprise. He was taken aback by her candor . . . and also how very far off the mark she was. He had done some research while they were apart. After hearing about her inventions and code-breaking skills, he couldn't help but be impressed by Anastasia Whittig. Woman or not, capable in the field or not, she was still an intriguing, talented individual.

"No," he said, treading softly. "Clearly you are not stupid, my lady."

Her eyes flicked up, but then back to her work.

"However, I do believe you are in over your head when it comes to this case." If she was going to be forthcoming, he had no choice but to be equally so.

Anastasia's lips pursed, drawing his attention to the fullness of her mouth for a brief, almost painful moment. But she didn't deny his statement. Her lack of false confidence impressed him.

It also left him with the strange sensation of wishing to comfort her.

"It isn't your fault," he added, getting to his feet and moving to the window. He stopped there and turned back. He found she had stopped pretending to look over the evidence and was now staring at him, her face devoid of emotion, though he could see it took effort to cover her feelings.

"You have hardly been in the field. You have been sheltered," he continued.

Her eyes widened as she slowly got to her feet. "Sheltered?" she said on the softest of breaths. Her voice dripped with renewed pain and even deeper indignation. "You have no idea about the circumstances of my life, Mr. Tyler."

Lucas watched her step closer. "I—"

She cut him off even as she came nearer. Once again her floral perfume wrapped around him. Gardenias perhaps, with a hint of jasmine. The scent called to his bloodstream and he suddenly felt hot as he slipped a finger beneath his cravat and tugged.

"My parents both died of a horrible fever," she hissed, her eyes telling a story of loss that even her words could not match. "It was sudden and infectious and I never got to say my good-byes to them. And just when I began to feel whole, my husband . . . the man I loved, my only remaining family that cared for me . . . *died* after a hunting accident. I was left all alone."

He drew a breath, but she kept moving forward. Now her body heat joined her perfume to twist its way around him. Lucas could no longer deny that the burning in his blood was desire. And if she came much closer, Anastasia wouldn't be able to deny it either. It would become perfectly clear to her.

"It was only when I was invited into the Sisters of the Heart Society for Widows and Orphans and was told of their real cause . . . female spies, that I felt like I had found a new family," she continued, her voice harsh and low. "For all this time, Mr. Tyler, I have fought to protect my friends in the field through my inventions, through my work deciphering their evidence. But I couldn't protect Emily, who is my best friend. The woman who took me in when I could no longer survive on the settlement my husband's heir allowed me."

She took another step and her body actually brushed

his. Tingling explosions erupted where she moved against him, and they rushed through him to heat every ounce of his blood. To make every nerve ending aware of her in the way men had been aware of women for millenniums. Powerful urges drummed through him. To pull her closer. To kiss her until she stopped talking. To stake some kind of claim.

Lucas sucked in his breath, trying to rein in his reaction to her. Trying to find some level of control in the face of her bald emotion.

"So don't tell me I have been sheltered," she whispered. "Because you do not know me at all."

The world came to a halt as she stood there, so close that his breath stirred the hair around her upturned face. He could find no words to say, and she had said so many that there seemed to be none left. But then the fire left her eyes and her face changed from the fierce champion back to timid society widow. Her eyes widened as she realized just how close they were, but to his surprise, she didn't move immediately.

His hand stirred at his side and he clenched a fist so he wouldn't lift it and stroke her cheek with his fingertips. His skin tingled to feel the satin of hers. Finally, she stepped back. A huge shiver rocked her small frame before she mumbled, "I—Excuse me."

Then she stumbled out of the room, leaving him alone.

Lucas shook his head as the paralyzing effect of Anastasia Whittig finally faded. But it was replaced by a strange emptiness now that she was no longer in the room, taunting him. Challenging him. Arousing him.

What had just happened?

He turned to look out the window and catch his breath. A better question was how could he keep it from ever happening again? Because such a powerful exchange could be nothing but dangerous in a case like this. And the case was all that mattered.

It had to be.

Chapter 4

A ball. How could she be going to a ball? Ana twisted her black handkerchief in her fist. The carriage rocked and she bumped against its wall.

Peeling back the curtain, she watched the lights of the city roll by. They were getting close to the home their hostess, Lady Westfield, had taken when her husband passed away a few years before and her son ascended to the title. Moving closer to the moment Ana had been avoiding since Gilbert's death.

Oh, of course it was well past the appropriate time to come out in Society again. Gilbert had died five years before. But it still felt like a betrayal to go to a dance. After all, as he lay dying, she had known things would never be the same for her again, and so she had preserved her life just as it was that horrible day. She had worn black and never taken it off. She had sequestered herself away. For the first few years it had been out of pure heartache. Her husband's death had left a hole in her very soul, and she felt no desire to fill it with the frivolity of Society, which had never given her much pleasure.

And now? Emily and Meredith often said she used her mourning to hide. She denied it, but she wasn't so certain that her friends were not correct in that assessment. Gilbert had always been the one to guide her into a room, to ease her natural nervousness around people whom she didn't know. With him, she had felt safe. Her life had been defined. She was Gilbert Whittig's wife.

Without him, she wasn't sure how she was defined or how she would manage. She certainly couldn't rely on Lucas Tyler to be her support. If she faltered tonight, he would be there to crow at her failure.

He didn't have faith in her abilities in the field . . . in any woman's abilities. Just the previous afternoon, he'd called her sheltered and hesitant and a danger to their case and their very lives. She blushed as she remembered her impassioned reply and the look of utter disbelief that crossed his handsome face.

Well, tonight was her first chance to prove him wrong.

She started as the carriage door swung open to reveal her footman, his hand extended to assist her from the vehicle. Her knees shook, and she couldn't seem to make herself move as the young man waited, blinking at her.

"My lady?" he finally ventured, his head cocking with confusion.

"Yes, Thomas, I'm just a bit slow." Tamping down her fear, she slid to the door and let him help her down. As he stepped away, she smoothed her gown and looked up at the large home. She had to show more than just Lucas Tyler that she could do this.

She had to show Charlie. To show Lady M. To show Meredith and Emily. They all had faith in her. She had to prove their faith to be well placed.

She had to show herself.

Somehow she moved into the crowd now entering the doorway and in a few moments, found herself inside the buzzing ballroom.

It had been a long time since Ana was in such a crush. When The Society for Widows and Orphans held events to raise funds, it was Meredith and Emily who took center stage. Ana normally stayed home, crunching figures and researching ways to increase attendance. The gatherings she did go to were teas and ladies' luncheons which consisted of twenty women, rarely more.

Truth be told, sometimes twenty seemed too many for her comfort. Yet here she was, in a ballroom with hundreds of people. They were laughing, they were talking, they were utterly comfortable in their fancy attire.

And Ana felt miserably out of place. Lost. Weak.
She longed for the ease of her day gowns and spectacles and inventions. Every fiber in her being told her
to turn around and run back to her carriage. Every
ounce of her soul reminded her how unprepared she
was for the field, that Lucas was right about her being
sheltered no matter how forcefully she denied that accusation.

The only thing that kept her frozen in place on the
edge of the ballroom floor was Emily. If Ana did not
do what she had come here to do . . . if she didn't
swallow her fears, then all of Emily's work would be
for nothing. The man who had nearly put her best
friend in a cold grave would very likely escape capture.

And the begrudgingly good name of the Lady Spies
would be tarnished in the eyes of the government forever. They might use her hesitation as proof that the
organization wasn't valid. God, they might even dis-
band the group. She wouldn't do that to Meredith and
Emily. She couldn't.

"Anastasia Whittig? Lady Whittig?"

Ana started at the sound of her name being squealed
from across the ballroom. She spun around in time to
see a pretty, plump woman in a blazingly violet gown
come hurrying around the perimeter of the dance floor
toward her at a shocking speed. Her face was flush
with color and her eyes danced as she reached Ana.
"By heavens, it is you!"

Ana stammered, looking for something to say when recognition dawned on her. "Victoria Nethercourt!" she exclaimed, numbly allowing the woman to grasp her hands. This was one of her friends, albeit a friend from another lifetime, long before she lost Gilbert, long before she became a spy.

"It's Victoria Brightoncraft now," Victoria laughed. "A Countess, can you imagine?"

"Of course." Ana nodded as the surprise of seeing someone she once called a confidante faded, replaced by an almost shy pleasure that she had been remembered after so long. "I heard of your marriage. Many felicitations. I hope you are well."

Victoria nodded emphatically and began to launch into a detailed accounting of the past few years of her life, but before she could proceed too far in her hurriedly spoken tale, yet another woman approached to reintroduce herself to Anastasia. And then another. And then another.

Within a quarter of an hour, Ana found herself surrounded by a flock of friendly faces, all welcoming her back to Society with excited glee. Even Lady Westfield herself, whom Ana had never been close to even before her self-imposed exile, stopped by to say hello and express pride that *her* invitation had been the first Ana accepted in so many years.

Ana listened to their giggling words, stored away the plethora of information she learned from their gossip, and generally marveled at their reception of her. These people not only remembered her, but they welcomed her back to their fold. Her old friends, ones she had lost contact with except in passing, *cared* for her.

It was shocking and thrilling all at once.

"Isn't that Lucas Tyler?" one of the women asked, rising up on slippered tiptoes to glance across the busy ballroom.

Immediately, Ana shook off her excitement as a new emotion flooded her. Dread. And when she looked deeper, anticipation. Lucas was here. She craned her own neck with as much subtlety as she could and immediately found him in the crowd, talking to another man.

But he was looking at her.

Her heart leapt into her throat where it cut off her air for a brief moment before she managed to control her reaction.

"My, he is a handsome one," Victoria said with a nod. "You probably don't remember him, Anastasia, as he wasn't in country when you came out and married."

Ana remained silent, unsure of how much she could or should reveal about her relationship with Lucas. Telling the women she knew him could either garner her much desired information or destroy her cover.

Another woman, Lady Taberton took up the story. "Despite his not having a title, he does have money. And just *look* at him. Why, he's one of the most sought-after bachelors in Society at present, Lady Whittig," she said with a smile that was a little more knowing than Ana wanted to think about. "He's considered a catch, several ladies have wagers running about who will snag him first, either for a husband or . . ." She trailed off with a suggestive wave of her hand.

Ana bit back a gasp. Of course she remembered how frank the talk of the married ladies and widows could become, but she never recalled it bothering her so much. These women were betting on who would bed Lucas first!

Assuming none of them already had.

"I don't suppose you would like to put yourself into the contest?" asked another woman, Lady Valleyton.

Ana turned her gaze onto the pretty redhead who was watching her with a teasing, playful grin. Her offer was made in all friendliness, but it grated along Ana's spine like metal on slate.

"No," she managed to say with what she hoped was a smile. It felt more like a grimace.

Victoria patted her hand and gave the women a shushing glare. "Come now, ladies. You know how attached to the late Lord Whittig Lady Whittig was."

Lady Valleyton's cheeks colored dark crimson as she glanced down at Ana's mourning gown. "My apologies, my lady," she stammered. "I never meant to offend."

Ana nodded stiffly. Actually, for the first time in a long time, she hadn't been thinking of Gilbert at all. "It's fine, of course."

"Well, those of you still in the running, get ready,"

Lady Taberton interrupted. "Because he's coming this way!"

The group of women caught their collective breath, and Ana was ashamed to admit she caught her own with it as she watched Lucas shoulder his way through the crowd, dodging footmen and overly eager mamas with the grace of an athlete. All the while he moved toward *her* . . . not the group of giggling women, but *her* with all the focus of a hawk hunting a field mouse.

When he got nearer, she saw that he was smiling, a friendly, rakish expression that made more than one woman around her blush. But the smile didn't reach his eyes. In fact, there was a dangerous, almost angry light in his gray stare that put her on notice. She had done something wrong, and Lucas wasn't pleased with her.

"Ladies," he drawled as he reached their group.

Clearly he was acquainted with at least one of the women to approach them all so boldly. Her gaze darted around her as she tried to determine which one . . . and how. She prayed it wasn't Lady Valleyton with her pretty pale skin and silky auburn hair, not to mention the philandering husband who probably wouldn't care who she took a tumble with since his legacy had already been insured by the birth of twin boys a year before. Drat the woman for already having her figure back.

The women smiled, but no one answered. Ana waited

as the awkward silence stretched and finally realized that Lucas was staring at *her*, eyebrows raised. He meant for *her* to be his conduit in introduction.

"Er—Yes, good evening, Mr. Tyler," she managed to croak. The women in the group spun on her with surprise mirrored in every gaze. After all, she hadn't spoken up about an acquaintance with Lucas when they were fawning over him like debutantes. "How—How nice to see you again."

He smiled, but again she noticed the tightness around his mouth, the tension in his forehead. "Yes, it has been a while. Since your last charity ball, was it not?"

Ana nodded, following his lead. "Yes. You were quite"—she swallowed hard—"helpful in obtaining funds at the last function."

He nodded in encouragement, and her pounding heart began to slow to a more normal rate. "I beg your pardon, how rude of me. Have you met these ladies?" she asked, motioning to the staring group.

"I have seen many of them, but I don't believe I've been formally introduced." Lucas flashed a winning grin that showed off the dimples Emily had mentioned. Despite herself, Ana's heart did a strange little flip.

Gripping her hands into fists, she gave the introductions and watched as Lucas exhibited every asset he had as a spy. He actually listened to each name, staring at the women long enough to recall their faces, but not so long as to be forward. He repeated their names as if he were putting them to memory, just as she sometimes did with tricky elements in a code.

"Well," he said with a bow when the pleasantries had been exchanged, "I hate to be rude, but may I steal Lady Whittig away from you? I have longed to speak to her about her next event for the Sisters of the Heart Society. Perhaps I could beg the next dance, my lady?"

He met her gaze evenly, and she saw his order in his eyes. *Don't refuse*. She was about to follow that order when she caught sight of her own black gown and remembered her reasons for wearing it. A woman in mourning did not dance.

She sucked in a breath. "I have no intentions on dancing this evening, Mr. Lucas," she said, ignoring the soft sounds of surprise made by the women in her party. "But I would be more than happy to discuss the details of our next Society event with you on the terrace if that would please you."

His eyes narrowed before he gave a curt nod. "Yes, of course." Offering her his arm, he said, "Perhaps your friends will be more amenable to dancing later."

With their enthusiastic murmurs ringing in her ears, Ana took Lucas's arm and allowed him to lead her past the dance floor to the terrace doorways in the distance. But as soon as they were out of sight and earshot of her renewed friends, his grip on her arm tightened and his steps filled with purpose and emotion.

"You needn't manhandle me," she said as she tried to pull herself free of his grip.

"Not a word," he ground out as he maneuvered them onto the wide terrace and away from the others outside. "Not yet."

"When then, Mr. Tyler?" she snapped, yanking her arm free when he brought her to a stop in a shadowy corner at the end of the terrace.

His eyes narrowed and a dangerous gleam lit up in them. "Now. *Now* you will explain yourself."

Lucas folded his arms as he waited for Ana's answer. Instead of doing as she'd been told, she gave him a withering glare and stomped over to the terrace railing to look down over the gardens below. Her hand snaked up and she began to rub her arm . . . right on the spot where he'd touched her.

He tilted his head. His grip hadn't been tight enough to hurt her, so the reason for her to touch herself there intrigued him.

"Well?" he asked, trying to bring his focus back to matters at hand.

She spun on him, eyes flashing in a way that made the brown come alive with lighter color. "Why don't you begin by explaining *yourself*, Mr. Tyler? What purpose did you have in dragging me away from those women? You created a spectacle."

He barked out a laugh. "I created a spectacle?" He drew in a breath and lowered his tone. This was not the time to lose control over his emotions. "What are you wearing, Anastasia?"

She flinched at the inappropriate use of her given name, but glanced down at herself nonetheless. Her eyes came back up, filled with confusion.

"A gown." Her lips thinned. "They are all the rage with proper ladies this season, you know. Someone came up with the silly notion that we shouldn't run around in our underthings."

He bit back both a retort and a sinful image of Anastasia in far less than a chemise. "No."

He took a step toward her as he lifted a hand to point. She stumbled back. Clearly, she did not fear him . . . what she feared was that he would touch her again. His breath caught at the idea as he watched her track his extended finger like it was a weapon.

"You are wearing a *black* gown, Ana. A mourning gown."

Her stare broke away from his finger and moved to his face instead. Her forehead crinkled and she looked at him like he had gone completely mad. He was beginning to think she might be right in that assessment.

"And?"

He rubbed his temple as he tried to keep himself together. This woman was the most frustrating and tempting piece of skirt he had ever met.

"You are wearing a black mourning gown . . . at a ball," he ground out through clenched teeth. "Between that fact and your stunning little return to Society, you are drawing far too much attention to yourself."

"Wait, you call ten or twelve women approaching me to say hello a 'stunning little return to Society'?" She shook her head.

He sighed. After years hiding herself away, she was so blind. "Only a few people may have approached you, but those who didn't are talking about you, Ana. Your name was on the lips of every woman and man in that room and probably still is."

Her face drained of color at that thought. "Perhaps some of the women mentioned me, yes, but I cannot believe what you say is true. You're exaggerating."

Lucas shut his eyes and slowly counted to ten in his head. "The women mentioned you. A large portion of the men are plotting to bed or wed you."

"What?" she cried, her voice elevating sharply before she remembered herself and looked around. Thankfully, most of the people on the terrace had gone back into the ballroom.

"It is true, Ana, whether you like it or not. Men of a certain age and disposition like pretty little widows. And since you have been out of Society for a while, you are a novelty. You are a woman the men want because you have been out of their reach for so long." He fisted his hands at his sides. It hadn't been easy hearing snippets of conversation about Ana's "attributes." Only his training and cover had kept him from busting a few of the cruder heads.

She stumbled back, but there was nowhere else to

go on the narrow terrace. She leaned against the railing like it was the only thing keeping her up.

"Before I married, none of those men even looked at me. I cannot believe I'm the topic of such conversation," she said softly, dropping her chin to stare at her slippered feet.

Her forlorn look touched Lucas in a place buried deep. Ana had actually *liked* being the belle of the ball, even if only for a few moments. She had enjoyed the fact that so many people remembered and welcomed her. Now her memories of the evening were tarnished as she realized the ramifications of them.

He drew in a breath and gentled his tone. "I realize garnering attention wasn't your design, but you must understand the fact that you are wearing black only magnifies the reaction to you. At the very least, it makes you instantly recognizable in a crowd. That is why you must start wearing color."

Her chin lifted slowly and the defeat was gone from her stare, at least for the moment. Ana straightened up and folded her arms across her chest. His heart gave the strangest little ache at the sight, the way her chin wobbled in indignation.

"Mr. Tyler, I am a widow. Widows wear black."

If a tone could wither, Lucas would have been curled up on the stones at her feet, ready to blow away with the next stiff breeze. Instead, he narrowed his eyes.

"Your husband died many years ago, my lady," he

said with a scowl. Normally he wouldn't have been so harsh, but damn it! The woman kept calling on the memory of a man dead so long ago. It irked him to no end.

Her eyes fluttered shut, but not before he saw the flash of sadness and loss in their depths. His chest tightened. She might be using her husband's death to hide away from the world, but her grief was real. He wasn't sure whether to shake her back to life or pull her into his arms for comfort.

Her voice was soft and even as she said, "Regardless of the time that has passed, I loved my husband, Mr. Tyler. A love like that doesn't happen more than once in a lifetime, so I will wear black to honor him . . . whether you approve or not."

With that, she turned away from him. Lucas held back a growl of growing irritation. And not just for the sake of his case. He shouldn't *care* what some repressed widow wore or her reasons for doing so.

He shook off the reaction as he took a step toward her. Grasping her elbow, he spun her back around to face him. "No—" he began.

But he didn't get any further. Ana lifted her chin in defiance and met his eyes. His angry orders fell away from his lips as he stared down at her. Moonlight danced off her sleek chestnut hair and made her eyes sparkle from emotion and the life within her that she repressed out of misguided guilt and lingering grief. He found himself longing to coax that life and emotion from her. To remind her not just how to be a good spy . . . but a woman again.

Her lips parted as if she had read his thoughts and her eyelids drooped slightly when her gaze focused suddenly, powerfully on his mouth.

By God, after everything she'd said, did she actually want him to *kiss* her?

"Very— Oh my!"

Lucas froze at the sound of a voice behind them. His gaze flitted to Ana. Her face had grown deathly pale with shock and fear. They had been discovered . . . and she was practically in his arms.

Slowly he let her go and backed away, knowing with each step that it was too late to pretend that whatever woman had seen them was mistaken in her assumptions. He turned with a wince. It was Lady Bellingham, the young wife of the old Viscount, notorious for her penchant for gossip. She wouldn't be able to resist telling the world what she had seen. Or almost seen.

Ana straightened up from the terrace railing, her lips pursed. "Good evening, my lady," she said, her voice as calm and carefree as if nothing out of the ordinary had transpired. "Isn't it a lovely evening?"

Lady Bellingham gave a sly smile as she glanced from Ana to Lucas and back again. "Very lovely. Quite *romantic*, don't you think Mr. Tyler?"

He cleared his throat and took another step away from Ana. "I hadn't really noticed, my lady."

The young woman let out a giggle. "Of course you

didn't, sir. How could you when you had a far more appealing subject to look upon in Lady Whittig?"

Ana shifted and some of her cool exterior slipped away. "You misunderstand, my lady—"

"Pish posh!" Lady Bellingham waved a dismissive hand. "I am not one to judge."

"Yes, well," Ana stammered. "I should return to the ballroom, I've been outside quite too long. Th-Thank you for your thoughts on the Society for Widows and Orphans, Mr. Tyler. I shall keep everything you have said in mind as we plan our next event."

"Yes, good evening, Lady Whittig," he replied, inclining his head.

"And I'm sure I will speak to you further inside, Lady Bellingham." Ana made her way toward the ballroom doors. "Good evening."

Lady Bellingham wrinkled her brow as she watched Ana slip away, then mumbled her own good-byes as she followed . . . to tell the story to the entire room, no doubt.

With a curse, Lucas turned to the terrace railing and gripped the steel with both hands. How could he have been so distracted? He hadn't done something so foolish in a year . . . and the last time he had done so it had resulted in tragedy.

But something in Anastasia Whittig made him reckless. Made him think of nothing but her. And he could only wait to see what the ramifications of his slip in propriety would be.

Chapter 5

A discreet visit could do no harm. Her driver could be trusted and she was sure she hadn't been followed. No, there was *no* harm in being at Lucas Tyler's town home. Ana paced the luxurious parlor as she tried to convince herself of that fact. At the very least, it could be no worse than being caught on the terrace with Lucas two nights ago.

She shivered as she thought of that night. Of Lady Bellingham's triumphant face. Of her own inability to cover her emotions . . . worse yet, her inability to stop herself from feeling those emotions entirely. No matter how she tried, she couldn't deny she had reacted to Lucas. When he pulled her close and then just stared down at her, an undeniable hunger in his eyes, she had responded. Her body had swayed toward his, and she had found herself wondering, for a wicked moment, what would happen if he leaned down and kissed her.

She shook her head to clear the unwanted memory away. Why in the world did she react so strongly to Lucas? He was pompous and arrogant and had no faith in her. He thought he could tell her what to do like she was a soldier in his own private regiment. And he acted like the mere passing of time could dictate when emotions faded.

Yet despite all those reasons not to like him, there was something about the man that—well, fascinated her. When he was near, all she could do was watch his mouth move. Inhale his musky, clean scent. Marvel at how his body heat surrounded her even when he wasn't touching her, and burned her when he did.

What in God's name was wrong with her? Was what Lucas said true? Was she so bloody sheltered that the first handsome man she had any kind of close contact with since Gilbert's death sent her into a trembling mess? What kind of woman did that make her, that she was so easily moved by an infuriating stranger?

She let out a sigh as she collapsed into the closest chair and looked around. Handsome and arrogant or not, the man had very nice taste. Understated, yet elegant. Not a frill or flower in sight, so he probably didn't have a woman's input in his décor.

Despite herself, she smiled, but the expression fell the instant the parlor door opened and Lucas stepped inside.

She sucked in a breath as she stumbled to her feet. Would she ever stop being surprised by how handsome he was?

"Good afternoon." His complete ease as he strolled into the room made her all the more aware of her own discomfort. "I admit I was surprised to hear you had arrived, Ana. And without a lady's maid to boot."

She pursed her lips partly at the hint of teasing in his voice and partly at the use of her nickname. He should be calling her by her title, yet she didn't correct him. She'd been thinking of him as Lucas for too long to start calling the kettle black now.

"I took great care in coming here, I assure you, Mr. Tyler." She folded her arms.

He stared at her for a moment. As always, his gaze gave her the impression that he was sizing her up. And as always, she wondered how she fared in his estimation.

Undoubtedly, very ill.

"I am certain you were careful." He motioned to the chair she had been occupying when he entered. "Won't you have tea?"

She hesitated. Was this how business was conducted? Over tea like they were discussing the weather? It seemed so civilized and *mundane*. She had always pictured the work of spies being done by dim candlelight in darkened rooms, not in a parlor at two in the afternoon.

"I did not come on a social call."

He sighed as he took a seat himself and stared up at her. "Does it then follow that we must be unsociable?"

"I—" Oh, how he flummoxed her! She expected one thing and he invariably did the other. With a purse of her lips, she sat down and shrugged. "I suppose not. Yes. Tea would be lovely, thank you."

He rang for the service to be brought in and then tilted his head. "Very well, I can stand the suspense no longer. Tell me, my lady, what brings you here on this 'not social' call?"

She retrieved her reticule from the floor beside her chair and carefully withdrew the folded newspaper within. She smoothed the creases before she held it out toward Lucas. Her hand trembled. She tried to stop it, but failed.

"Did you see this?"

He took the paper and she watched as his slate gray eyes darted over the article in question. "Ah yes, Blighton's weekly Society paper. Very good for starting fires. Otherwise, it's complete rubbish."

"That may be, but it is well-read rubbish." Ana glared at him and he blinked back in innocence as if he were waiting for her to explain her upset. "We are in the paper."

He nodded. "I see that." With flourish, he shook out the pages and began to read, " 'And Blighton's is pleased to announce the return to society of Lady A.W. at Lady Westfield's soirée this week. And though she is still wearing her widow's weeds, an intriguing report says she will not be wearing them long. We've been told another lady saw her entangled in the arms of Mister L.T. on the terrace in the moonlight. Has Lady W. found love again?' " He paused for effect, though his face was calm as still water. "Scintillating."

"Oh, you frustrating man!" she burst out, getting to her feet. She snatched the offending article from his hands and paced to the fire where she took one final glance at it, winced, and tossed it into the flames. "Everyone will know this refers to us. Lady Bellingham made it common knowledge that she stumbled upon us at the ball."

"I imagine you're correct," Lucas said on another sigh. "But I don't know why this is a surprise to you. After all, I told you that your return caused a commotion. If you add the element of a potential romance to the mix, the *ton* will swarm around you just to see what will happen next. Society adores a good love story. Or a bad one."

Ana looked at him, dwarfing the chair he sat in. A lock of dark hair had fallen rakishly over one eye. He looked like the hero of every story she'd ever read. And yet Society believed it was possible she could find love with a man like him. She, who had only ever captured the attention of one man in her entire life. She, a woman who locked herself in the cellar of her best friend's house for days at a time. The idea gave her a treacherous thrill.

She tamped it down with a stern reminder of her

place. "You also told me that my being the center of attention would harm this case. How are we to continue our investigation if I am being watched and judged every time I pass through my front door? Our affiliation was supposed to be kept quiet."

He gave a little shrug as he leaned back in the chair and draped one elbow over the back with casual ease. "Supposed to. An interesting choice of words, Ana. You see, one thing you must learn about the field is that you cannot always control the turn of a case. There are no 'supposed tos' when it comes to an investigation. You must adapt, change when the circumstances surround you change."

She drew in a breath as he met her eyes. Though he seemed jovial and relaxed, she saw for the first time just how involved he was, how interested he was in how she handled herself. And how would she? She had never liked change. Rules were made so that everything went according to plan. That was the life she led.

And Lucas was now telling her that rules and regulations had no place in the field.

"What are you suggesting?"

He didn't answer, but very slowly he rose to his feet. Step by step, he came toward her. She wanted to back away, but she stood her ground. She had to. Partly because she needed to prove a point . . . and partly because the hot fireplace was at her back.

He stopped less than a foot in front of her and tilted his head. "If we ignore the report and are not seen in any more"—he smiled wolfishly—"compromising positions, then the interest in you will fade." His smile fell as he reached out and fingered a black ruffle at the shoulder of her mourning gown. "Especially if you insist on wearing widow's weeds everywhere you go."

She lurched back from his questing fingers and would have gone down on her backside in the process if not for the steadying hand he reached out and put on her arm. Once she regained her balance, he pulled away, leaving her bereft and relieved in almost equal measure. Confusion was her only constant.

"Ah, Fannie, tea. Thank you," he said with a smile toward the door. Ana turned and watched a maid quickly set a tea service on the sideboard. He waved her away and poured two cups himself.

"Does that answer your burning question, my lady?" he asked as he put a bit of cream and sugar in one cup, then motioned to the other.

She nodded without speaking. She couldn't really find words after the strange encounter. He had touched her, she had recoiled, and yet, she felt anything but horror. Damn this entire blasted situation.

"Is that yes to cream and sugar or yes that I've answered your questions?" he asked with a chuckle.

She couldn't help but be eased by his smile and laughter. Her shoulders relaxed. "To both, I suppose."

"Good. Since you're here, perhaps we can go over some evidence while we share our tea."

She cocked her head. It was as if the heat between

them had never existed. To him, it probably didn't. An unwelcome disappointment touched her. A man like Lucas Tyler was used to the power he held sway over women. And hadn't Emily said that he would use any method in his arsenal to control the turn of their case? Perhaps that included taking advantage of her attraction, of her loneliness.

That she could not allow.

She set her mouth into a thin line as she forced an attitude more befitting business. "Yes. I would be happy to review the evidence."

She took the cup of tea he offered and followed him through an adjoining door to another room. She realized this was his office, a private place in his home where Lord knew how many secrets were hidden. She watched as he unlocked a compartment on his desk and withdrew a pile of papers.

"Here." He motioned his elbow toward a large table on the opposite side of the room. "Let's spread these out."

She took a few of the items and they spread them across the tabletop until it was covered by notes, reports, and a large map she had last seen when Charlie briefed her on the status of the case. One by one, the places where spies had been attacked were marked on the map.

Ana drew a long breath and stepped closer. Lucas leaned down and his shoulder just brushed her back.

With a jolt at the contact, she cast a quick side glance at him. He didn't even notice as he focused on the items before them. She set her jaw. If he could be unaffected by their proximity, so could she.

"I've been thinking about the attacks," she said, happy that she could form words at all.

"And?" His gaze flitted to her.

"What kind of patterns are there to the attacks themselves? Is there some order the spies are being chosen in? Perhaps if we learn the reasons behind those who are harmed and those who aren't, we could trace the attacks back to their source."

Lucas straightened up and stared with open admiration that warmed Ana to her very toes. "A very interesting proposition, Anastasia."

He ducked his gaze back to the map. He pointed to a cluster of four markers on the East End in Southwark. "The first three were all in the same general area surrounding a rough little pub called Wickerbys. Not a surprise, really. It is a well-known place for spies to gather and exchange information."

Ana cocked her head. "Well known to whom? The general public could not know such a thing or else all the spies in His Majesty's service would be easily unmasked."

"Known to others within my organization," he corrected. "That information might be easily ascertained through good intelligence."

"What about these two?" She pointed to two other markers on the map. This time they were both within the confines of Hyde Park.

He glanced at a sheet that told which incidents had happened when and where. "The first was an attack on a spy who was meeting a contact at the park. The second was a spy who was not on assignment. He was simply there for personal reasons, meeting with friends, and was attacked." A shadow passed over his face. "He was the first spy to die. The others were merely wounded and taken out of service."

Ana thought of Emily with a shiver. Having one friend attacked was difficult enough. Lucas must have known so many of these men who had been cut down in the field. To be helpless against such atrocities had to wear on him. Especially considering the kind of man she knew him to be even after such a short acquaintance.

"Could his attack have been mere coincidence?" she asked, watching his face as he cleared the emotions away. How she wished she could do the same. It was something she'd never really been able to do, despite all her training.

Lucas shrugged, his stare holding on the marker that represented the dead spy. "It's always a possibility, but he didn't live the kind of life that would lead to such violence outside of his work. And the attack was so much like the others that we must assume it was related."

She nodded once. "What *are* the common elements of the attacks, Lucas?"

He started before he spun to face her. She felt the blood drain from her face. Had she really just called him by his given name? Damn it!

"I—" she stammered.

He lifted a hand. "I like to hear my name from your lips."

She sucked in a breath before she turned away. Her cheeks burned as she moved blindly to the window. She was shaking as she tried to regain calm without success. Cover her reactions? She wished she didn't have them at all. Especially these unexpected reactions of heat and desire and fear that mixed in a potent brew in her mind.

"May I ask you a question?"

Ana felt his stare burn at her back and she forced herself to turn. She hoped her expression was somewhat in control. "Of course."

"Why haven't you ever entered the field?" He cocked his head. She wasn't sure of what kind of answer he wanted to hear by the tone of his voice or the look on his face.

She hesitated as her gaze drifted down to the black mourning gown she wore. Lucas followed her line of vision and his face tightened. The moment stretched out between them uncomfortably as she searched for a way to explain herself without giving him too much personal information. It was far too dangerous to explain her inner emotions, her battles with her grief, to a man like this. He was trained in twisting those things to use against suspects. He could easily do the same to her.

She was still struggling when the office door suddenly opened behind Lucas, and a footman rolled a man in a wheelchair inside. He seemed startled by her presence for a moment, as did Lucas when he turned.

"Am I interrupting something?"

Chapter 6

Lucas winced. He couldn't help it. Although it had been a year since his best friend, Henry Bowerly, was cut down in one of the first attacks on the spies, he still wasn't used to seeing him in that contraption. It stung with the same intensity it had the first time.

"Tyler?" Henry said with a tilt of his head. His gaze slipped to Ana.

Lucas shook off his reaction and forced a smile. "Of course you aren't interrupting, Henry. Lady Anastasia Whittig, may I present the Marquis of Cliffield?"

Lucas turned toward Ana to find her staring at his friend. Her eyes were wide, her cheeks pale as she gave a nod. She stared just a moment too long at the chair, then her eyes darted away as high color replaced the pallor of her skin.

He sighed. There was no blaming her. It was rare to see a man so young in such a device.

"I—I—" Ana clenched her hands in front of her, trembling as she fought for breath. Fought for words. "I can explain why I am here."

Henry tilted his head, but before his friend could interrupt, Lucas stepped forward.

"It is all right, Ana," he said softly. Her eyes flitted to him, questioning, pleading and his heart stirred in a strange, unwelcome way.

"Yes, Lady Whittig," Henry said. She jolted at the sound of her name from a man she didn't know. His friend continued hurriedly. "I know your purpose here very well. I have been assisting in making assignments for the spies in the War Department since I was injured." A shadow crossed Henry's face before he covered it with his usual jovial mask. "I know who you are. And about your group."

Ana stared in speechless hesitation. Lucas saw the wheels turning in her mind as she digested what Henry had to say. The doubt that flickered in her eyes stirred his admiration. She didn't just accept what she was told because someone she trusted—or at least he *hoped* she trusted him on some level—hadn't denied it. She was perfectly able and willing to come to her own conclusions about Henry.

Lucas stepped forward to place a comforting hand

on her forearm. Her gaze snapped away from his friend and up to his face at the unexpected motion. Heat flashed between them again, surprising him, though it shouldn't. Heat was the only thing he could depend upon when it came to Ana. Otherwise, she was an utter surprise at every turn.

He drew his hand away. "What Henry says is true. He works for the War Department, and he has helped me with my investigation thus far. You don't need to fear that he would reveal your secret."

Her face relaxed just a fraction at Lucas's statement, but he noted her wariness did not flee completely.

"I see." Her tone was even. Noncommittal. Then she stepped forward and held out a hand. "It's a pleasure to meet you, Lord Cliffield."

Henry took her offering and they shook. Then he glanced behind her at the table. His face grew somber. "Looking at the evidence, are you?"

Lucas nodded. It was good that Henry was here. Not only could he contribute to their investigation, but his presence put cold water on whatever desires Lucas had a hard time fighting when he was alone with Ana.

"Yes. Anastasia was just looking at the order of the attacks and wondering about common threads between them." He glanced up and smiled at her.

She seemed stunned that he was giving her credit for the notion, but then a little blush colored the apples of her cheeks and her lips tilted. "I hoped if we could establish some kind of pattern, it would lead us to the origin of the attacks and the person behind them."

Henry's eyes snapped up for a brief moment, then returned to the map. He lingered on one flag in particular and his frown lengthened. Lucas shifted as he awaited his friend's response.

"It would be a good idea," Henry finally said, his voice distant. "Except we've already done such an analysis."

"You have?" Both Ana and Lucas answered together. Ana's brow wrinkled as she shot a glance his way. Lucas ignored her questioning stare.

"When? Why wasn't I involved?" he asked.

Henry shrugged before he placed his hands on the large, metal front wheels of his chair and pushed until he moved backward, away from the table and the map. Lucas resisted the urge to assist his friend. Henry was independent and didn't like to be aided.

"Sometimes a man must investigate his own tragedies, Tyler," he said softly.

Ana cleared her throat. "Can you explain, my lord?"

Henry glanced over to her. "She doesn't know? You haven't told her?"

Lucas shook his head.

Henry returned his focus to Ana and Lucas saw his friend's grim determination. "Look to the map, my lady."

She hesitated, then did as she had been told.

"The green flag there beside Wickerby's . . ."

She nodded as she motioned to the little flag. "Yes?"

"That flag represents me. The attack that put me in this chair and ended whatever future as I had as a spy. Whatever future I had, period."

Ana fought not to allow her natural reaction of horror and sympathy to flash across her face. For Henry's sake, but also for Lucas's. While he'd been able to hide his emotions toward everything else, when his friend talked about his attack, they had become so clear they almost made her wince.

She looked at the benign marker that represented so much pain. *This* was Lucas's vulnerability. His drive. His reason for wanting to solve this case. And suddenly she wanted to help him. Worse, to touch him. But she couldn't. Partly because Henry was in the room, partly because it was wrong to do so, and partly because he was standing so stiffly that she feared if she did, he might break. His jaw was set with anger and frustration, his eyes hard as cold flint.

She turned away from the draw of him and focused on Henry. "I am very sorry," she said softly. "I cannot imagine what you have gone through."

He smiled, but the expression was thin. How often did he hear those same empty platitudes? She wished she could take them back.

"Thank you, my lady. But that is why I have been so involved in this case. There are no common elements to the assaults, I assure you. Just that all the men attacked were spies. And all have either died or been removed from the field due to injury or discovery." Henry sighed.

She nodded, but her mind continued to whirl despite his reassurances. Why hadn't the Marquis included Lucas in his private investigation of common threads? Or even mentioned it to him before?

"How is your friend, my lady?"

With a start, Ana refocused. "My friend?"

"Lady Allington." Henry's mouth twitched with an emotion she could not place. "She was recently hurt, was she not?"

Nausea rose in Ana's throat, choking her as she thought of Emily. Dear God, what if she ended up in a contraption like Lord Cliffield's chair? Adam reported she was improving each time he saw her, but who could be sure of the long-term effects of her devastating wound?

"Yes," she said softly. "In an attack that could be related to this case."

She was surprised when Henry's eyes widened and Lucas straightened up behind her as he stared at his friend.

"You believe the attack might be related to the other spies?" Henry asked, his voice low and deceptively cool considering the light of emotion in his eyes.

Lucas hesitated and Ana felt him searching for a way to answer. Finally, he nodded. "It very well may be."

"I wish you had told me your suspicions," his friend

said, hands clenching in his lap. Then he smiled at Ana like the exchange hadn't occurred. "I should probably get back to my own affairs. I simply wished to see one of the mythical Lady Spies."

She nodded, uneasy now that Lucas had turned away and paced to the window. Was he angry with her? Or did he simply believe she was a fool for revealing something about their case? And why did she still want to go over and touch his arm? Comfort him?

"I hope I did not disappoint you, my lord," she said, continuing to glance at Lucas from the corner of her vision.

"No," Henry said with another smile as he rang a little bell that was attached to his chair with a golden rope. Immediately, the door opened and the Marquis's servant appeared to wheel him away. "You did not disappoint, my lady. Good afternoon to you both."

The door shut behind him and immediately Ana turned to face Lucas. "I am so sorry."

He kept his back to her for a long moment, then turned. "Why?"

"I let our thoughts about the cause of Emily's attack slip out when I wasn't aware of how much information Lord Cliffield already knew. Clearly you had not shared that assertion with him. I should have known better." She wrung her hands as every curse word she knew— and that was quite a few thanks to Emily's education— ran through her head to abuse her.

Lucas stepped toward her and she was pleased to

see a shadow of his usual smile tilted his lips. "You were told that Henry was an ally in our investigation, why would you think I'd be angry you shared something with him?" He sighed. "It is my fault that my friend doesn't know all my thoughts on the subject, not yours."

She watched him for a moment as he moved to look at the map again. "May I ask you a question?"

He nodded.

"Why didn't you tell him that Emily's attack could be related to this case?"

He hesitated, then turned and looked her in the eye. It was such a sudden move that she hadn't time to prepare herself or temper her reaction. A blast of something she could only describe as pure lust rocked through her, heating her to her very core when the steel of his stare locked with hers. She hated herself for it, yet a part of her welcomed the heat. Welcomed the way just a look from this man could make her feel alive like she hadn't felt for so very long.

But then she saw the same sadness in his expression that she'd felt when he looked at Henry Bowerly. And the same empathy and desire to make his pain go away touched her in a place deeper than lust.

"Lucas?" she prodded softly.

He shrugged one shoulder. "Perhaps for the same reason he kept his investigations private. We have been friends for as long as I can recall, Ana. We try to protect each other."

Her heart thudded so loudly she could scarce hear anything else. "May we declare a truce?"

He grinned but the tension around his eyes remained, as did her desire to smooth it away. There was so much more to this man than the cocky spy Emily had described. So much more than the infuriating devil who captivated Ana's attention despite herself. There was loyalty in him. Powerful ability as a spy. There was also more emotion than she wagered he ever wanted anyone to guess.

"Were we at war, my lady?"

"Perhaps not openly, but I will admit I have not made this easier for you." She cleared her throat uncomfortably. "And you have fought me, as well."

He tilted his head in acquiescence, but did not answer verbally. His stare was growing more focused by the moment and she found it difficult to continue.

Swallowing, she said, "After meeting your friend and hearing the story of his attack, I have realized that you and I should not battle each other. On the contrary, we have more in common than perhaps I allowed myself to believe."

"How so?"

His face was unreadable. Damn, but he was a good spy. Right now she wished she could turn off her disturbing emotions and only let him see a mask.

"We each have a personal stake in pursuing this case."

She swallowed hard when he took a long step toward

her. Everything in her told her to run, but she held her ground. She trembled, but not from fear as he stopped just a breath in front of her.

"I—I am bound to protect Emily. And you wish to avenge Lord Cliffield. We are working toward the same goal, whether we wish to work side by side or not."

Dear Lord, but he smelled good. Like soapy water and clean male skin. And his voice was rough as sandpaper when he said, "But we also both know how dangerous it can be to allow personal issues to influence a case."

She managed to lift her gaze to meet his and immediately wished she hadn't. He wasn't just talking about their mutual hope to see a friend's potential killer brought to justice anymore. What he was referring to went deeper. Right to the heart of the desire she kept trying to deny.

"Yes," she squeaked and wished her voice was stronger.

His hand lifted, and for the first time, she noticed just how big it was. How big he seemed to be. Why hadn't she noticed that on the terrace a few days before? His fingers swayed toward her cheek. To her horror, she found herself fighting the urge to lean toward his hand. Then he seemed to remember himself, for his hand dropped to her shoulder instead where it burned against the thin satin of her sleeve. His heat rolled through her like a fire across dry wood until she feared she would combust then and there.

"If personal desires are dangerous," he said quietly, his voice low and husky and bubbling with the same need that brewed inside her, "then perhaps we should keep them out of this."

She felt herself nodding, even as she stared at his mouth. He was going to kiss her. Even before he started to lean in, she knew it as clearly as she knew her name. The fact didn't even surprise her. What did surprise her was that she *wanted* his kiss.

So very, very much.

That treacherous thought hit her like a physical slap and she recoiled from it by pulling away.

"I—We—Yes." Idiot! She spun for the door. "Good-bye. Just—good afternoon."

Then she all but ran from the room, heart racing and body shaking. And wanting in a powerful way she had never experienced before.

Not even with her husband.

Chapter 7

❦

S he was the only woman wearing black, but that wasn't why Anastasia was surrounded by people. Despite the fact that she had not danced all evening, she was the belle of the damned ball. Lucas swigged a gulp of his drink, eyes narrowing.

Since she had entered the room more than two hours before, she had been swarmed by old friends, social climbers . . . and men. Oh, so many men. Probably the same ones who his contacts had reported sent bouquets to her home every day. His jaw popped as he clenched his teeth.

Currently she was talking to the very handsome, very rich, very *titled* Earl of Rawlingworth and smiling away like she was having the best time ever. He'd never hated the man before, but now Lucas's blood boiled as she glanced up and laughed at something the gentleman said.

It wasn't just that she was surrounded by admirers that made his fists clench and his frustration rise. It was that *he* hadn't gotten within a breath of her all night. No, Ana had been avoiding him. Just as she had been since the afternoon in his office when he was so close to kissing her. She had responded politely enough to his note asking her to meet him at the ball, but she had not approached him, and her words hadn't indicated she felt anything for him but a businesslike acquaintance.

Which burned in his belly like fire. He had felt her desire that day as strong as his own. Whether she denied it or not, it was there. And he felt a very intense, very strange need to pull her into a dark corner and prove that to her. Pull her out of those widow's weeds and . . .

Enough!

Rawlingworth raised her gloved hand to his lips and bowed before he moved away into the crowd, leaving Ana unaccompanied for the first time in hours. Now was the perfect time to make his move. Making his way around the perimeter of the ballroom, Lucas measured his breath and slowed his steps. The last thing he wanted to do was let Ana see how much she affected him. Or the rest of the *ton* since the gossips were already on the alert when it came to the two of them.

She noticed his approach when he was fifteen paces away. Her eyes widened and she thrust her shoulders back, as if preparing for a battle rather than conversation. He sucked in a breath before he gave her a smile.

"Good evening, my lady," he drawled.

She nodded briefly. "Mr. Tyler."

He sighed. "We're back to that, are we?"

"It may be for the best. It's certainly proper."

She didn't meet his gaze, but instead looked out over the ballroom as if searching for a more interesting companion. He wasn't sure if that display was for the benefit of the watching eyes around them or for him. Either way, he clenched his teeth in annoyance.

"I hope you recall that you are here to work tonight, not amuse yourself," he said and immediately wished he had tempered his peevish tone.

Her gaze swung to him and he was surprised how cool her expression was. Unhurt by his harshness. She arched one brow. "I'm very well aware of why I'm here. I have been waiting for *your* move."

With a purse of his lips, Lucas held back a curse. This little slip of a woman, with her spectacles and her damned mourning gowns, set him on his heels like the most experienced courtesan never had. She infuriated and aroused him in equal, powerful measure. And he didn't understand either emotion. Nor did he wish to feel them, not if they provided such damned distraction.

"In ten minutes, slip away from the party," he directed with military precision. "When you leave the ballroom, turn left down the long hallway and then right into an adjoining hall. I shall meet you there. Don't let anyone follow you or notice your departure, do you understand?"

She nodded once before she walked away, leaving him with only a hint of her enchanting scent as a reminder that she'd been there at all. He gritted his teeth as he set out through the ballroom. After this investigation was over, he was definitely in line to go over his training methods. He obviously needed to remember what a spy was and was not supposed to do.

Of course, when this case was over he could finally breathe easy again. He would forget Anastasia completely.

Right.

He stepped into the shadow of an ornate statue that was in the hallway where he was to meet Ana and counted to ten in his head. Slowly, calm returned to his body. His blood stopped rushing in his ears. He remembered who he was and why he was here. For the spies who had been cut down, for Henry, he would control himself.

Perhaps a visit to a brothel was in order. It had been a few months since he had bedded a woman. Likely that was the real reason for his distraction when it came to Ana.

Of course, he hadn't ever felt like such a lusty animal

around Emily Redgrave, who was equally pretty. Just not irresistible to him.

"Damn it," he muttered. Then words fell away as Ana came around the corner into the side hallway.

She held the skirt of her black gown in her fist as she crept into view. Her brown hair, which had been done in a simple style, was beginning to droop after a night in the hot ballroom. Little strands of it framed her oval face. She would be beautiful in red. Blue. Gold.

Nothing at all.

"Lucas?" she whispered and it startled him from his thoughts.

"I'm here." He stepped out from behind the statue and she gave a little jump of surprise before she collected herself and stepped forward.

"I'm sorry it took me so long. I was waylaid by Lord Evenport on my way out of the ballroom."

His eyes narrowed at the mention of the dandified womanizer's name. "Just come with me."

She tilted her head at the harsh tone, but did as she was told, falling into step beside him as he approached one of the doors in the hallway. He looked around.

"Keep watch," he ordered as he fished in his pocket for a lock pick.

She looked at him evenly for a moment before she reached out and turned the doorknob. To his surprise, it swung open.

"How did you know it was unlocked?" he asked as he ushered her inside.

"I didn't." She shrugged. "But protocol reminds us to check a door before we start utilizing other means of entry."

His lips thinned and he wasn't sure which emotion inside him was stronger: annoyance or begrudging amusement. "I've never been one for protocol," he said.

A laugh was her reply as she shut the door behind them. "Clearly. Will you now explain to me what we're doing snooping around our host's home?"

"How much do you know about Lord Sansbury?" he asked as he glanced around the private office. Nothing seemed immediately suspicious, but he wouldn't expect a man to put his lowest deeds in plain sight.

"Not much," she admitted as she folded her arms. "He's given to the Society's charity for Widows and Orphans on several occasions, otherwise I hear little of his activities. But if you have suspicions about the man, why don't you share them?"

He sat down at the desk and carefully tugged the drawer. The top one opened without hindrance and he began a slow search through the various papers as he talked.

"I've received some new information in the last few days about Sansbury. He may be involved in the attacks on the spies."

She cocked her head. "Who did you receive your intelligence from?"

He lifted his gaze. An odd question. "From Henry."

Her brow wrinkled. "Where did he get it from?"

He got to his feet and came around the desk, distracted from his search by the incredulous expression on her face. And by the fact that he didn't know the answer to her question.

"From research, I suppose. Like you, he deciphers information, only he has been forced by circumstance, rather than inclination."

She shook her head, still unconvinced. "But how did he get new information? This is your case. If he is conducting research for you, wouldn't he do that research based on information you brought him, rather than giving *you* new information? Did he tell you its source?"

"You sound as though you doubt him." He folded his arms. "You've only met him once."

She shrugged, but she was watching him closely. "I neither doubt nor believe him. As you said, I have no relationship to him. But I do know that it is unwise to make searches of the house of an otherwise respectable man without knowing the basis of accusations against him."

He opened and shut his mouth. Heat burned inside him, but he wasn't sure of the reason. Was it frustration that he didn't have answers to her questions? Or anger at himself that he hadn't ever thought to ask them?

That was ridiculous! He knew Henry. He trusted his friend. Ana was simply being contrary yet again. So much for the "truce" they had made a few days before.

"Would you rather let a potential traitor go because

you doubt a valid source?" He stepped closer so he didn't have to raise his voice.

She shook her head, though her eyes widened at the way he moved. "Of course not, I only—"

Before she could finish, Lucas held up a hand to silence her. There was a very faint sound from the hallway. He strained to hear it again.

Ana scowled. "Don't you raise your hand at me! I'm—"

He tossed her a glare as he stepped to the door and pressed his ear to the wood.

Blast! The sound he had heard were footsteps coming toward them at an even, sure clip.

"What is it?" Ana whispered, moving toward him.

He cast a side glance at her. "Someone is coming. Stay there."

Her eyes widened and the blood drained from her face as she watched him, but she did as she had been told. In fact, he was surprised that the slight tremble of her hands was her only reaction. She didn't faint or go into hysterics, she merely waited.

The footsteps grew closer and Lucas moved away from the door. Whoever it was, they were likely about to burst into the room and there were no alternative escape routes. Alone, he could have managed to squeeze out the window in time, but he didn't think both he and Ana could.

"Come here," he whispered.

Ana tilted her head in question, but followed his di-

rection. Behind them, the doorknob rattled and she
stiffened as her frightened gaze flitted up to his.

Lucas didn't think. He didn't ask her leave. He caught
her arm, hauled her against his chest and dropped his
lips to hers.

It had been five years since Ana had been kissed.
And it had never been like this. Gilbert's kisses ca-
ressed, a gentle expression of the tender love they felt
for one another. Lucas *possessed*. Every bit of strength
and power that flowed through his body was equaled
in the way his lips pressed to hers. And then the tip of
his tongue traced the crease of her lips and he claimed
even further.

He demanded entry into her mouth, and she acqui-
esced without a hint of hesitation. The world was getting hot. It was shrinking. A fog clouded her mind as
Lucas stroked her tongue, bringing back faded memories of pleasure and heat and sin. Her body tingled
and her fists, which had been clenched at her sides,
slowly opened as she slid trembling fingers to his fore-
arms. She clung to him for dear life, riding out all the
wild, new sensations.

It was utterly amazing how quickly matters could
spin out of control. But they were. Or she was. At that
particular moment, she could remember nothing, feel
nothing, desire nothing but more. More Lucas. More
kissing. Just more.

And then the sound of a throat clearing reminded

her of all the things she had forgotten. Immediately, she fought the tidal wave of desire that choked her rational mind and shoved back against Lucas's chest. He pulled away from her lips, but his arms stayed around her in an iron grip as he tilted his head toward the door. Their host, Lord Sansbury, was standing staring at the two of them with an equal amount of interest and disdain.

Ana's cheeks burned as she struggled in Lucas's arms, but he refused to release her, despite the precarious nature of their position. It was almost like he didn't want to hide what they had been doing.

But that was just it, wasn't it? He hadn't kissed her because of some overwhelming passion he could no longer deny. It was done because he heard Sansbury's approach. The kiss was part of a ruse. It meant nothing to him. She tilted her head to look at him. That was why he seemed so calm. So unmoved, even as her heart raced and her thoughts were heavy and slow with desire. She had *liked* kissing him.

And if she were honest with herself, she wished she were still doing it. Horror flooded her, matching need with equal intensity. What had she done?

"Ah, Sansbury. Sorry, didn't see you there," Lucas drawled, finally allowing her out of his hot, confusing embrace. She backed away a step, taking natural refuge behind his larger frame as she tried to look anywhere but in Sansbury's direction.

"Quite." The other man's voice was cold, dismissive. "This is my private office, you know."

Lucas grinned, a cocky gleam in his eye even as Ana felt the tension in his body. "Is it? My apologies, my lord, I wasn't really paying attention when I came in."

Sansbury seemed to relax at Lucas's demeanor. Ana couldn't help but watch him in wonder. Charlie was right, he was a good spy. Just sheepish enough to be believable and cocky enough to fulfill his reputation. She shook her head. She had a job to do, too, and that was to follow Lucas's lead.

"Our apologies, my lord," she added, dipping her gaze. Her embarrassment wasn't hard to pretend, at least. She felt it in every pore. That and a lot of other feelings she didn't want to fathom or name at present. She had no doubt they would plague her for many days to come.

"Yes, well," Sansbury motioned for the door. "No harm done, I suppose. But I would appreciate if you returned to the ball."

Lucas turned to her with a small smile as he offered her an arm. She stared at it for a moment. What had once seemed innocent was now very dangerous. Touching him had a new meaning after that kiss, and she was actually afraid of doing it. But when his eyes widened and he stared at her expectantly, she did what she feared and slipped her hand into the crook of his elbow.

She was greeted by heat, but fought her natural

urge to pull away and run as fast as she could. At least until they were alone, she had to keep up the ruse. She gave a demure nod as they passed into the hall.

As soon as Sansbury closed the door behind them, she pulled her hand away from Lucas. To her surprise, he caught it and pulled it back into his arm.

"Our cover," he hissed, tone terse even as he managed to keep his expression open and bland.

She blinked back unexpected tears as they moved down the hallway back to the ballroom. The ramifications of what they'd done were beginning to hit her now. Dear God, if Sansbury spoke, even just to one other person, the news could spread like wildfire. She had betrayed Gilbert's memory and soon everyone would know it.

"I cannot believe this is happening," she whispered, more to herself than to Lucas.

He rewarded her statement with a sharp glare, but that was the only indication that he felt any emotion whatsoever about their kiss. "It was do that or be caught in a situation that would have been difficult to explain. I made a choice."

She dared a glance at him from the corner of her eye. His lips were thin with grim determination. He really didn't care. He really hadn't felt anything. For him the kiss had been an act, nothing more. Her heart sank. She had been the only one to lose herself in desire and emotion. God, she was an idiot of the highest order to think it might have meant something.

No! She shook off her deepening despair. What did she care that he wasn't moved? The last thing she wanted was for him to be moved! The kiss was a mistake. If Lucas felt nothing when he touched her, all the better. That would only ensure it would never be repeated and she could bury her reaction away where she wouldn't have to face it ever again.

The buzz of the ballroom drifted into the hallway, and Lucas suddenly released her. He glanced around before he said, "You go back inside first. We might as well not draw even more attention to ourselves than we already have."

She nodded, avoiding his eyes as she started back into the ballroom. He caught her arm and she looked up. To her surprise, he wasn't smiling. Even the normally cocky light had faded from his stare. And that scared her.

"No matter what happens, Ana, you mustn't behave as if anything out of the ordinary occurred tonight. If we're lucky, Sansbury will exercise discretion."

It had been a long time since she was in Society. She didn't know Sansbury's disposition well enough to know if he was the kind to spread tales.

Blood rushed to her cheeks as reality hit home yet again. "What do you think the chances of that are?"

Lucas hesitated just long enough to answer her question without ever saying a word, then shrugged. "Whatever happens, do not react. I'll come to you later and we can discuss it."

Numbness took over, spreading throughout Ana's body. She didn't even fight the tide. It was too overpowering and at least it helped her ignore her urge to run away.

"Very well," she whispered as she slipped back into the ballroom. As she walked, she lifted a hand to her mouth. She still tasted Lucas on her lips. And it was good. Drugging.

And despite everything, she wished she could kiss him again.

Chapter 8

Ana's head spun as she slipped into the house. She gave a brief nod to Benson as he took her wrap and made polite, empty inquiries about her evening, but she was only going through the motions. While she smiled and talked, her mind was spinning.

That kiss. That stupid, dratted, unexpected kiss still burned her lips when she allowed herself to think about it longer than a brief moment. And she had been forced to think about it. Because Lucas was correct in assuming Sansbury would be free with his telling of the tale.

The news had started as a whisper, and by the end of the evening, her passionate kiss with Lucas had been the topic of conversation throughout the ballroom.

At least it had been passionate on her part.

"Are you well, my lady?"

She started. "Yes, of course, Benson. Just—well, I am not used to these events and I think I've tired myself."

He nodded and his stern countenance seemed almost sympathetic before he snapped back into propriety. "Should I call for a bath to be drawn?"

She hesitated. That did sound heavenly, but it was so late. And with her nerves frayed and skin still jumping from Lucas's touch, she wasn't sure it was the best idea. The last thing she wanted was sinful fantasies of him in the vulnerability of the bath. "No, I think not tonight, but thank you."

"As you wish, good evening."

She waved her good night as she trudged up the staircase toward her chambers and what she knew would be a long and sleepless night tormented by memories of Lucas's mouth swooping down on hers, demanding and claiming desires she had no right to feel. And Society had eaten it up! The idea of a romance between the "sad widow" and her "dashing rogue" enthralled the masses. By tomorrow, the news would have spread to every corner of the *ton*.

Her temples began to throb at the thought, and she lifted her fingers to press against them. Oh, it was too much to fathom. Their case had been threatened and so was her very sanity by the strange feelings that now bubbled inside her.

She stumbled up the hall until she reached Emily's

door. Her friend was probably asleep, but Ana turned the knob regardless. She had developed the habit of checking on her each night before she went to her own bed. Nearly losing her made Ana wary of Emily's condition.

She stepped inside and was surprised to find Emily's candle lit. Her friend was propped up just slightly, her tangled blonde hair spread across the pillows, and she held a book in her hand, though she didn't seem to be focusing on its pages. At the click of the door, Emily glanced up.

"Hello!" Her face registered relief as she set her book aside.

"My goodness, I didn't know you'd be awake," Ana said as she stepped inside. "I didn't mean to interrupt your reading."

Emily waved at the novel with a wince of pain that shot through Ana like the bullet that had felled her friend. Emily was so strong. To see her like this was heartbreaking, despite how much she had improved in a short period of time.

"Oh, it was a ridiculous story anyway. Something my lady's maid gave me to pass the time. You know Bonnie, she's a romantic, so of course it's a lot of rot about love and forever. I would much rather talk to you."

Now it was Ana's turn to wince. Love and forever. She'd had it once and thought it was a once-in-a-lifetime experience for her. Tonight had turned those beliefs on their head and everything was suddenly confused.

"What brings you home so early?"

Emily's question brought her out of her reverie and she tilted her head in surprise. "Early? Emily, it is after three."

Her friend's frustration was plain as she clenched her coverlet in her fingers. "Oh. I have no sense of time anymore. Every moment is the same for me. I hate being confined to this blasted bed. I hate not being useful!"

Ana smiled her sympathy. For the first time since she met Meredith and Emily, she was beginning to understand their desire to be active. To be in the field. She had once feared investigations, but now she could see why her friends craved the thrill. Why they thrived on the adventure and danger that waited around every corner.

"Perhaps I could be of some help!" Emily's face lit up. "I could assist you."

Ana started at the thought. Emily wasn't well enough to be out of her bed, let alone work. Aside from which, she wasn't certain she wanted anyone else involved in the case, lest her friends see how deeply involved she now was with her reluctant partner.

"How?" she asked.

Emily's eyes sparkled with the possibility of being occupied again. "I could do research like you used to do for Meredith and me. Or we could talk through the case together."

Anastasia stiffened as a sudden, unpleasant thought

occurred to her. "Do you not trust me to work on my own?"

Emily cocked her head. "Of course I do. Why in the world would you say such a thing?"

She turned away from her friend's intense stare. "I have little experience in the field. Perhaps you don't think I'm handling myself well."

That was certainly her own fear. Especially after tonight.

"I have no idea how you are or are not handling yourself," Emily said with a shrug that was immediately accompanied by a sharp intake of breath that indicated pain. Ana stepped toward her, but her friend warded her off with a raised hand. "No."

A moment passed as Emily rested back on her pillows, her breath shallow as she struggled for control over the ache. Tears rushed to Ana's eyes as she watched helplessly. Finally, the gray pallor of pain faded from Emily's face, and color returned to her cheeks.

"I'm fine. It's passed."

"Perhaps you should take some of your—" Ana began, moving toward the bedside table.

"No." Emily's sharp tone stopped her. "No. If I take that poison, I won't be able to think. Please, Ana."

Her eyes went wide. She'd never heard such a mournful tone from her best friend. Emily's eyes were wide, unshed tears glistening in them.

"Please. I'm asking you to involve me in this case for *my* sake. Not because I doubt your abilities. Not because I doubt your strength. Please. Let me help in some way."

Any argument Ana would have made faded as she came to the bed. She sat down in the chair beside Emily and reached for her friend's hand. For a moment, they only sat together in silence before Ana said, "Of course. Of course I desire your help and your counsel will be very useful, I'm sure."

As long as Emily didn't figure out *too* much, that was. But Ana could control what she said and didn't say to her friend.

"So what can you tell me?" Emily asked.

"There isn't much to tell. Lucas and I have investigated several options when it comes to who could be attacking the spies. We've mostly reviewed the evidence and tonight we were at Sansbury's ball. Apparently he is a suspect in the attacks."

Emily wrinkled her brow. "Sansbury? He might be a bit of a lecher, but I don't see him as a traitor. His loose tongue alone would do him in."

Ana nodded. The man certainly did have that, as she had learned from bitter experience.

"That was my thought, as well. But Lucas had the information from his friend within the War Department, Henry Bowerly."

"The Marquis of Cliffield?" Emily peered up at the ceiling.

"Yes. Did you ever meet him? They're old friends."

Ana thought of her first impression of Cliffield in his

wheelchair. And the way he had refused to consider her thought that the attacks were linked somehow.

"No. But Tyler and I didn't meet more than a few times before I was hurt." Emily sighed. "Cliffield was injured, was he not?"

"Yes. In one of the first attacks on the spies." Ana sighed. "He is in a wheelchair. It bothers Lucas."

Emily's eyes narrowed. "I thought I heard you say that a moment ago, but now I'm certain. Did you just call Mr. Tyler *Lucas*?"

Ana stopped herself from babbling. Had she called him by his given name? Dear Lord, she had.

"I—"

Emily pursed her lips. "It took you two years to stop referring to Charlie as Mr. Isley! And I thought you didn't want to work with Tyler, so why do you care if the injury to his friend causes him pain?"

Ana sucked in her breath. Why had she said that? It didn't matter in the scope of the case. Not only did it reveal too much about how close she'd grown to Lucas, but it betrayed him, as well. She shouldn't have shared her thoughts on the subject.

"I—I don't care, of course," she lied. "It was merely an observation."

Emily looked less than convinced, but she shook her head. "So what does Cliffield believe, if he is involved in this case?"

Ana shrugged, trying to cover her earlier slip by being detached now. Unlike Emily or Meredith or Lucas, she wasn't practiced enough at covering her emotions to believe she was successful.

"It was strange. Lucas and I were discussing the possibility of common elements in the incidents. Of finding links and letting those links lead us back to the source of the assaults."

Emily nodded. "A very good idea."

"But Henry dismissed that. He said he had already investigated that possibility and it was a dead lead." She thought of Lucas's reaction. "Lucas was surprised. He wasn't aware Henry was doing any private investigation. It seemed odd to me that Henry wouldn't share such vital information with the spy actually assigned to the case, even if this case is personal to him because of his injuries."

Emily nodded. "That is strange. Those War Department spies are so stuck on protocol. Not Tyler, necessarily." Emily rolled her eyes. "He flouts the rules. But generally those who work in the home office have the 'rights' and 'wrongs' pounded into them daily. For Cliffield to neglect to mention such an important fact isn't ordinary. Do you intend to pursue that?"

Ana started. She hadn't even considered investigating Henry further, despite her surprise over his reaction. He was a member of the War Department. He was Lucas's friend.

"I— But how would I do such a thing?"

Emily smiled. "You know how, Ana. You've been doing it for years. Have Meredith do some background checking on the man. Now that she is in Town, I'm sure she'd be happy to help. And ask Lucas. Subtly, of course. Talk to Henry. Press the issue."

"Do you really suspect he's involved in wrong-doing?" Ana asked, thinking of the empty sadness in Lucas's eyes when he looked at his fallen friend.

Emily began to shrug, but stopped herself with a grimace. "I doubt it. It's probably just as he says. A dead lead he followed for his own purposes. Nothing more than a break in protocol between friends. But still . . . if it's out of the ordinary, it warrants some research."

"I suppose." Ana got to her feet and moved to the window across the room. From her position on the bed, she doubted Emily could see her face. That made Ana feel a little safer from her seeing stare and knowing questions. "Lucas would be angry if he knew I was questioning his friend's motives. He would be . . . hurt, I think."

"Again, I must ask, do you care?" Emily asked and Ana heard the incredulous tone of her voice.

She pondered that. Yes. Sadly, she did care. She'd seen a torn and tattered part of Lucas's soul the first afternoon she met Henry. He hadn't meant to share it, perhaps, but his intentions didn't change the outcome. And the worst of it was that she understood his pain. She had felt it herself. She did not wish to cause him more of that pain if he found out she was pursuing an inquiry into Henry's motives.

And she shuddered to think of what he would feel

if, by some strange chance, Henry really was involved in some kind of wrongdoing.

"Ana?" Emily craned her neck, trying to see her. "Has something else happened?" She hesitated just long enough that Emily's tone changed. "It has! What has happened?"

She considered the question. Soon enough, Emily would hear about the kiss, either from a gossip sheet or from Meredith, but she just wasn't ready to face her friend's comments . . . her potential censure, yet.

"I—" she began, avoiding Emily's searching eyes.

"Anastasia!"

Moving back to the bed, Ana forced a bland smile. "It's very late and if I'm to get Meredith on the case, I'll need to send a message to her early tomorrow. I had best be on my way to bed and you need your rest, as well."

Emily glared at her, unable to get up to pursue her questions. They both knew it. "Fine. But don't think I'll forget that this conversation was left unfinished. At some point, I won't be confined to this bed and then you won't be able to avoid me."

With a laugh, Ana came to her friend to press a kiss against her forehead. "I never wanted to. Good night."

With Emily's muttered curses echoing in her ears, Ana walked into the hallway and shut the chamber door behind her. But her bravado and good nature faded the moment she was alone. Emily was right. The questions she had asked, the points she had made, they were all good ones.

Ones Ana would have to answer. Especially if she intended to go behind Lucas's back and do a little investigating of her own.

Lucas strummed his fingers along the top of his desk, pouring all his nervous energy into the rapid tap-tapping. It didn't help. He still felt uneasy, restless.

And he still saw Anastasia Whittig's face instead of the notes he was supposed to be encoding.

"Damn it!" he growled, tossing his pen aside. It splashed a jagged line of ink along the parchment, but he didn't care. Since last night, he hadn't cared about much but remembering the kiss he'd sworn was just a cover for Sansbury's benefit.

It wasn't. That was becoming clearer every time he remembered the way Ana's eyes had fluttered shut just before his mouth met hers. The way her body trembled and then her mouth moved with such sweet passion. He had felt her melt. That was real, pure, not some act for Sansbury.

And if he really looked hard at his own reaction, it hadn't been part of an act for him, either. He burned from her touch. And if there hadn't been the matter of their case and the interruption between them, he would have taken that simple kiss much further.

That was a very dangerous and equally foolish desire when it was clear she wanted nothing more than to be a pious widow for the rest of her days.

The door to his study opened slightly and his butler

stood in the entryway. "Lord Cliffield to see you, sir."

Lucas sighed. That was probably best. He wasn't getting any work done, and perhaps Cliffield had something to share about the case from other agents in the field.

"Very good. Send him in."

As his servant left to fetch Henry, Lucas took a moment to compose himself. Last night there had been murmurings . . . very well, *rumblings* about the kiss between Ana and him, but that didn't mean the news had spread past the ball. Or at least, he had faint hopes that it hadn't.

Very, very faint.

"You look troubled."

Lucas looked up as Henry was wheeled into the room. He waved his servant away. Once the man had shut the door behind him, Henry pushed himself forward.

Lucas turned away from Henry's focused stare, from the ever-present reminder of how he'd failed the best friend he'd ever had. Lucas couldn't hide facts from Henry when he looked right at him.

"Not troubled," he reassured him. "Simply tired. And frustrated that this investigation is not progressing. I should have discovered the truth by now!"

He slammed a palm down on the desk top.

"Are you certain that is the only cause for your frustration?" Henry asked.

Lucas turned around to find his friend staring at him, arms folded. He met his gaze evenly, and Lucas thought he saw the barest flicker of anger in his eyes.

"Yes, of course. This case has been the most important thing in my life for nearly a year, Henry."

"Well, I heard there might be another distraction." Henry cocked his head. "There were rumors about a kiss."

"Damn it."

Lucas pursed his lips. It had been folly to believe that the sensational gossip at the ball could be contained. Clearly that was not to be. Which meant his attempts to cover up one mistake in this investigation had only caused a deeper, more pressing problem. The case could only be hindered by focused attention.

"Did you plan to keep this from me?" Henry asked.

Lucas arched an eyebrow at his tone. "I had hoped to keep it utterly quiet!"

His friend's face twitched with annoyance, and immediately Lucas felt himself go on the defensive. It wasn't as if he was the only one with secrets! What about Henry's covert investigation behind his back? What about his unnamed resource that said Lord Sansbury was involved in the attacks on the spies even though Lucas had no intelligence that pointed in that direction?

Henry sighed and Lucas looked at him. His best friend. Confined to that wheelchair for the rest of his life. Blast! Why was he even considering those things? Damn Ana for creating questions in his mind.

He softened his tone. "Kissing Anastasia was only a

way to keep our cover when Sansbury came upon us in his study," he admitted quietly, even though the voice in his head taunted him with what a liar he was. He stifled it with violence. "But now that action will only hinder my case."

"It's the talk of the town," Henry said with a nod.

Lucas raked a hand through his hair. "This is exactly why I resisted this partnership! Something like this never would have occurred if I were alone or even with a male partner!"

Henry laughed. "Well, I should hope not."

Lucas tried to glare even as a grin tilted his lips.

Henry's own smile fell and he stroked his chin. "However, it doesn't necessarily follow that your investigation must be hindered. You could turn this to your advantage."

Lucas hesitated. That idea had crossed his mind, as well. After all, the gossip about the kiss with Ana had not been malicious or cruel. In fact, Society seemed enamored with the idea that the two of them were falling in love after all her years of mourning and all his attempts to dodge the marriage mart. He had his own ideas about how he could take advantage of the situation.

Of course, they also involved taking full advantage of the desire that had sparked into a wildfire with Ana last night. And he wasn't sure if that was the best idea considering how powerfully he reacted to his timid little widow.

Still, it couldn't hurt to hear Henry's thoughts on the subject. He took a seat at his desk and folded his hands. "How do you propose I do that, Henry?"

His best friend smiled in the same way he always had when the two of them were boys and Henry was about to lead him into all kinds of trouble. And Lucas had a sinking feeling his friend was poised to lead him into even more.

Chapter 9

"**C**oncentrate," Ana ordered herself through clenched teeth. "You can do this. You've done it a thousand times before."

She stared at the encoded piece, but the words and symbols swam before her eyes, and she couldn't find the concentration to make out the very simple code. Finally, she pushed the paper aside with a curse.

Emily was right. Swearing *did* make her feel better. But the relief was fleeting. The moment she stopped pretending to work, her mind returned to the subject she'd been pondering and dreaming of and tormented by for two days.

Lucas. Lucas's dimples. Lucas's lips. Oh, and of course, Lucas's kiss. Her greatest hope had been that a few days away from his company would make her come back to her senses. But instead of making the strange ache she felt when she recalled the kiss go away, the distance she'd put between them had only served to sharpen the longing, the desire that woke her from restless dreams. And she found herself reliving that kiss more, not less.

She covered her eyes with a groan of frustration. "What the hell do I do now?"

There was nothing to do, was there? Except try to fight the desire that seemed to swirl within her.

The sharp rap of a knock at the door above her rattled her from her troubling thoughts and the equally troubling roads they led her down. It was a relief to be interrupted from both.

"What is it?" she called out.

The door opened and a footman appeared at the top of the stairs. "I'm sorry to disturb you, my lady, but you have a visitor."

She wrinkled her brow. "Who is it?"

Meredith would have just come below stairs without announcement, and she didn't expect Charlie until tomorrow. Her servants had been given strict orders that the men who were suddenly leaving cards at her doors were to be told she was not in residence. So that only left—

"Mr. Lucas Tyler, my lady."

Ana's heart fluttered wildly as she stared up at the

benign face of the servant who had no idea what turmoil that announcement put her in.

Still, some of her unrest must have been reflected in her face, for he cocked his head and asked, "Should I tell him you are not in residence at present?"

That was a tempting thought, but she doubted Lucas would believe her footman. Aside from which, she had been avoiding the inevitable for too long. There was their case to be considered. She had to work on that for Emily's sake. If she could only rein in her reactions to Lucas, she might even be able to garner a bit more information on Henry Bowerly.

"Tell Mr. Tyler that I will be up to meet with him momentarily."

"Very good. He is waiting for you in the East Parlor." With that, the young man bowed away and left her alone.

Ana slowly smoothed her dress. In the wavy reflection of a mirror on her work space, she made sure she didn't have any ink on her face and removed her spectacles. But then she couldn't find any other little chores to keep her from going upstairs, so she trudged up to the main house and down the hall.

She had to be calm. Lucas would be. Certainly *he* hadn't been pondering that little kiss. He hadn't seemed at all affected after it happened. There was no use showing how shaken it had left her.

She paused at the sitting room door, took a deep

breath, and walked inside with a smile. "Good morning, Mr. Tyler."

He was sitting in the green settee by the fire and he seemed to dwarf the feminine piece. It was a slow, sensual unfolding of muscle and sinew as he shoved to his feet. She thought she saw a flash of something in his gray eyes, but then it was gone and he was cool and calm. Just as she had expected.

"Good morning," he said, his voice gruff. "How is Lady Allington?"

She smiled despite her nervousness. "Improving a small bit every day. The doctor says she is out of danger from the initial injury, though the risk of infection is always hovering. But we have every hope she will make a full recovery in time."

"Very good." He nodded once, shifting his weight from foot to foot as if he was nervous. Her eyes narrowed. She hadn't seen him like this before. Like he wanted to say something, but was trying to find the words.

What if her actions had given Charlie no choice and now Lucas was going to ban her from the case?

He cleared his throat and her heart sank. "Certainly you know that word of our kiss has become public?"

Heat rushed to her cheeks, but Ana forced herself to stand in place and continue looking at him evenly. This was no time to wilt away. She was beginning to learn that.

"Yes. It was the talk of the ball and I saw mention of

it several times in the various gossip sheets." She sighed. "I did my best to follow your order that night and not react—"

He raised a hand to stop her from speaking. "None of your actions caused this, Anastasia."

She stopped, surprised by the kindness in his voice and the strange expression on his face as he tilted his head and looked at her. Long and appraising.

Now her urge to turn away was doubled by the emotions beginning to stir in her chest. "I suppose all we can do is minimize the effect. It will make our investigation all the harder, but I'm sure we can work something out." She shrugged. "Perhaps you can attend one event while I make an appearance at another."

He shut his eyes with a quiet sigh. "Do you really believe separating will stop the talk?" Before she could answer, he continued, "It won't."

She bit her lip. He was right. And if he had come here to tell her she'd been removed from the case, that was probably for the best, too. But how it stung! She hadn't wanted this, but now the idea of giving up the investigation tore at her.

"So, is this over?" she whispered, fighting the tears that were starting to sting her eyes. The tears he surely saw. "Have I failed?"

Lucas took three long steps toward her and caught her hand. She wasn't wearing gloves because she'd been doing work in her cellar, so his rough fingers touched her own with no impediment. Instantly, her body melted the same way it had the night he kissed her. The ache of need started in her bloodstream and settled between her legs where it began to pulse in a most shocking way. Every limb felt heavy, useless, and she couldn't help but lick her lips as she stared into Lucas's eyes.

"Listen to me," he said softly, but she felt his gaze burn on her mouth. "This is *not* your fault. And this case, this investigation and your part in it doesn't have to end if we use the situation to our advantage."

Ana shivered. Somehow this didn't sound like she was going to like it.

"How can we do that?"

He let out a low breath. "For some reason, society is fascinated by the idea of a romance between us. So . . . let's give them one."

The blush that had darkened her cheeks bled away as she stumbled back a step, pulling at her hand. "What?"

He wouldn't release her. "Think of it, Ana. If we pretend an engagement, that will allow us to hide in plain sight. If we are caught together talking, whispering, people will believe it is because we're in love. And if the initial interest and the increase in my invitations is any indication, the *ton*'s matrons won't be able to resist inviting us to every event. That kind of access could be pivotal in this case."

Ana could hear his words, she understood what he was saying, but it seemed like his voice had been slowed to half time. There was a dull ringing in her ears matched only by the racing of her heart. That was *not* excitement churning in her stomach. There was nothing thrilling about this!

Yet it thrilled her.

"An engagement?" she whispered, reaching her free hand up to cover her eyes. "This is not happening."

Lucas released her hand immediately and when she dared to peek at him between her fingers, she saw his jaw had suddenly set with frustration. Almost like her denial irritated him.

"Do you have a better suggestion, Ana?" he snapped, folding his arms across his broad chest and making the heavy fabric of his overcoat flatten against the muscles there. For a moment she was mesmerized, but she forced herself to look away. "Please, do tell me if you have an alternative that is less distasteful to you than pretending to be engaged to me for a few weeks."

"A few weeks!" she cried, backing away another step. Dear God, she wasn't sure she could pull off such a deception for a few *days*, let alone a few weeks.

His lips thinned. "Don't overwhelm me with your enthusiasm."

She let her hands drop to her sides. "You don't understand what you are asking of me."

Her thoughts drifted to Gilbert, just as they had been the past few days. It was bad enough to go around kissing this man . . . but to involve deeper emotions . . . even if they were pretending? Gilbert had been the one great love of her life. The only man she had ever wanted and certainly the only one who had ever wanted her back.

Shoving that away was like denying that powerful, once-in-a-lifetime feeling had ever existed.

Wasn't it?

"I am asking you to do your job," Lucas snapped. "And yet you are behaving as if I'm taking you to the gallows, not a few balls."

"To do this would be such a betrayal," she whispered.

He moved toward her one step and his eyes were lit with fire. "Of whom?"

His voice was so cold, she ventured he'd already guessed.

Lifting her chin, she forced herself to meet his gaze. "My husband."

His jaw twitched as he clenched it. There was something almost . . . proprietary, territorial in the way his shoulders stiffened and his back straightened. "You cannot betray a dead man."

She flinched at the harshness of his words. Tears stung her eyes a second time, but she blinked them back. She would not let Lucas see them. "I already have."

His brow wrinkled. "With that kiss?"

Slowly, she nodded. There was a long moment of silence, and she did not dare to look at Lucas so she shifted her focus to the floor.

Finally, he spoke. "This engagement wouldn't be real, Ana. Once we have completed our mission, you can return to your basement. You can go back to being the mourning widow and use your grief to hide from the world if that pleases you so much."

She snapped her gaze up at that mocking tone and met his fiery stare. Every fiber of her being told her to snap back. To argue. But she couldn't. Lucas might be cutting her to the very quick, but he was only stating the truth. She *was* afraid to live again.

Without answering, she started to turn away, wanting to escape that knowing stare. Wanting to separate herself from the burning anger and equally potent desire that so reflected her own faithless heart. But he didn't let her escape so easily. He caught her arm and forced her to turn back. Pulling her in, he surrounded her with sudden heat.

"It is only a betrayal if you feel something," he whispered.

Then his lips came down to crush against hers.

The first time he kissed her, it had been a surprise. Not gentle, but not forceful. This time, his lips waged a war against her resistance.

She was lost the moment he swept his tongue over her lips.

Ana opened to him, reveling in the thrusting heat of his tongue, arching into the hard angles of his body as her hands came up to fist the arms of his jacket. She clutched the heavy fabric, clinging to him for support and longing for more. More. More.

What was happening to her? Need and desire had

been there with Gilbert. She had enjoyed his kiss, his touch, the moments they shared in and out of their marital bed. But it had never been like this. This heat that suffused her every pore. This aching, driving need that made her want to tear at Lucas's clothing, bare herself to him shamelessly.

His hands stroked her back, sparking the nerves along her spine until her knees actually shook. Dear God, if he laid her back on the settee right now, if he lifted her skirts . . . she wouldn't resist. And despite that shocking insight that rocked her to her very core, she did not pull away. She couldn't.

But apparently, he could. Breaking the contact of their lips, Lucas took a long step away. His gaze flickered with serious danger, and she realized she had barely escaped the very fantasy she'd been entertaining. Unlike the first night they kissed, she knew for certain that this meant more. That her touch enflamed him as much as he made her burn.

"Tell me, Ana," he asked, his voice rough. "Did you feel something?"

She swallowed hard. Did she feel something? She felt everything! It was like her nerves had never been fully alive until the moment he touched her. Like she had been sleeping and he woke her from that slumber with a kiss.

"No," she whispered and the tremble in her voice was so pronounced that she knew he would hear it and realize what a liar she was.

He smirked and she was right. He knew. A man like him had probably made a hundred women tremble like that in the past. Of course he knew.

"Well, as much as that pains me, my lady, I can tell you the only feelings you inspire in me are desire." He looked her up and down, and she felt stripped under the intensity of his gaze. "Which I can master. So if you feel nothing and I am able to keep whatever I feel in check, then there can be no betrayal of your *beloved* husband."

She winced at the mocking that had entered his tone again. She hardly knew this man, yet his opinion of her somehow mattered. And right now he clearly believed she was a simpering hypocrite.

And wasn't she?

She refused to meet his gaze. "But the plan—"

He shook his head. "It changed, Ana. The plan changed. If we want to have any chance of continuing this investigation, you'll have to adapt."

Ana shut her eyes. There was no arguing. She didn't want to give up the chance to catch whoever caused Emily's attack. And she had no alternative to Lucas's suggestion. Even if she did, she was shaking too hard to formulate a reasonable argument.

"Very well," she whispered, her voice barely carrying.

Lucas stared at her for a long moment, then turned on his heel to go.

"I'll make certain an announcement is circulated to a few of the papers and that the news makes it to some key ears. In the mean time, I will send over some snippets of code that were intercepted by agents in the field. Perhaps those will give us clues. Good afternoon."

Ana lifted her gaze in time to see the door close behind him. With a shiver, she sank down into the nearest chair, clutching her hands over her chest.

It was only then she realized she'd been holding her breath.

So much for not feeling anything.

"I don't have time to accept an invitation." Ana moved to her work table and carefully laid out another page of encoded symbols and signs. Some of the items Lucas had sent over to her were incredibly complicated.

Meredith leaned back against the edge of the table and looked at her. "Yes, I can see you're very busy."

Ana looked up at the tone of her friend's voice. Meredith was watching her so closely. For the first time, she realized just how she must appear, flitting from code to her notes and over to a long-forgotten invention she'd been working on. A lady's compact mirror with a strip of putty hidden behind it for making impressions of keys, coins, or other items.

"I *am* very busy!" she insisted. There was no way she was going to admit to Meredith that for the second time in as many days, she was hiding from Lucas. That he'd sent her three notes since their "engagement" that she had left unanswered. It was better to blame her work for her hibernation.

"Could you explain all this again?"

Ana sighed. Meredith seemed so cool. So pulled together. She knew her own hair was a sloppy bun. That she looked like an owl with her spectacles perched on her nose. Versus Meredith, with her sophisticated sleek hairstyle and calm disposition. *She* had probably never felt like this. Out of sorts, confused on a case.

Ana hesitated. No, that wasn't true. Meredith had married a man she once investigated. She'd fallen in love with Tristan even while wondering if he was a traitor. Certainly that must have been much harder than feeling unexpected and unwanted lust for a fellow spy.

Except Ana had no hopes for a happy ending like Meredith's waiting for her at the end of this case. Not that she wanted one.

"I don't know what part you don't understand," she snapped, peevish at herself more than her friend. "Society heard about our . . . our kiss in Sansbury's private office. Lucas felt an engagement was our only remaining cover."

Meredith shook her head. "That part I grasp fully, Anastasia. After all, this Lucas Tyler does his work very well. Word of your engagement is in"—she reached over and snatched up a pile of papers she had brought with her to Ana's work room—"*The Times*, *The City Herald*, and Blighton's gossip sheet is heralding its own foresight by claiming it knew of your secret love nearly a week ago."

Ana winced. She'd been avoiding the papers. Trust Meredith to force the truth down her throat.

Meredith set the items aside and folded her arms. "I was asked about your engagement no less than five times at various teas and luncheons in the past few days. Even Tristan entertained inquiries at Whites. A few of the gentlemen have some rather unsavory bets riding on these supposed nuptials."

"Bets?" Ana repeated, horror rising in her.

Meredith ignored her outburst. "What I don't understand is why you're hiding away two days after this engagement was announced? And why you haven't yet been seen in public with Lucas Tyler?"

Ana hesitated. How could she explain how frightened she was to Meredith, who had never feared anything?

"I told you," she said softly. "I have been busy."

Meredith shook her head as she pushed away from the table to catch Ana's hands. "This is a golden opportunity! The pile of invitations and calling cards waiting for you upstairs should tell you that. Society is enamored. Your work with the Sisters of the Heart Society for Widows and Orphans is being praised by all! We've even seen an increase in donations."

"Really?" Ana blinked with shock. How could such a small thing cause so many ripples?

"Yes." Meredith grinned. "I have heard your face

described as 'uncommonly pretty' and 'classically beautiful,' both of which I agree with wholeheartedly."

Blood flooded Ana's cheeks. She met her best friend's eyes. "I never asked for the spotlight."

Meredith's face softened with understanding. And Ana knew she did understand. Both her friends knew her so well. "But you have it, Ana. You must take advantage of it! Emily and I don't understand why you aren't. If she wasn't confined to that bed—"

Ana yanked her hands free and walked away. "She would be down here railing on me as you are. Why do you think I'm down here where she can't reach me?"

When she turned around to look at Meredith again, she found her friend staring at her, eyes wide and mouth open.

"I've never heard you use that tone. What is it? This is more than mere shyness at your newfound fame." She looked at her for a long moment, then Meredith's face registered a glimmer of understanding. "Is it because of Tyler?"

Ana hesitated a fraction of a second too long. Long enough that Meredith lifted a hand to cover her mouth. "That is it! Why didn't I see it?"

Ana dipped her head with shame. There was no use hiding the truth. "I liked it when he kissed me." She heard Meredith's sharp intake of breath. "I know it's only part of the case, but it's been so long since I felt that way. Maybe I've never felt that way."

Meredith nodded. "He is very handsome. And charming from everything I've seen. It's understandable why you would feel something when he touched you, Ana. It isn't wrong to want."

Ana lifted her gaze. "Yes, it is. It is for me."

Her friend pursed her lips. "Because of Gilbert?" Ana didn't answer. "It's been five years, dearest."

Ana shook her head. Lucas kept telling her that, too. As if time alone could change her heart and her past. Could make her forget.

"Do you know how long I loved Gilbert?" she asked.

Meredith shook her head, but Ana could see her shock. Ordinarily Ana's grief was not something she discussed, not even with her two best friends.

"Since I was twelve years old," she admitted softly. She thought back and was frustrated when all she could conjure was a blurry image of what her husband had been like then.

"Our families had estates close to each other, so we grew up together and I loved him from afar," she whispered. "But he never noticed me. No one ever noticed me except for my parents. And then, one day, he did."

Meredith smiled sadly, but didn't interrupt.

Ana fiddled with the items on the tabletop as she continued, "No one had ever been interested in me before. I was a wallflower the first few months after I came out. But when he began to court me, it was like every fairy tale I'd ever heard come true. I had never thought I'd have a love match, and yet, somehow, I did.

I knew that was something rare. Especially for me. Something that would only happen once in a lifetime." She sniffled as tears began to sting her eyes. She looked at Meredith evenly. "So that is why it is wrong for me to *want* Lucas. Why this engagement, false though it may be, feels like such a betrayal."

Meredith shook her head. "*Why?* I still don't understand."

Ana let out an exasperated sigh. "If I feel something for another man, it is as if I am forgetting that once-in-a-lifetime love with Gilbert." She clenched her fists. "Like I'm saying it wasn't special. As if I believe the vows I made on my wedding day were interchangeable."

Meredith covered her mouth and now tears sparkled in her friend's eyes, as well. "Oh, Ana. No . . . No—"

Ana shook her head. "Please don't argue. You don't understand! You didn't love your first husband, so when you found love, you were free to accept it with all your heart. But tell me, if Tristan were gone, can you imagine going on with your life as if his existence meant nothing to you?"

Her friend hesitated. "I—I—"

"Then please don't judge my feelings," Ana said. She swiped at her tears and lifted her chin. "Now, that is enough of this talk. Let us get to the matter you came here for. Did you find any information about Henry Bowerly?"

Meredith paused and Ana could see she was struggling, wanting to press further on the subject of Gilbert, but finally she let out a sigh of reluctant acquiescence.

"The Marquis of Cliffield is not an easy man to investigate," she admitted. "He has used his position in the War Department to mask his life, especially since the attack on his life a year ago."

"What did you find?"

"On the night Cliffield was injured, Lucas was there. But he wasn't supposed to be."

"No?" Ana asked and relaxed as the painful subject of her past gave way to the comfort of the particulars of her case. She'd never thought she could find peace in an investigation.

Meredith shook her head. "Although Tyler and Cliffield were often partners in investigations, for the case Cliffield was working on, he'd asked to be paired with another man. A man of no title named George Warfield. But Warfield took ill the night of the attack and Tyler stepped in. It was very last minute. Apparently, even Lord Cliffield didn't know about the switch until he saw Tyler. When the shooting began, Cliffield pushed Tyler out of the way and he was struck instead."

Ana lifted a hand to cover her lips. No wonder Lucas was so guilt ridden over the injury to his friend. Cliffield's protective interference had caused him to be confined to the wheelchair for the rest of his life.

"My God."

Meredith nodded. "But if you look at your map that

Charlie provided, you'll see that George Warfield, himself, was attacked soon after. His was the second death."

Ana drew back. That could very well mean that Warfield had been the target that night. In the darkness, the assailant had probably mistaken Lucas for the other man. A dark, sick feeling churned in her stomach at the thought of Lucas being cut down.

"I'm working on getting more information," Meredith finished. "But—"

Before she could finish, there was a commotion at the top of the stairs and her basement door flew open. Both women spun on the intruder. Ana gasped.

Lucas. And he did not look happy.

Chapter 10

Lucas knew who the woman with Ana was. Lady Carmichael, Meredith Archer, another of the Lady Spies. She'd married nearly a year before, but was still active with the group. She arched a fine brow at him as he came down the stairs, relaxing from her ready-to-fight stance.

Ana didn't. She remained rigid, staring at him like she was ready to give him a good punch and run like the devil was at her heels. Not a stellar beginning to their "engagement."

He tossed a dismissive glance at Lady Carmichael. "I am sorry to intrude, but this is between us. I would appreciate a moment with Ana."

His brow furrowed. When the hell had he started

thinking of them as an "us," rather than him and the leg shackle he was forced to endure? Probably the same moment he first tasted her lips.

Lady Carmichael's eyes went wide with surprise at his forward demand. Then her mouth twitched into a small, knowing smile. "Very well." She turned to her friend. "I shall say farewell to Emily before I go. And I'll be back with more information for you as soon as I have any."

Ana spared a brief nod to her friend, then returned her pointed, furious glare back at him. Fire burned in her eyes. The same kind that boiled there when he kissed her. And that put his traitorous body immediately at the ready, despite how irritated he was.

The door above them closed and she stepped up at once, surprising him by closing the space between them and poking one slender finger against his chest.

"You have no right to barge into my home and be rude to my friend and partner!"

His eyes narrowed. "Rude? Ha! You want to tell me about being rude? Rude is ignoring notes and invitations and making a general muck out of a perfect opening in this case."

Her expression reflected how that comment stung. Now that she was so close, he looked down into her face. Her pretty hair was pulled into a clumsy bun and little tendrils of soft locks twisted around her cheeks and neck. She had a smudge on her left cheek and a blotch of ink on her thumb and the finger that still hung, hesitating in the air mid-poke.

Emotion welled up in him. The desire he wasn't surprised by. He had come to expect that he would want Anastasia. That the mere sight of her would call to his blood. But the other emotion shocked him— tenderness.

Seeing her like this, in her private room, with her papers and inventions and work scattered all around, brought up a soft feeling he wasn't sure he'd ever experienced before.

He couldn't stop himself from reaching out. She watched with widening eyes as his hand came closer, but she didn't flinch when he wiped the smudge of dust from her cheek.

"I was worried about you, my little fool." He chuckled. And that was true. When she ignored his notes, he had become concerned.

"You needn't be. I'm fine."

She pulled back. It was just as well. Tenderness was the last thing he needed or wanted. Clearing his throat, he forced a more businesslike manner.

"Go upstairs and put on a gown," he ordered. "*With color*, Ana, and come with me. There is a meeting this afternoon in Hyde Park I want to watch. We've arranged it in the hopes it will draw out an attacker."

Ana tilted her head. "Why must I wear color?" She looked down at her gown. "I could—"

"If you were really falling in love with me," he said, stepping a little closer, "you would no longer be in mourning. If you wear black, it will arouse suspicion that this engagement is not real. Please, no arguments. Put on a gown with color."

Ana's entire face scrunched up with displeasure, but she grunted out either "fine" or something far less ladylike and stomped up the stairs to do as she had been told.

Once she was gone, Lucas shook his head. The woman was a trial, but there was something undeniably attractive about her. Something that went beyond her obvious physical beauty. She was . . . open. Honest. Loyal. And beneath her nervous exterior, there was a strength of spirit and will that appealed to him.

There was also no denying her intelligence. He looked around the large, open room she had turned from some kind of cellar into a work area. Snippets of code were tacked to the walls. Many were complicated enough that he would need assistance in deciphering them, and he had always thought he did passably well in encoded work. There were glass beakers filled with mysterious, pungent liquid and everyday items in the process of being transformed into tools of the trade for a spy.

He made his way up the stairway to the main house, then down the hallway to the parlor where he had waited for her every other time he'd visited. He entered the room and sat down by the fire with a sigh.

"I was hoping to see you before I departed."

Lucas started. He'd been so caught up in his thoughts about Ana, he hadn't noticed Lady Carmichael standing beside the window that faced the gardens outside. Her arms were folded, and her dark blue eyes held his own. Appraising him.

He leaned back in his chair and gave her his most dashing grin. "Hello again, Lady Carmichael."

It was clear she was less than impressed by his charm when she snorted out a bark of laughter. "Much more polite now, aren't we?"

He tilted his head in acknowledgment. "I do apologize, of course. I needed to speak to Anastasia on a matter of great importance."

"Yes." Lady Carmichael came closer. "Your engagement. I would congratulate you, but I wager you realize I know the truth about that ruse."

He nodded. "I doubt you ladies keep many secrets from each other."

A shadow of concern fluttered briefly over her face. "Not many."

He wrinkled his brow. From her expression, he would almost guess she feared Ana did hold some part of herself back, even from her closest friends. An idea that intrigued him. What made her hide behind the veil of grief and rules? What made her deny the parts of her that wanted him? Wanted more than a staid existence of a widow who only played at being a spy rather than embraced that life. She was really rather good at it. Yet she feared it, still.

Feared him. Or at least, he thought she did when she trembled in his arms.

"I want you to know that if you ever hurt Ana, Emily and I will find a way to destroy you." Meredith Archer gave him the sweetest smile in the world. "I would cut your heart out before I saw you harm her in any way."

Lucas drew back at the unexpected statement from the pretty, proper woman before him. But then his shock faded. If her friends needed to resort to threats, that most definitely meant Ana harbored some feelings for him. And that gave him a powerful thrill of triumph.

It also made him realize just how fully he wanted to pursue those desires. He'd been trying to deny them because she clung to the idea of staying true to her late husband.

But deep in his soul, in the hot blood in his veins, he wanted to act on the need that sparked so powerfully between them. He wanted to feel her pulse quicken. To push past her reflexive denials and make her face the heated wants he tasted in her kiss.

He felt his smile widen. They were engaged now. Perhaps it was time to make the act a very realistic one. She would never give him her heart. There was no risk of that. No risk of anything deeper than an affair to last the duration of the case. She was a widow, so she could not be ruined. And he had wanted her from the first moment she rushed up on him, her eyes ablaze with fire as she accused him of causing Emily's attack.

He wanted to make those same eyes blaze with surrender.

Lady Carmichael was staring at him, gaze focused and irritated. Deadly serious.

Tilting his head in acknowledgment, he said, "I understand your desire to protect Ana. But I think you underestimate her ability to protect and make decisions for herself."

The lady began to laugh. "Trust me, Mr. Tyler. I don't underestimate Anastasia in any way. Nor should you."

Before Lucas could retort, the door behind him opened. Lady Carmichael looked past him to the entryway, and her eyes widened. Then she smothered a giggle in her hand. Heart sinking, Lucas got up and turned to face Ana.

He almost stumbled back at the sight. She was wearing a hideous green gown that was at least six seasons out of fashion. Clearly it had last been worn before her husband's passing, and she had pulled it from the depths of her armoire and had it hurriedly pressed. The collar was high, with ruffles along the neck that covered the delectable slope of her throat. The waist was far too high, as well. And to make matters worse, Ana had clearly lost a little bit of weight since her husband's death, so the entire contraption hung around her curves like a sack.

It was, in a word, horrific. Even to him, who rarely noticed a lady's clothing unless he was determining the best way of removing it. There didn't seem to be a best way to remove the fluffy, ill-fitted gown she was wearing at all.

If this was how she had dressed during her marriage, no wonder she feared her desires. If she had been his six years ago, he would have wanted her wearing daring, bold gowns. Ones that brought out the sparkle in her eyes and the golden highlights hidden in the rich length of her chestnut hair.

Ana glared at Meredith. "Oh, hush! It's the only gown *with color*"—she glared at him—"that I have. It will have to do."

Meredith smiled. "I did not say a word."

Muttering something under her breath, Ana spun on him with narrowed eyes. "And you had best keep your comments to yourself, as well."

Lucas lifted his hands in surrender. "I wouldn't say a thing." He forced a smile and offered her an arm. "Shall we be off, then?"

Ana nodded her good-bye to her friend, and he led her from the room and off to the waiting carriage and whatever their afternoon in the park would bring.

Ana shifted. Wasn't there a way to hold a man's arm without actually touching him? Smelling the faint hint of his shaving soap? Being wrapped in his heat?

If there was, she had not yet determined it. Even if she barely clung to Lucas's arm, electricity still zinged up her fingertips. Normally when they were this close, he was kissing her.

She pursed her lips. Those were exactly the wrong kinds of thoughts to be having. They were performing an important part of their duty. Guarding over a spy as he took a meeting in the crowded park.

The afternoon promenade was in full swing. Hyde Park was crowded with ladies and gentlemen on horseback, in carriages, and on foot. All were jockeying to see and be seen.

She craned her neck to peer over the crowd. Along the edge of the lake, she saw the man they were following. He wasn't someone she knew, but a rich merchant. He was waiting for another spy while he fed the ducks that flocked around him. He blended in perfectly. No one would have suspected his true purpose in the Park.

"Mr. Tyler, Lady Whittig!"

Ana jolted from her concentration as a large woman wearing a feathered bonnet came rushing across the grass toward them.

"Smile," Lucas ordered through clenched teeth, then did the same.

"Lady Hickman." Ana forced a smile.

"I heard of your engagement." The boisterous woman reached out a hand. "Many felicitations to you!"

Lucas and Ana each shook her hand in turn, though Ana's heart sank. Dear Lord, word really had spread.

"I am so very pleased for you," the lady continued. "After all, my dear daughter lost her husband a year ago, herself. I hope she can find some happiness again just as you have, my lady. Well, I must be back to my party, I only wanted to wish you joy!"

With that, the woman gave a quick nod and headed back through the crowd. But no sooner had she gone than another couple strolled by and called out their congratulations. People were waving, stopping to say hello.

Ana's cheeks were starting to hurt from all the smiling and a horrible thought was forming in her mind. If everyone in Society seemed so aware of how she had supposedly fallen in love and agreed to marry Lucas Tyler in just a few days, that meant her late husband's family had likely heard the same. Though she had not visited them in the past few months, she still felt a closeness, especially with her mother-in-law. And she could only imagine how pained the news would make her.

"If you continue to hold yourself so far away from me," Lucas growled, his face suddenly pinched as he moved her toward the perimeter of the lake so they could get a better view of their mark, "then no one will believe our engagement. Anyone paying any kind of close attention at this moment would peg us for false."

Ana stole a glance out of the corner of her eye at

him. He looked as irritated as she, herself, felt. It was as if he delighted in vexing her, knowing she was resistant to this engagement, yet forcing her to act like it was true. Forcing her to lean in closer and feel the desire she was trying to fight.

Her thoughts strayed to Emily's comment. That Lucas might use her emotions . . . even the need she felt for him, against her if he felt it would get him what he wanted. Was that what he was doing now?

"Here comes the other man," Lucas said, low and close to her ear.

Emily welcomed the interruption and watched as a second man approached. This man she did recognize. A country gentleman who rarely came to town. Dandified to the hilt. She was shocked that he would be in the King's service.

"But that is Sir George Thornton!" she gasped.

Lucas nodded. "Yes. And a fine spy."

"But he—he is a fool." She stared as Sir George sat down on the bench next to the other spy. They never spoke, never even acknowledged each other. For a moment, Sir George mopped his forehead as the other man continued to feed the ducks. Then he got up and started away. Ana's eyes widened as she caught a quick glimpse of the other spy sweeping up a small packet and thrusting it into his pocket. No one would have noticed such a thing if they weren't sharp eyed.

"Sir George is a fool," Lucas said with a smile as the first spy got up and started out of the park at a slow

•

gait. "But you are a shy widow. And you and I are hopelessly in love."

She started at that statement, and her gaze flashed up to him.

"Things are not always what they seem, Ana." Lucas tugged her to move. "Remember that."

She bit her lip to keep from retorting. "Is that all, then? Are we finished?"

"Yes. If someone was going to attack, they likely would have done it before Sir George left his evidence. Now it's too late, our man is lost in the crowd." He pursed his lips. "Damn. I really hoped to apprehend one of these bastards today. If we could only catch one person in this plot, we could out the rest."

She stared off into the crowd of watching eyes and smiling, laughing faces. As they walked along the path, her mind drifted to what he had said a moment before.

"You and I are not hopelessly in love."

Lucas sighed. "As I said, things are not always what they seem."

A glimmer of hope brightened inside her. "But why do we have to *seem* like we're hopelessly in love? Why couldn't we let everyone believe this is a marriage of convenience instead?"

That would solve everything. No more close encounters. No more stolen kisses. No more of the graze of Lucas's hand on her waist as they walked.

His fingers tightened on her arm and his pace quickened as he lead her out of sight of the main promenade of the park and into a more densely wooded . . . and less-populated area. Once there, he grasped her shoulders and turned her to face him.

"No one would ever believe this was a marriage of convenience, Anastasia," he said, and his fingers burned even through the heavy, frilly fabric of her gown.

"Why?" she asked as she pulled away, but he wouldn't let her go. His gaze held her in place as much as his hands. It was dark as stormy skies.

"I have no title, so I am not in immediate need of heirs. I do not require money, so I would not marry for the settlement I would obtain." His eyes narrowed. "And even if I did, your 'beloved' husband provided very poorly for you on that score."

Ana jolted. "What right do you have to delve into my finances?"

He shrugged. "Isn't that why you live with Emily?"

Her heart stung, but she couldn't deny it. Gilbert had never been very good with money. He had died so young, he'd never thought to prepare a decent settlement for her when he was gone. She had never resented that, but she couldn't deny it.

When she didn't answer, his mouth set with cocky triumph. "And there is one more reason."

She folded her arms and glared up at him. "And what is that?"

He cupped her chin with one big hand and tilted her face up. "Anyone who knows me knows I would not marry unless I felt passion, desire for the woman."

Her lips parted as his mouth came down, but any weak protest she would have attempted was silenced by his kiss. He smiled when she shamelessly allowed him entry.

And he took it, tasting, teasing, even as he guided her back into the little grove of trees and out of the prying view of any passersby. Her backside hit the trunk of a tree, but she hardly noticed. All she could feel was him. His arms coming around her, his hard, solid chest pressed against her own. His mouth doing such wicked things, things she had forgotten. Things she'd never known, yet she craved like an oasis in the desert.

The kiss deepened as they both reached for . . . something. Something primitive and wanton. It was as if the very air around them shifted, grew heated and heavy. Ana forgot that they were in the park, in the open, she even forgot all her protests and fears and memories. All that mattered was that she wanted Lucas to keep kissing her.

She wanted more. Her back arched and her hips brushed his. She felt the hard thrust of something against her thigh and she realized, with a jolt of shock, that it was his erection. He *wanted* her. Really wanted her. Now.

If his body hadn't told her that, his hands would have when they started to move. He inched his fingers up her side, sliding in a slow, seductive trail until he teased the curve of her breast. He shoved the ridiculous ruffles aside to cup the mound and his thumb began to circle her nipple through the fabric.

Ana gasped, breaking the kiss as a shot of hot want blasted from the tip of her nipple and settled between her legs. Dear God, how had he done that? It was like he set her on fire, awoke her long sleeping senses. She should stop him.

But she didn't. Instead, she let her eyes flutter shut and expelled her breath in a long, jagged sigh.

Suddenly the swirling pleasure of his thumb stopped, the rock of his hips stopped. Everything stopped. She opened her eyes to find his face just inches from hers. He was staring at her, gaze wild and intense in the shadowy, filtered light of the trees.

Shaking his head, he pulled back. "You see, Ana? A marriage between us could never be one of convenience. If we were married, we would have passion. Desire. Everything in your kiss tells me that. The way you react to my touch confirms it."

He pulled away, breaking the embrace as he ran a hand through his hair. Ana continued to lean back against the tree, her trembling legs unable to move as she watched him put more distance between them.

She hadn't wanted him to stop. It was wrong. It went against everything she had told herself she was. But there it was. The truth, like it or not.

"Take me back," she murmured, smoothing her twisted ruffles into place. She lifted her chin and hoped he wouldn't see how shaken she was. "You have proven your point, so take me home."

Lucas stared at her for a long moment, his gaze focused on her own with disconcerting vision and clarity. Then he gave her a formal bow.

"Whatever the lady desires."

Chapter 11

Lucas watched Ana disappear into her home and slam the door behind her. She hadn't even allowed him to get out of the carriage and escort her. Not that he blamed her after what had happened in the park.

He hadn't intended for the kiss to go so far. Well, perhaps he had, but not in such a public place. And he certainly hadn't intended to lose control of himself. He'd only wished to test Anastasia's boundaries.

Instead, he'd put her against a tree and nearly rutted with her in full view of a hundred or more of Society's finest.

And what had he been thinking going on and on about marriage? He rubbed a hand over his face. A *real* marriage? Why in the world would he want that? His relationships with women had always been about pleasure. Brief and satisfying, yet easily forgotten.

Yes, he resented the hell out of Ana's lingering devotion to Saint Gilbert . . . a man who had not even bothered to ensure his wife was taken care of after his untimely death. But Ana thought the damned moon and sun set over his grave! Still, irritation over her continued commitment to a corpse was one thing, but trying to prove *he* would be a perfect substitute by groping her in the middle of the park at five in the afternoon was quite another.

"Idiot," Lucas muttered to himself as the carriage halted at his doorstep. He pushed open the door and climbed down. He needed a willing woman. Or a cold bath. Or anything that would get his mind off Ana and back on the case where it belonged.

His butler opened the door. "Good afternoon, sir."

"Is it?" Lucas growled as he shrugged out of his coat and handed it to the man.

"Sir, you have—"

"Not now." Lucas waved him off and started down the hallway toward his office.

"But Mr. Tyler—" The man was at his heels, insistent.

Lucas came to a sharp halt and turned on the man with barely repressed fury. "What is it?"

"Your mother is here, sir. Waiting for you. And she seems rather annoyed by—"

Before he could finish, Lucas's mother's own voice pierced the quiet of the hallway. "Lucas Ian St. John Tyler."

Lucas winced as he turned toward the parlor. His mother stood in the doorway, arms folded. Though she was only five feet tall, she actually terrified him more than any traitor. Especially when she used all his names.

He smiled. She did not return the expression. She had the "you have a lot of explaining to do" look in her eyes. The same one she'd had over many years and countless pranks.

"Mother, I thought you were in Bath enjoying the waters with Aunt Grace for at least another two weeks."

He stepped forward to place a kiss on her cheek before he motioned to the parlor. Closing the door behind them, he faced her. She still had her arms folded. That was a very bad sign.

"I would have been doing just that, except that I heard some news. About an engagement." Her eyes, slate gray like his own, narrowed. "How long did you intend to keep your family in the dark?"

Lucas swallowed. Plan for all contingencies. That was a golden rule for spies. Be prepared for everything. Only . . . he wasn't. Not for this. Not for the little light that brightened her eyes, pushing away her annoyance and revealing itself as hope. Joy.

"Mother—" he began.

"Oh, never mind! You are hopeless and I love you for it." She opened her arms and enveloped him in a hug. "I won't lie and say I'm not pleased, even if I was shocked by the news at first. But I've heard nothing but good about Lady Whittig. I recall a little about her from before her first marriage."

He blinked, his world spinning. This was a very bad thing. Very, very bad. He couldn't explain the truth about the ruse without outing himself as a spy. He could only imagine his mother's reaction to *that* news. She'd always been protective. She'd probably have an apoplexy if she knew he was shot at on a regular basis.

"And now that we are all here, we will meet her and—"

He hadn't thought it possible, but his heart sank even further into the depths of his stomach.

"All?" he repeated weakly.

She nodded. "Of course! Your brothers and sisters and their wives and husbands are all very anxious to meet the woman who has finally captured your attention for more than ten minutes together. I think Peter and Martin may actually have a wager of some kind about when you would marry, so you'll make one of them very happy, indeed."

She laughed at the idea, and Lucas couldn't help but smile. He was certain his two older brothers did have some kind of bet. With his luck, they'd involved his brothers-in-law, as well. And his two older sisters were no doubt knitting baby booties for his future children already.

"When is the earliest date we can arrange for a family dinner party?" his mother asked.

Lucas opened his mouth to protest, then shut it again. There was no use arguing with her. His mother would have her way. His thoughts drifted to Anastasia's widow's weeds and outdated clothing. He couldn't bring her into his mother's home looking like that. Not without rousing suspicion.

"Lucas?" His mother tilted her head. "Is there something wrong? You're just *staring* at me, darling, and you have the strangest pale fishy face just now."

"Three days," he said, hoping he could manage to do what he needed to do before that time. "She will meet the family in three days."

His mother nodded, satisfied, at least for the moment. "Very good. Now I must return to Huntington Circle. The servants are in an uproar at my early return, and now we have a lovely party to plan. I shall send along all the details by tomorrow afternoon."

She pressed a kiss on his cheek as she moved for the doorway. Meeting his eyes, she said, "I so want to see you happy, my dearest. I hope this marriage will do that."

He smiled, though he guessed the expression was somewhat pained. In the field he could cover his heart without even trying. But with his mother, his family, he had never mastered that ability. "I will see you very soon."

She waved as she slipped away. As soon as he was sure she was gone, out in her carriage being whisked off to make God knew what kind of diabolical plans, Lucas threw the parlor door open.

"Wallis! I need a *modiste*. The best *modiste* in London! And I need her now!"

Ana set a card down on the rumpled coverlet and grinned at the way Emily's face scrunched.

Meredith laughed. "We put her in the field for a couple of weeks and she becomes a conqueror!"

Emily shook her head as she placed the next card on the pile. "Well, we always said she had hidden talents."

Heat filled Ana's cheeks. "Stop teasing."

"Who is teasing?" Meredith asked as she played her next card. "It's true."

"I have yet to accomplish anything on this case to merit your esteem," Ana argued with a sigh. "I have only managed to get myself into a false engagement that I have no idea how to explain to Gilbert's family. So I'm hiding from them. I follow Lucas around like a puppy, but he may or may not be keeping me from the biggest details of the case. And I have my questions about the Marquis of Cliffield, but I haven't found an opening to ask those questions. In all, it isn't a remarkable beginning."

Emily's stare met hers and held with intensity.

"Working a case involves patience as often as it involves adventure. Keep looking for the moment, for the opening. You'll find it. But for heaven's sake, don't be discouraged. I think your theory about tracing the culprit of these attacks by finding out how they are related is a good one."

Ana smiled, despite her self-deprecation. "Perhaps today I shall find that precious opening. Lucas sent me a note demanding an audience in . . ." She looked at the little clock behind Emily. "A quarter of an hour."

Butterflies began to flutter in her stomach when she said those words. After that heart-pounding kiss in the park the previous afternoon, she hadn't heard from Lucas. His cryptic note had her on edge. And so did the fact that every time they were alone of late, it ended in a passionate embrace and the sinking feeling that at some moment she wouldn't stop him and she would end up in his bed.

Actually, the feeling that accompanied that inevitability wasn't particularly sinking. In actuality, it was thrilling. And guilt-inducing. And unexpected.

"Are you going to play?" Meredith asked.

Ana looked up to find both her friends staring at her. The two women exchanged a knowing glance before they returned their attention to the game. Ana put down a card.

"Ha!" Emily played her last. "I win!"

Meredith shrugged. "Perhaps we let you win because you're a convalescent."

Emily glared at her with mischief sparkling in her eyes before she swung her stare back on Ana. "So . . . any more kissing you'd like to tell us about?"

Ana's heart lurched. "What did you hear?"

Meredith sat up straighter. "Ha! There has been kissing! Tell us about it."

Ana shoved off the bed and turned toward the door. "No kissing!" she cried. "I misspoke. No kissing."

Emily laughed. "Too late, we'll wheedle it out of you eventually, you know."

Ana stopped at the door and looked over her shoulder at her two friends. In reality, she knew that comment to be true.

"Perhaps," she teased, although the idea gave her little pleasure. "But not today."

With that, she closed the door behind her and headed downstairs where she knew Lucas would be waiting in a moment. She entered the parlor where they always seemed to meet and was surprised to be greeted by the very man himself.

Her heart skipped in a suspect fashion. "Lucas! I didn't know you'd arrived."

He smiled and the skipping turned to throbbing. She really needed to find immunity to that look. Those dimples. Emily was right that he thought they were a weapon.

"We only just did."

"We?" she repeated and only then noticed a middle-aged woman standing beside the fire. When Lucas was around, it seemed her peripheral vision was non-existent. "I'm terribly sorry, I didn't see you there."

The woman smiled at the two of them. "It's quite all right, my lady."

"Lady Whittig, may I present Miss Catherine Mullany."

Ana inclined her head in confusion. The name seemed familiar but she couldn't place . . . wait. Catherine Mullany was a *modiste*. In fact, she was one of the most sought-after dressmakers in London. Meredith and Emily had talked about her.

She shot Lucas a look. "What's going on?"

"Miss Mullany, have Benson take you to . . . darling, where would you like to be fitted?" He met her stare with an unquestionable message in his eyes. *Play along.*

She bit her lip and then did so. "I think Meredith and Emily would like to watch. Miss Mullany, ask Benson to take you to Lady Allington's chamber. If you have any materials to carry with you, I'm sure he can arrange for that."

The woman bobbed out a quick curtsey and exited the room, leaving Ana and Lucas alone.

The moment the door closed, she backed a step away. "I repeat my earlier question: What is going on? Why is the most sought-after garment maker in the city in my house?"

"Do you recall how I told you that you must adapt to the changes in a case?" he asked, taking his usual seat by the fire.

She folded her arms. "Yes."

"I'm afraid we are about to face yet another adaptation. You see, my mother and the rest of my family were on holiday in Bath. I had hoped we would be able to finish our investigation before they got wind of our 'engagement' but that was not to be. They are now in town and they, er"—he hesitated—"they want to meet you."

She stumbled back. "What? When?"

He shifted. "The day after tomorrow."

Her ears began to whoosh with blood until she could hardly hear anything but the throbbing of her own heartbeat.

"Obviously you cannot meet with them wearing mourning gowns or things that are seasons out of date," he continued.

"I cannot meet with them at all!" she argued, pacing away. "You told me yesterday that if anyone was watching us that they would see our engagement is a farce. Well, your family will be watching us, watching *me* very closely."

He came toward her. Reaching out, he caught her hands. The normal flood of desire sprang to life in her body when he touched her, but this time that need was pushed to the background. Something else came to the front.

Comfort.

"Ana, you can do this," he said softly. "Regardless of

what I said yesterday, I have seen you merge seamlessly into an act before. I believe in your abilities."

She swallowed. Desire and the comfort fled, replaced by a giddy joy and swelling pride. Drat! Perhaps Lucas *was* only saying what he thought she wanted to hear. Perhaps Emily was correct in her warning that Lucas would use emotions against her.

Regardless, she couldn't help a thrill that he saw her as a capable partner. No one, not even her husband, had viewed her in that fashion before. She wanted to live up to it.

"Then I'll do it," she said softly. "If you think I can, then I will."

His face softened, and this time it wasn't a cocky smile, but something more gentle. Something just for her. "I know." He brushed a lock of hair away from her eyes. "Now, go upstairs and be fitted. I will send you more details about the dinner with my family to-morrow."

He pulled away and slipped to the door. There he paused and looked at her one last time before he was gone.

"You will look beautiful in that one," Meredith breathed as the *modiste* held a bolt of crimson fabric up to Ana's body.

"It's so bold!" she protested as she looked at herself in the mirror, fingering the soft material.

"You should be bold," Emily argued, shifting on her pillows. "I like it."

Ana shrugged and nodded to the woman. Miss Mullany set the fabric on the ever-growing pile Ana had agreed to. She assumed the woman would then choose one color, perhaps two, to design the gown she would wear to meet Lucas's family.

She smiled as the dressmaker began to pack up her things. In actuality, it had been *fun* to be fitted. She and her friends had giggled like schoolgirls. And Ana had almost forgotten what it was like to choose fabric that wasn't harsh black or dark gray. What could it hurt to have *one* dress with color? It was only for the sake of the case, after all.

"Thank you again for coming to have me fit on such short notice," Ana said as she rang for footmen to come and fetch the woman's things.

The dressmaker smiled. "I will return the day after tomorrow with a new gown for your meeting with Mr. Tyler's family. And by next week, I shall bring you your new wardrobe in its entirety."

Ana came to a stop, her hand frozen at the bell pull. "A new wardrobe? No, that cannot be correct. I only need one gown."

Miss Mullany gave her a quick, subtle glance from head to toe that brought a blush to Ana's cheeks. Clearly, the woman was making note of the severe black of her mourning gown. Lucas was correct when he said her clothing drew attention to her and threw doubt on their courtship.

"I assure you, my dear, Mr. Tyler was very clear on the point. I have been paid to provide you with a season's worth of new gowns as soon as I am possibly able."

Ana shook her head. "That—that will cost a fortune!"

The *modiste* laughed. "For a man as in love as Mr. Tyler seems to be, it is of little matter."

The breath left Ana's lungs as she stared. Lucas, in love with her? Her mouth was suddenly dry and her head spun. It wasn't real. It wasn't real. And now she had to react for her case. Pretend her world wasn't spinning, tilting off its axis.

"Mr. Tyler is very kind, indeed."

"Very kind," the other woman agreed. "I will send a messenger to arrange a time for your final fitting tomorrow afternoon."

"Good day, Miss Mullany," Ana choked as the lady moved past her and followed a stream of footmen into the hall.

The second the door closed, Meredith was on her feet.

"I saw that," she said, casting a glance at Emily. "I saw your face when she commented about Lucas being in love with you. Are your emotions becoming involved in this case?"

Ana stared at her friends. Both of them were focused entirely on her, and this time she knew walking away wouldn't be an escape. They were no longer teasing her about a few stolen kisses. They were truly concerned.

And about something she didn't want to think about.

"Of course not," she lied. "That would be foolish, wouldn't it? I already told you why I am still dedicated to Gilbert. You know I would never allow myself to feel something for another man."

Emily slowly forced herself to sit up, her eyes flickering with pain and worry in equal measure. "Ana, you're still very young."

"So was Gilbert," Ana snapped, tired of the argument about her age. "Too young to die. Should I forget he lived? That I loved him?"

Her friend winced, and Ana wasn't sure if it was because of physical pain from her injury or a reaction the raw emotion coursing through the room. "I don't agree with you that feeling something for another man equates forgetting your husband. But Tyler? That could be so dangerous."

Ana turned away without answering.

Emily continued, "He could be manipulating you, Ana."

She flinched as her thoughts turned to their interaction just a few short hours ago. She'd recognized he might only be saying he believed in her in order to stroke her ego, to make her carry out his wishes. But she had still allowed herself to slip under the spell of his gentle reassurance.

"If he is showing you tenderness, it isn't because—"

She spun on her friends. "A man like him could never want a woman like me, is that it?"

Emily shook her head. "No, I—"

"I'm a mouse, and he is strong and filled with adventure. He would want a woman like *you* instead. And if I let myself think otherwise, I might end up brokenhearted." She shook her head. "Don't you think I remember what it was like to be a wallflower before Gilbert realized he could care for me? I know I'm dull with my little spectacles and my inventions. I know I get ink on my fingers and sometimes forget what to say when I'm in a crowd of people. How foolish do you believe I am?"

She blinked as the words fell from her lips. Her husband had always forgiven her for those things. Assured her that he cared for her despite all that.

But Lucas . . . Lucas never seemed to notice those failings at all.

Emily stared at her, gape-mouthed. Meredith stepped forward. "Emily doesn't mean that at all, Ana. If Lucas wants you, I have no doubt that is real. But your reaction proves that you are involved already. It could be very dangerous for you. It could even get you killed if you end up more focused on Lucas than your case."

Ana clenched her fists. "Like you were with Tristan."

"That was different!" Meredith protested.

"Yes, it was." Ana nodded. "I am *not* falling in love with Lucas like you did with your husband. And I cannot listen to these wild accusations any longer."

She turned her back and walked away.

Emily and Meredith exchanged a glance of worry as the door shut behind her.

Chapter 12

Lucas shifted his weight from one leg to another, leaning on the banister in a way he hoped would appear nonchalant when he felt anything but. Anxiety curled in his stomach, made his muscles twitch. And all for one woman. One infuriating, intriguing, dream-haunting woman.

Anastasia Whittig. The carriage he had sent for her earlier in the evening would be arriving at his mother's home in a matter of moments.

Why was he so nervous? He was *never* nervous. Granted, his family could be a lot to handle, especially when they were together in a loud, boisterous group. But he didn't doubt Ana would come through their interrogation with flying colors, so long as she remembered her purpose in being there.

No, the reason his stomach was in knots had more to do with seeing *her* again. Something about Ana called to him, awakened his blood. There wasn't any use denying it. That would be akin to denying the sun rose and set every day. His desire for her was just a fact of life now. And he had to decide what to do about it. Sooner rather than later.

There was a knock at the door, and he straightened up as his mother's butler opened it. Lucas sucked in a breath as a woman he hardly recognized entered the foyer.

Was this Ana? *His* Ana of the lopsided hair and the smudged cheeks and the spectacles? There were hints of her in the person who stood before him, like the nervous smile she cast in his direction as she handed over her wrap to the servant, but this woman was more goddess than bluestocking.

He owed Miss Mullany an enormous bonus when he delivered his final payment, because the gown Ana wore was like something out of a fantasy. It was a deep, dark rose color that made her chestnut hair and brown eyes look richer and brighter. It had been fitted perfectly to accentuate the figure she normally hid behind staid mourning gowns. The neckline swooped to reveal the top swell of her breasts, then cascaded over her body in a smooth, flowing line.

Lucas moved toward her, hands itching with a desire

to touch her. Not just touch her, but kiss her, hold her, make her groan with need and gasp with pleasure. The only thing that kept him from doing just that was the fact that he was in his mother's foyer with an entire family waiting expectantly for him to return with his "intended" in tow.

He reached for her hands and lifted one to his lips. A little tremble was his reward and her brown eyes sought his.

"You are beautiful, Ana," he whispered.

She smiled and he forgot to breathe again. It was only then he realized how infrequent that smile was. Oh, she let her lips tilt up from time to time, but that wasn't like this. This warm, open, utterly enchanting expression that doubled his desire to kiss her until neither of them could think straight.

She looked down at her gown. "This is too much, Lucas. One gown is bad enough, but I've been told you ordered an entire wardrobe!"

He stifled a moan. Dear God, an entire wardrobe. It would be like unwrapping a present every time he saw her. Learning which color brought out the glow of her complexion or the sparkle in her eyes. Yes, he owed the seamstress a bonus.

Ana was still talking. "I must insist that you—"

He held up a hand. "What you wear is important to the case, Ana. A new wardrobe is part of our investigation."

The smile that had so enchanted him fell away,

replaced by a flash of hurt and a tinge of embarrassment. Her chin dipped.

"Oh. Of course. I didn't mean to imply that you bought me these things out of any pleasure to yourself."

He slipped a finger beneath her chin. "Actually, it gives me uncommon pleasure to see you in color. Probably more than it should."

Her eyes widened and then her smile returned, along with a pretty pink blush that matched her rosy gown. He offered her an arm. As she slipped her hand into the crook of his elbow, he said, "Come, my family awaits us in the parlor."

He felt her stiffen, tremble at that statement. Reaching up, he covered her hand with his own and was warmed by the brush of her bare arm against his fingertips.

"You will do perfectly fine, Ana. They have no intention of eating you alive."

She gave a brief nod. "I have no choice but to do perfectly fine. For Emily." She let her gaze slip up. "For you."

Lucas didn't wait for the shock of that statement to sink in. He opened the parlor door and led her inside.

The buzz of conversation in the room ceased the moment they entered. Heads swiveled and his entire family stared, along with Henry Bowerly, whom his mother had invited. Lucas girded his loins for the explosion of energy about to come.

"Lady Anastasia Whittig." He squeezed her arm for comfort as he led her forward to where his mother waited on the settee, staring at Ana with a soft expression. "May I present my mother, Lady Dannington."

His mother got to her feet in one smooth, elegant motion and reached out both hands to Ana. She slipped her hand from the crook of his arm and took his mother's offering.

"My dear, my dear," his mother whispered as she enveloped Ana into a brief, fierce hug. "Welcome to our family."

Lucas winced. The complication his family introduced had been keeping him up at night the past two days. Of course they would instantly accept Anastasia. He knew them well enough to realize they would be deliriously happy he had finally chosen a future bride. And yet, at the end of the investigation, the false engagement they had perpetrated would be over. His family would be hurt. They wouldn't understand.

It was a sacrifice he loathed to make, even for King and Country.

With a smile of approval for him, his mother immediately drew Ana away and began to introduce her to the rest of the clan. He watched as Ana shook hands with his older brothers, Peter, who had inherited the title of Earl when their father passed and Martin and their wives. His two older sisters, Elizabeth and Charlotte, and their husbands were next. Then she hesitated before Henry.

His friend looked Ana up and down and his eyes went wide. Lucas knew why. Who wouldn't be shocked by her new appearance after seeing her in widow's weeds? Henry shot a glance at him before he smiled at Lucas's mother.

"Ah, but my lady, I have had the pleasure of meeting Lady Whittig before."

His mother shot a playful glare in his direction. "Of course you have Lord Cliffield, Lucas *would* introduce his future bride to his friends before he recalled his family might like to know her, as well." She patted Henry's arm. "But you are like family, so I forgive his transgression."

His eldest brother Peter laughed as he put an arm around his own wife, Eleanor. "Just this once."

Lucas watched Ana as she laughed with the group and quickly fell into a comfortable rapport with the entire family. It was as if she *belonged* there, sitting amongst his sisters, laughing at his brothers' awful jokes, and exchanging knowing smiles with his mother. Any fears she had expressed about being able to perform the act of his fiancée were unfounded. She performed the part with little trouble.

In fact, as he watched her, he sometimes forgot it was pretend at all. It was too easy to picture her like this forever. A part of his life, a part of his home and family.

He shook off that thought as a footman appeared

to announce that dinner was served. The family began to gather itself into order. His mother walked beside Henry into the dining room and his brothers and sisters followed behind. He trailed his way across the room to where Ana awaited him. He held out an arm wordlessly, and she smiled that real smile she had gifted him with earlier. And as it had earlier, the expression captivated him as he led her into the dining room.

Ana pressed a hand against her aching belly as she tried to catch her breath. It was impossible when laughter kept bubbling up from deep within her and spilling out. Tears of mirth burned her eyes, and her cheeks ached from smiling all evening long at the stories and jokes Lucas's family had shared.

"I swear to you," Lady Dannington said, gulping back her own gasps of laughter. "He took ten years off my life disappearing like that."

Lucas's oldest brother, Peter nodded. "But he was always roaming off, causing some kind of trouble. Eventually we stopped looking. He came home when he was ready."

She met Lucas's stare and was surprised to find he wasn't really involving himself in the story. Instead, his elbow was propped up on the table's edge, his chin resting in his hand, and he was watching her, a small smile tilting his lips.

Her laughter stopped abruptly at the sight of him. This was all an act. It seemed real, but she had to keep reminding herself it wasn't. It simply wasn't.

She forced herself to keep a benign, unaffected face. "I am learning all kinds of new things about you, Lucas."

His smile broadened and those distracting dimples appeared. "You see why I wanted to keep her away from you all."

His family laughed.

"When you ran away," she asked. "Wherever did you go?"

A flash of emotion crossed his face, intense and fierce. She straightened up in surprise to see it. Normally he was so controlled. But, of course, it was gone as swiftly as it had appeared. She had seen it, though, and it made her realize that he, too, had secrets. Buried deep, but there.

Why did she suddenly wish she could ferret them out?

"I couldn't begin to tell you," he said with a shrug. "Don't even recall."

Her brow furrowed. That was a lie. He remembered where he went. Clearly the times he spent alone as a child were important to him. And despite how utterly inappropriate and stupid it was, she wanted to know more.

"I remember!" Henry chimed in with a grin. "There

were plenty of times he came to my parents' estate to hatch all kinds of little plots against his sisters."

There was a cry of mock outrage and laughter amongst the siblings, and the table dissolved into more stories about Lucas's frequent pranks against the lot of them. Whatever deeper emotions she had briefly seen were now gone as he argued his case against their laughing accusations.

Anastasia watched them interact. As entertaining and amusing as the family was, as much as they ribbed each other, what was clear was their love for each other. Their close bond. Lucas's brothers were protective. His sisters adored him. Even Henry, of whom she was unsure, obviously loved Lucas and his family. And from the light in his eyes, those feelings were returned by Lucas completely. He wasn't anything like the stubborn, demanding man who pushed past her boundaries, both physically and emotionally.

Seeing him so at ease with his family made her . . . jealous. That was utterly ridiculous, but there it was. Her parents had died just as she entered adulthood. Her siblings were much, much older than she. They had never been close to her, and they rarely came together now that they each had their own busy lives. She had always been an afterthought to them. Even when her husband died, none of them had offered her deeper comfort than what she would expect from a mere acquaintance.

Being here with this boisterous, affectionate family only made her all the more aware of her own lack of the same.

It also made her wish, for a blinding, terrifying moment, that the ruse of the engagement with Lucas was real. Then she *would* belong to this family. Then all the love they showed each other would also come to her.

And so would Lucas. Permanently.

She flinched at that thought as it skipped traitorously through her mind.

"Why don't we retire to the parlor?" Lady Dannington said as she got to her feet. "I would love to hear more about Lady Whittig now that we have regaled her with our family stories."

Ana started, pleased to be drawn away from the dangerous trails her thoughts were taking. She gave Lucas a quick glance and was relieved he wasn't staring at her. What was it this man did to her that made her long for things she could never, would never have? Made her forget herself?

This case needed to be solved. And not just because of the increasing danger to the spies. Not just for revenge against whoever attacked Emily or struck down Henry. Now her very sanity was in danger. The sooner they caught the culprit, the sooner she could return to her inventions and research and forget Lucas.

"My lady."

She jumped as she turned to find Henry had wheeled his chair beside her. He was staring up at her with an unreadable expression.

"I'm sorry, I was woolgathering."

His smile was thin. "I believe Lucas's mother intends to take him aside for a moment to discuss some family business before they retire to the parlor. Perhaps I may have the pleasure of escorting you instead?"

Lucas looked up from the conversation he was having with his mother. "Yes, would you mind going with Henry? We'll join you in a few moments."

"Of course." Ana forced her thoughts back to the case. Just as Emily had predicted, the chance to question Henry had come, and now she could take it without it seeming forced or obvious.

"That would be lovely. Thank you." She nodded to Lucas and his mother before she walked away with Henry pushing himself along at her side.

"Lucas tells me you accompanied him to the park to observe Sir George make contact with another spy."

Ana's heart leapt as she lifted her gaze. Lucas's siblings and their spouses were just a few feet in front of them. How could Henry bring up such a sensitive subject? Certainly they did not know Lucas's true profession.

She cast him a side glance and found he was watching her just as intently. Perhaps this was a test.

"Lord Cliffield, surely you do not wish to broach such subjects in this place."

Henry's eyes narrowed, and his fingers tightened to white knuckles as he pushed the chair along. "I think I know when my tone is safe and when it is not, my lady," he said, then his eyes softened. "Though I do appreciate your desire for discretion. It serves a person of your position well to always be careful. You never know when a slip in propriety will put you in danger."

Ana did not reply as she watched him. The anger she'd seen at her admonishment was gone now. What had been its cause? Mere frustration over his inability to investigate cases in the field any longer or something else?

"That is very true," she finally said, since he seemed to require an answer. "And these are very dangerous times for . . ." She hesitated again as she stole a glance at Lucas's family. They were engrossed in their own energetic conversation as they entered the parlor. "These are very dangerous times for a person in my position, in any position that protects the Crown. Until we solve this case."

Henry pulled his chair to a stop in the parlor and smiled. "I'm sure you'll do your best, Lady Whittig."

There was something condescending in his tone. Something that raised Ana's hackles. Of course, she knew she had to push that reaction away. There were many spies who thought less than nothing about the Society and their abilities. Even Lucas had his doubts.

"I'll make a few drinks," Lucas's oldest brother, Lord Darrington said. "Lady Whittig? Henry?"

"Sherry," she said with a smile.

Henry inclined his head. "The same."

Once the attention had shifted from them, Henry looked up at her. "You'll be fine, as long as Lucas is there to guide you. He is a talented spy."

She nodded. "Very talented," she agreed and did not have to force that answer.

"His creation of this 'engagement' was genius," Henry continued, his voice dropping so no one else would hear. "And those emotions he showed tonight, they *seemed* so real. He's always been especially gifted when it came to the playacting required by our position."

Ana fought the urge to turn away from Henry's words like they were a physical slap, although his statement wasn't a surprise. Emily had said the same thing many times. Lucas was a gifted spy. Lucas could use emotion to his advantage. And she had been telling *herself* all night that this ruse wasn't real.

Drawing a calming breath, Ana forced a smile. "I suppose we all have to play a role in our profession." She hesitated as Lord Dannington handed over their drinks, then backed away. Once they were alone again, she continued, "You are a good example."

Henry's eyes darted up, wary. "What do you mean?"

"Well, some might dismiss you because of your injury, but clearly you're just as active in your organization as any other man. You know a great deal about this case." She hoped she looked merely interested, not suspicious.

He frowned as his gaze slipped briefly to his legs. "It is very personal to me, of course."

"Yes, I can imagine. After all, you were attacked, and you are as involved with those who were injured or killed as anyone."

Now the frown lengthened, and his grip on the tumbler in his hand strengthened. "I would say I'm more involved than most," he growled. "I sent the spies who were killed or injured to their final assignments."

Ana felt her eyes widen and she forced herself not to react to that surprising outburst. "I did not realize."

Henry blanched, his eyes going strangely wild as he stared up at her. His other fist curled around his chair arm as he opened his mouth to speak. "Well, I have many duties, you know."

She tilted her head, chasing his gaze. "But were you responsible for sending *all* the injured spies to their final duties?" she pressed.

His eyes narrowed. "You were correct, Lady Whittig. This is not the appropriate place for such discussions."

Ana stiffened as he abruptly wheeled himself away. Henry had been so adamant that there was no common element to the attacks. He'd struck her theory down so swiftly. But he had not been correct. The men who had been attacked *did* have one thing in common.

Henry.

"You are lost in thought."

Ana jumped and spun around to find that Lucas had come into the room, walked practically into her arms, without her ever noticing. Some spy she was. Her gaze darted to Henry. He was across the room now, but he was watching them, his expression unreadable.

"Yes, I was just . . ." She hesitated. What to say? That she believed his best friend had just let loose with information he hadn't meant to share? That her intuition was going mad?

"Ana?" Lucas murmured.

"I was just thinking about what a pleasure it has been to know your family better," she said with a stiff smile for the group.

Lady Dannington nodded. "I agree, my dear."

Lucas also smiled, though the expression didn't quite reach his eyes. Still, he offered her an arm and led her closer to the circle of his family.

"Can you tell us more about yourself, Lady Whittig?" Lucas's eldest sister Elizabeth said as she threaded her fingers through her husband's. Ana looked at the comfortable closeness the two shared with a twinge stinging her heart.

She shook the feeling away and tried not to look at

Lucas. "I grew up around Dorset, in a tiny little village called Risenwich."

Lady Dannington smiled. "Ah yes, a lovely place. And your parents were Lord and Lady Horchester, were they not?"

Ana fought to keep her own smile. "Yes," she said softly. "They died of a fever just before I turned twenty."

As the family murmured their condolences, Ana found her attention drawn back to Henry. He had positioned his wheelchair outside of the circle the Tylers had formed and was simply watching the group. Actually, watching Lucas. And now, as his gaze moved, watching her.

Her thoughts returned to his comment about the spies who had been attacked and his admission that he'd assigned them all. He hadn't meant to share that fact, of that she was certain. But why would he want to hide it? Unless . . .

What if the attacks were orchestrated by someone inside the War Department? Someone who knew the identities of the spies and the kinds of cases they were on . . . perhaps because *he* was the one who assigned them, himself.

She broke the stare when Lucas put a gentle hand on the small of her back. When she looked over at him with a start, he smiled. Comforting her. His gaze was full of encouragement.

What would he do if she told him her suspicions?

Would he embrace her theory and help her investigate it, or push her hypothesis . . . and her . . . away?

Shaking her head, she pulled herself together. His reaction didn't matter. He was her partner in this case. She needed to talk to him in private. As soon as possible.

The clock on the mantel dinged out the time. Ana was surprised that it was already midnight. How had the hours flown so quickly? She had enjoyed her time with Lucas's family, ruse or not. Folly or no.

"Is it that late?" Lucas's sister Charlotte asked, getting to her feet. "My goodness. We should get home, love. The children expect an outing bright and early tomorrow."

The rest of the family were already getting to their feet and Ana let out a sigh. She had survived their questions, their hopes for a future with her in their family.

"It is very late," Ana agreed as she gently squeezed Lucas's arm. "But I had a wonderful time. Thank you, my lady, for having me."

Lady Dannington crossed the room, her smile as wide and bright as the sun and just as warm. She enveloped Ana in a second hug and clung to her just long enough that tears sprung to Ana's eyes. That loving contact was something she'd tried to believe she didn't miss. But she did. Desperately.

"Good evening, my dear. You will hear from me in a few days. I hope you'll allow me to call."

Ana nodded immediately. "Of course, I look forward to it." She said her good-byes to the rest of the family, then took the arm Lucas offered.

"I will escort Lady Whittig to the carriage and return in a moment."

Ana followed his lead into the hallway. But the moment he closed the door and they were alone, she half turned toward him.

"I must speak with you alone," she whispered. "Tonight."

There was a flash of something in his eyes. Dark. Dangerous. Sensual beyond words and her body clenched in unwanted and wanton reaction. She could scarcely catch her breath when he looked at her that way.

"Of course. Tell my driver to take you to my home. I shall meet you there in half an hour."

She leaned away and gnawed her lip. The last thing she needed was to be caught in yet another compromising position.

He seemed to read her worries. "My driver is discreet, I assure you."

She nodded. There was no choice. Her thoughts couldn't wait until morning and she couldn't tell him her tentative theory in the hallway of his mother's home with Henry mere feet away. There was no telling how Lucas would react.

"Very well. I will see you in a short while."

But as she ducked out the door and slipped into the

carriage, she realized her heart was throbbing and a thrill had begun to stir low in her belly.

In a very short time, she would be alone with Lucas. With no one to interrupt them, no one to stop them, nothing between them except her wavering resolve.

Chapter 13

Lucas cleared his throat before he opened the door to his parlor where Anastasia awaited him. But as soon as he saw her, he realized what he should have tried to clear was his head. Every erotic fantasy, every inappropriate dream he'd had of her since the moment they met came roaring back to taunt him.

She was standing in front of the fire, staring into the flames with a faraway look in her eyes. She didn't seem to notice as he stepped inside and closed the door. Instead she reached up and caught a loose lock of chestnut hair between her fingers. He watched, mesmerized as she slowly twirled the curl around and around her delicate finger. Then she parted full lips and let out a sigh.

He was taken aback, just as he had been earlier in the evening, by how drawn to her he was. How mesmerized he'd been by her smile that night. How her laugh enchanted him and made him long to hear it as often as possible. And how natural it was to see her with his family, like she had always been there in their loud and teasing ranks.

And now here she was in his home. And it was just as easy to imagine she'd always been here, too. In his life. He wanted more of that. More of everything.

Meeting with her alone in the middle of the night was a mistake. A very bad mistake. He should have been thinking about their case and whatever mysterious thing she wanted to reveal to him about it. But he wasn't. Instead, he was pondering how there was nothing to stop him from what he was about to do: cross the room, draw her into his arms, and kiss her.

It was inevitable.

So he did. In a few long steps he made his way to her, grasped her shoulders and turned her. Ana gasped at the unexpected touch, but she didn't pull away. She didn't run.

"I've been waiting to do this all night," he admitted before he brought his lips down on hers.

He meant for the kiss to be slow, gentle, in the hopes that he could keep it from exploding out of control. But Ana had no such plans. Instead, she parted her lips and took more, demanded more. Lucas was strong in many ways, but not against that kind of assault.

He speared his tongue between her lips, tasting the faint hint of sherry mixed with her natural sweetness. For a wicked moment he wondered if she tasted like that everywhere else and groaned at the unbidden thought that made hot blood rush to his ever-hardening erection.

He slid his hands down the curve of her back, feeling her shiver in response as he pulled her closer and let her know how much touching her affected him. When he gently stroked against her, Ana gasped and pulled back, eyes glazed with need and dark with desire that she too-often repressed out of respect for a dead man he currently hated more than anyone else in the world.

"Lucas," she whispered, a plea, a question, a prayer for a lifeline more than anything else.

But he wasn't noble. He wanted her. And he wouldn't pull back just because she feared what her late husband would think. He owed that man no allegiance. In fact, in his mind, neither did she. If he touched Ana again, he could see that she would surrender. Taking her, loving her until the dawn, it wouldn't ruin her. She was no blushing virgin.

There was no disadvantage to taking what he wanted. Nothing to stop him unless she said no.

Which she wouldn't. Because no matter how she trembled, no matter how many times she put Gilbert Whittig up as a shield between them, she wanted him. With as much fire as he felt in his own body. She might not want to admit it, or even fully recognize it, but it was there in the way she darted her tongue over her lips, in the way her back arched, just the slightest bit, when his arms tightened around her waist and he pulled her closer.

"Just say no, Ana. If you don't want this." He brushed his lips against hers and she tilted her chin up for more.

But she didn't say no. Not when he delved deeper into the kiss. Not when he pulled her in closer, not when he rocked against her a second time. Her fingers curled into his coat, her breath hitched, and her groan was so low he wouldn't have heard it if he wasn't so utterly focused on her and nothing else.

Lucas's hands were moving and gliding in ways Ana had all but forgotten existed . . . and a few she'd never experienced before. There was a little voice inside her screaming to tell him to stop. To run away.

But the voice was very tiny. And every time Lucas stroked his tongue over hers, it grew fainter. When he slipped his fingers up and found the ten little pink buttons that fastened her gown in the back, the voice disappeared entirely.

Her dress drooped forward in a matter of seconds, then fell away. The point of no return had come and gone. She knew what would happen next. If she was honest with herself, she welcomed it. From the first moment she saw Lucas, she had been drawn to him in ways that terrified and excited her. Why couldn't she have just one night?

Lucas stepped back, leaving her cold. He stared at her and heat filled her cheeks as she lifted her hands to cover her barely clad breasts. What was she thinking? A man like him couldn't want her. Now that she was standing in nothing but her chemise, he would come to his senses and send her away.

Instead, he lifted a hand and pushed her protective fingers away, making her stand before him with no barrier but the thin fabric of her underthings.

"Dear God, she even made you a new chemise."

She glanced down. She'd all but forgotten the pretty chemise Miss Mullany had brought along with her new gown. It was soft and pink and matched her dress perfectly. Now she blushed with the realization that Lucas was looking at her with pleasure, not disdain as she had feared.

He wanted her. His eyes told her that. And even if they hadn't, there was no denying the sharp ridge of the erection she'd felt against her belly when he held her close. She saw it now that he had pulled back.

God help her, she wanted him, too. Which was why she didn't step away when he kicked her rumpled dress aside and drew her back into his arms. It was why she didn't resist as he turned her toward the settee and lowered her down on its cushions. It was why she sighed with anticipation as his heavier weight came down beside her.

His mouth explored, teased, tempted and she found herself reaching for the kiss, chasing the pleasure he could give. Every fiber of her being seemed focused on the stroke of his tongue, the fresh taste of his breath and the way his hand was suddenly on her hip. His fingers branded her as they inched up, up the bodice of her chemise, and finally he cupped one breast.

A shudder worked through Ana. His hand was so hot, so big that it covered her entire breast, so rough that she could almost feel the ridges of his fingertips even through the silk garment. Her head lolled back and she shut her eyes with a quiet groan. It was heaven.

Then he moved his hand, and the sensation was better than heaven. Heat sparked from his fingertips as he stroked her breast, his thumb gliding over her hard nipple until a steady throb started between her legs. She arched and pressed her thighs together to relieve it, but that only made the needy feeling more pronounced.

He watched her face, studying every reaction and motion as he tormented her with fingertips, knuckles, his flat palm. No move was rushed, each was designed to have her slipping under his spell.

But she was already lost to it. Lost to him.

And as he lowered his dark head and caught her distended nipple between his lips, she didn't care about being lost. For the first time in years, she felt alive.

She gripped his shoulders as he sucked her nipple through the thin scrap of silky fabric. She could feel that touch through every nerve in her body, but the pressure and pleasure seemed to gather between her thighs. She needed release, craved it like opium.

"Please," she gasped as she pulled at his jacket. "Please."

He lifted his head and smiled down at her. That cocky, sure smile that usually made her blood boil with frustration and desire in equal measure. Now all it did was stoke the need low in her belly. She glared at him, yanking his coat away from his shoulders in a silent order and praying he wouldn't force her to voice what she desired. She didn't think she could manage that. Not when she was shaking, not when her body's wants were roaring through her, clouding her mind.

But he didn't demand she beg. Instead, he shrugged out of the jacket and made quick work of the waistcoat and shirt beneath. As he tossed them away, she stared.

Her husband had been a pampered aristocrat. He hadn't done a day of manual labor in his life. In fact, he hadn't even enjoyed sport all that much. His body had been masculine, but paler . . . softer.

Lucas, despite his upbringing, had the body of a pugilist. Clearly, he used his body as a weapon in the field, trained it with physical exertion. It showed in the way the ropes of muscles shifted beneath his skin. In the way his broad shoulders worked as he slipped his arms beneath her and lifted her into a sitting position.

"Touch me," he whispered. His voice was dark and husky in the quiet room. "Show me what you want."

Her gaze darted to his, and Lucas realized that was both a terrifying and exhilarating order for her to follow. *Want* had never come into the equation when it came to her body before. Perhaps her husband had been what some women called a "considerate" lover. Which Lucas surmised almost always meant the kind of man who asked his woman to close her eyes, think of her duty to the Empire, and did his business with swift efficiency.

If that was the case, what a waste. Ana was so responsive. The lightest touch in the most benign places could make her shake with pleasure. And when he dared to touch her in more intimate ways, her expression alone told him it wouldn't take much to bring her right over the edge of release.

She reached out, delicate hands trembling, and placed a palm flat on his pectoral muscle. He sucked in his breath. He'd thought her touch was electric before. Now it was lightning charged. Hot and soft and unsure, but naturally skilled as she glided her fingertips across muscle, down over his stomach, then hesitated at the waist of his trousers.

Her brown eyes came up, soft and misty, but also questioning.

"Touch me," he said with a nod of encouragement, even though he could hardly hear his own voice over the rush of blood in his ears. "There is no 'wrong' way.

Do what you want, what your body tells you to do."

She drew in a shuddering breath, as if she was gathering her strength to follow his order. Then she met his gaze with a surprising flash of feminine power and let her fingertips drift down and over his throbbing erection.

Lucas tried to remain stoic, but it was just too much. He growled out a curse as he clenched his fists against the settee cushions.

She withdrew her hand immediately. "I'm sorry."

He shook his head. "I don't want you to stop," he managed to pant. "I just want more. More of you."

Her eyes widened, but beneath the surprise was a light of understanding. She knew what he meant. And she understood full well what would happen next.

Lucas leaned toward her, catching the edging of that pretty little chemise between his fingertips. He lifted, inch by inch, taking his time to reveal the fine, gentle curves of her thighs, the soft swell of her hips, the flat plain of her stomach and finally, pulling the article over her breasts, her head.

Ana shifted. He could see her fighting her natural urge to cover herself, but she didn't do it. Instead she sat straight up, watching him look at her. Her nipples tightened under his observation. Her stomach quivered.

She was even more beautiful than he had imagined she would be. Her body was soft and lush, but he could see the benefits her training had given her in the delicate curves of muscles in her arms and legs. He could easily imagine those limbs wrapped around him and he shuddered with the thought.

He bent his head to capture the ridge of her rosy nipple a second time, but this time there was no barrier of fabric between his tongue and her flesh. She arched, her fingers coming up to comb through his hair, a soft cry escaping her lips as he suckled.

His hand found her knee and he cupped it, then his fingers roamed, inching up her thigh until he felt the warm, humid heat of her core greet him. Gently, slowly, he parted her legs and stroked along the crease of her outer lips.

She jolted with a gasp of surprise and pleasure. Her fingers dug deeper into his shoulders, but she didn't refuse him. Her legs fell open and he pushed a finger into her clenching sheath. She pulsed around the digit in welcome.

"Oh my God, Ana," he groaned. "You feel like heaven."

She moaned an answer as her hips lifted and it was too much for him. He needed to be inside her. He needed it more than breath or water or food. And he needed it right now.

He pulled away long enough to yank his boots and trousers off, then returned to his position on the settee. He pulled her down the cushions until she was flat on her back, legs spread, and settled between them.

"Look at me," he whispered.

Ana opened her eyes and met his stare, so wild with the passion he was holding back. The desire she was about to get the full benefit of. All she could see was gray-blue depths, like stormy seas.

"Ana, I can't wait."

It was a lifeline he offered. A way out. She could say no. He had told her that at the beginning. She could say no and he would walk away. Frustrated and angry, probably, but he would not force her hand. He wasn't that kind of man.

But instead of taking the lifeline, she reached for him, urged him into her embrace. She felt the hard, heavy tip of his erection probing her entrance, and she instinctively arched toward the heat of that touch. He growled out pleasure as he moved forward.

And then he was inside her, gently urging her long neglected body to open to accept him. And she did. Her body sang with pleasure as he filled it, filled her. For the first time, she realized how empty she had been in the past few years. Now she felt . . . complete.

She didn't have time to register the shock of that realization because Lucas moved. He thrust, lifting her backside from the settee and steadying her as he moved. Her mind emptied of all thoughts except for the focused pleasure of his touch. She found her back arching, her hips lifting to meet his invasion. Every nerve, every feeling went into sharp focus, centering around the place where their bodies met. Her breath was short as she raced toward release. She had been there before, but never like this.

And then Lucas touched her at the spot where their bodies were locked. His thumb bore down on the button of her pleasure and she bit back a scream of pleasure as her body began to tremble and tremor around his. He seemed to have been waiting for that moment, for her release, because his spine stiffened and he growled out a low, feral sound of pleasure before he pumped hot into her sheath, then collapsed down on top of her, panting.

Ana put her arms around him and held tight, smoothing her palms across the strong planes of his back. He felt . . . right. Making love to him had felt right, lying tangled in his arms felt right. A sense of peace, contentment washed over her. A feeling unlike any she'd ever felt before.

She stiffened at that thought. That couldn't be true. She had been at peace with her husband. He had pleased her. She loved him with all her heart. How could she compare what had just happened with Lucas to her life with Gilbert . . . and have her marriage come up short?

All the worries and fears she had set aside while Lucas touched her came rushing back in one horrible moment. She had always believed if she allowed another man any part of herself that it would cheapen

Gilbert's memory. But it was worse. She had forgotten him entirely.

She had betrayed everything she was. And she had liked it. Already her body craved more.

"Lucas," she said, sliding her hands to his chest and pushing while she tried to ignore how good it felt to touch him even now. "No, get off."

He lifted his head and his eyes locked with hers, dark with remnants of desire. But the moment he saw her face, the desire was replaced by frustration. With a sigh, he rolled away to let her get up. She snatched at her chemise, holding it as a shield before her.

Lucas had no such qualms about his nudity. As if to defy her modesty, he rolled onto his back and put his hands behind his head. He stared at her.

"You don't have to run away from what happened, Ana," he said softly.

She tried to avoid his stare as she pulled the chemise over her head. Now that her aching body was covered, she at least felt some level of control returning to her. Not that she wasn't fully aware that a thin scrap of silk was no barrier to her own desires.

As had been proven tonight.

"You did nothing wrong," he insisted.

She shook her head. "I did everything wrong," she murmured as she searched for her dress. The pretty new gown was now in a wrinkled pile a few feet away. "Oh, I've done everything, everything wrong!"

He sat up, the frustration replaced by full-blown anger. "Don't say that, Ana. Don't ever say that!"

"It was a mistake," she whispered as tears stung her eyes.

But somehow it didn't feel like a mistake. Even now, staring at Lucas, feeling the heat of his passion and his anger as he got to his feet totally nude, what they had shared felt anything but wrong.

"I told you that you could say no," he reminded her, his shoulders stiff.

She looked at him. "I know that. I don't blame you." She rubbed a hand over her face. "I blame myself. I should have taken that offer to pull away."

But it wasn't just that she *hadn't* said no. It was that, when Lucas touched her, she *couldn't* say no.

And that was why it never should have happened. Why it could never be repeated.

Chapter 14

Pain slashed through Lucas's body, so hard and harsh that it surprised him. He didn't think he could feel something so intense. Not when it came to a woman. But with this woman, everything was different.

This night had been powerful for him. He wasn't going to try to deny that fact. Touching Ana, taking her body, had been different from any other experience in his life. And despite her protestations now, after the fact, that it was a mistake, he knew it was powerful for her, too. That was why she was scared.

That was why she was running.

He watched as she struggled to get into her gown and frustration replaced the pain. Why, he didn't know. It wasn't as if he expected more from her. It wasn't as if he wanted more.

But he was still angry. He grabbed for his own discarded trousers and stepped into them.

"Does the memory of a dead man keep you warm?" he snapped as he fastened his waistband.

Ana had her gown halfway over her hips when she froze. Slowly, she turned to face him, her skin as pale as porcelain. He could see how deeply he'd cut her and regretted it, but he was too angry to withdraw the question . . . and too curious about her response.

"How dare you?" Her whisper was harsh in the quiet.

"No, I really want to know. Was your husband so damned perfect that his corpse is preferable to a flesh and blood man? Or is it that you are so afraid to want"—he took a long step toward her, crowding her on purpose—"to *need*—"

She stiffened as he reached for her and caught her shoulders in an inescapable grip.

"—to change, that you will use him as a shield any time your boundaries are pressed?"

"You don't know a thing." Her breath came in heaving gasps between each word.

"Yes, my dear, I'm afraid I do, despite your attempts to keep a wall between us." He yanked and she stumbled against his chest, her dress falling from her hands as she tried to push away. He held tight, keeping her pressed against him and loving the feel of her body against his, regardless of the circumstances. "I know that when I touch you, you quiver. That I can take you over the edge with just a flick of my wrist. That you surge up to meet me when I drive deep inside you."

"Stop," Ana whispered as she twisted in his arms.

But he couldn't let her go. He had been driven to the edge of reason, of sanity, a place he'd never been before. He was out of control. The gentleman inside him, the one that normally would have released her in frustration, had been crushed by her harsh words of rejection, and now he wanted to press her, push her, force her to see what she was so afraid to face.

No matter what the cost.

"Did *he* ever do that for you?" he demanded and found himself praying her answer would be in the negative.

She shook in his arms, her eyes wide and wild . . . but he saw want in them as well as fury and confusion. And the answer he sought also sparkled in the depths of her stare. Lucas knew, just by her expression, that he was the only man who had ever brought her to such heights. Had ever made her lose herself so completely.

That accomplishment brought powerful triumph crashing through him and tempered his frustration.

"He is dead, Ana," he said softly. "Climb out of the grave you have put yourself in beside him. You know you want more."

She shook her head and her voice took on an edge of desperation, like she was trying to convince herself of her feelings more than him. "No. No, I loved him. Pleasure is nothing compared to that. I can't let *wanting* make me forget."

With a shove against his chest, she wrenched herself free. Lucas could have caught her, but he let her go. He was too stung to hold her.

Pleasure was nothing to a dead love and she was driven to cling to it, even if it meant cutting off her life. Cutting him off.

Why did that hurt so much?

They stared at each other for a long moment and then he turned away so she wouldn't see just what those words did to him.

"I don't think you have anything to worry about." He stared at the dying fire with unseeing eyes. "You never let yourself forget for a moment that you are a widow. *His* widow. No one else can forget either."

Behind him, she gasped, but he didn't move. He could not stand to look at her and have her deny him. Deny passion. Deny whatever else was boiling between them.

The silence stretched for a long time, but finally she cleared her throat.

"I came here tonight because I thought of something."

Slowly, he turned. She had pulled her dress up and was in the process of buttoning it. Her mouth was still swollen from his kisses and her chest still flushed from the release he had given her, but her expression was detached. As calm a mask as any seasoned spy he'd ever worked with.

"Did you?" His voice was hard as ice.

She hesitated for a moment at his tone, but then nodded. "I am beginning to wonder if someone inside the War Department could be involved in the attacks on the spies."

Lucas froze, his anger and disappointment fading at that stunning statement. As much as it sickened him, he could not dismiss it immediately.

"Why do you believe that?" he asked, metering his tone.

"From the information I've been given, it seems like many of the attacks were on spies who were deeply hidden from public view. Their identities would be difficult to ascertain without inside knowledge. As would be their meeting places. Clearly there are common meeting arrangements in your organization, but some of these men were attacked at parties, even in their own homes. Places no one should have been laying in wait hoping to catch a spy off guard."

Lucas nodded. He hated to admit it, but her theory made sense.

"The attackers do always seem to be one step ahead of our spies," he murmured. "They often attack when our men are close to breaks in their cases. Someone on the inside would have access to that kind of information."

"Selling that kind of information to our enemies

could be very lucrative for a person in financial difficulty . . . or even someone who was just greedy," she said with a nod.

Her discomfort seemed to dissipate as they moved away from the subject of the sex they had just indulged in and toward the relative safety of their case, where they could pretend not to have any personal relationship. Bitterness surged in him, but he tamped it down. This was business now.

Pleasure was over.

"It's a plausible theory. I will do some investigation into the possibility."

She lifted her gaze to his. Her eyes sparkled with emotions, and he found himself drawn to her despite the knowledge that she was afraid of what they'd shared. That she wanted to deny it meant anything.

"I have an idea of whom you could investigate."

He started. "What? You don't know the War Department as well as I do. Who could you possibly suspect?"

She hesitated again, and it put every fiber of his being on edge. What in the world could she be holding back? What could make her shift her weight with nervousness and refuse to meet his eyes?

Finally, she whispered, "I believe it might be Lord Cliffield."

"Henry?"

Ana winced at the loud, angry, and incredulous tone of Lucas's voice. It seemed all she could expect from him tonight was passion, whether it be angry or otherwise. She shivered as he stared at her, blinking like he wasn't sure he had understood her correctly.

She nodded.

He barked out a harsh laugh. "Henry Bowerly, the blasted Marquis of Cliffield? My best friend? The man who was nearly killed in the first attack?" He stared at her. "And *that* is who you suspect is behind the attacks on the spies?"

She tensed under his mocking look, but didn't turn away. She'd expected as much, she even understood it, though she didn't like the way he looked at her like she had lost her mind. After all, Lucas had seen his best friend bleed. He'd held Henry and prayed he would survive an assassin's bullet.

Just as she had when Emily was attacked. She could only imagine that if the tables were turned . . . if Lucas came to her with accusations against Emily or Meredith, she would react with much the same disbelief.

She drew in a few long breaths to stay calm. It was all she could do. Tonight Lucas had tempted her with potent desire, challenged her with angry lust, and now he was denying her with utter contempt. And all the while he was standing mere feet away from her wearing only loosely buttoned trousers. His hands were firmly planted on trim, muscular hips, which only drew her attention to the subtle ripple of his stomach muscles each time he drew a harsh breath.

And made her recall, in vivid detail, the reason he

was standing with no shirt, no boots, his hair wild from the way her fingers had combed through it at the height of passion.

She blinked away the images of his mouth on hers, his body filling her. This was no time to allow distraction. Especially since she had so adamantly denied those things had meaning to her.

"I—I realize this is a shock to you," she murmured, trying to look anywhere but his half-naked body. "You may not want to believe—"

He cut her off by biting out, "I *don't* believe it."

"Lucas—" she started.

"No." He shook his head when she tried to speak again. "*No*, Ana. I have known Henry since I was eight years old."

"I'm aware of that." She stepped up to him and reached out before she considered the consequences of such an action. When her fingers touched his bare arm, a spark ran up her spine. His skin was warm beneath hers and more of those heated images flooded through her mind, unwelcome, but oh, so pleasurable to recall.

Lucas tilted his head and met her gaze. His stare was one of challenge, daring her to keep touching him. Daring her to pull away.

She did, yanking her fingers back as if he burned her.

"I am aware of that," she repeated, managing to keep some semblance of control. "But the fact you've known Henry most of your life is exactly why you may be blind to the truth."

"I am not blind, Anastasia. You have been in the field for what . . . all of two weeks? And yet you think you have uncovered the answer to questions my organization has been pursuing for a year or more?" He barked out a laugh that was anything but kind or humor-filled. The confrontation in his stare doubled.

She stiffened. He was mocking her and her abilities. "I may not have been in the field as long as you have been, but I *have* been involved in many investigations before. I have intuition, Lucas. And whether or not you want to see it at this very moment, I also have ability."

She froze as she heard the words come from her lips. For the first time, she believed them. For the first time since she'd been approached by Charlie, she had faith in her skills. When had that happened? And how?

Lucas's snort of disbelief cut off her thoughts. Tears sprung to her eyes at his look of incredulity. She hadn't realized until that moment how important his confidence in her had become. His praise was something she'd come to depend on. And even though she knew his present attitude had more to do with her reaction after they made love and her accusations toward Henry, it still tore through her with surprising pain.

Part of her wanted to run and hide, but for the first time, a stronger part of her made her stay.

"He kept facts of the case from you."

Lucas waved a hand. "Enough of this."

She trembled, but pressed on. "And he conjured up evidence for which you have no source."

"No—"

It took everything in her to continue in the face of his angry refusals, but somehow she did it. "He is the one who assigned the spies, Lucas! All of them who went to their deaths were sent there by him. *He* knew their movements. *He* had all the facts of their cases. He told me that himself tonight, but when he let that information slip, I saw panic in his eyes." Now it was she who stepped toward him and he who retreated back. "I may not know much, but I know what I saw."

He folded his arms. Gone was the gentle spark in his eyes. And the smile she'd come to anticipate was also long gone. The man before her was hard and cold as steel. Unbendable. Untouchable.

"There are other explanations."

Ana stared at him, surprised by how painful the distance he now put between them was. There would be no reasoning with him tonight. Not when he was so hell bent on denying her suspicions.

"I can see you are angry. You don't want to believe this to be true. Perhaps I should just go and leave you to consider what I've said."

His eyes narrowed. "Yes, that is probably best."

Shaking her head, she made for the door, but before she left, she looked over her shoulder.

"Please think about it, Lucas. Because even if you refuse to look into my theories, they have merit. And if you don't pursue them, I will."

Before he could answer, she left, shutting the door behind her. Outside in the hallway, she leaned against the barrier that now separated them. But even if the door hadn't been between them, they were clearly leagues apart. Tonight had changed the fragile relationship they'd been building. Not just the argument they'd had, but making love and his challenges regarding Gilbert, as well. Nothing would ever be the same again.

What did that mean? And why did it frighten her so much?

She wasn't sure. The only thing she was sure of was that he was the most frustrating man she had ever met. And she could not deny that he'd given her the most wonderful night of her life.

Meredith held up the tea pot in offering, first to Ana, then to Tristan. Both of them shook their heads. Meredith splashed a bit in her own cup, then returned to the little round table in her parlor. She sat down between her husband and Ana, and gave her friend a smile.

Ana wished she could return the smile with one so broad and free of tangled emotions, but it was impossible. As pleasant as it was to sit in Meredith and Tristan's home, her mind was constantly turning, burning with memory, aching with doubt and possibility.

From the light of concern in Meredith's eyes, her

friend noted Ana's state, though she had yet to say anything about it.

"I'm very happy you could finally stop by and pay us a call," Tristan said as he placed a gentle hand over Meredith's. "I have wished to see you very much since our arrival, though training and business have kept me away."

Ana nodded. Tristan had been preparing to become a spy for the War Department ever since he married Meredith. Her friend beamed with pure pride at her husband, and Tristan's hand tightened over hers in a silent message.

Turning her face, Ana concentrated on her cup of tea. The flush of jealousy surprised her. She did not begrudge her best friend any happiness. Meredith deserved every moment of joy she had now.

But Ana couldn't help but wish her own life were so uncomplicated. That her emotions were clear and well-defined. Up until a few weeks ago, they had been. She'd been a widow. She'd been in mourning. She knew who she loved. She knew who she was.

Thanks to last night, thanks to Lucas's accusations, now she knew nothing at all.

"Tristan is going to be a wonderful spy," Meredith said with a smile. "He has amazing instincts."

Tristan laughed as he got to his feet. "And my amazing instincts tell me that Anastasia wants to speak to you alone." Ana opened her mouth to protest, but Tristan shook his head. "No, no, I don't mind. You are in the middle of a case and need my wife's assistance. I certainly look forward to the day when I call upon it."

He smiled as he bent to place a kiss on Meredith's cheek, then patted Ana's shoulder before he slipped out of the room, shutting the door behind him.

Ana shifted uncomfortably as Meredith's blue stare settled on her face. "I didn't mean to push him out of his own sitting room."

"He understands. Soon enough we'll be working cases together." Meredith beamed with excitement at the prospect and Ana winced. The thrill of a case would bring her friends closer together, not push them apart as had happened to her and Lucas.

Not that she wanted to be closer to him. Or at least, that was what she kept repeating to herself.

She shook her head. "I cannot believe you will no longer be a part of The Society. What will Emily and I do without you?"

Meredith drew back in surprise. "I will always be a member of The Society, no matter how many cases I work on with Tristan." Her eyes narrowed. "And you are trying to change the subject before it has even started. Enough nonsense about my future, Ana. You have been troubled since your arrival. What is wrong? Has something happened?"

Ana plucked at the lacy edging of the tablecloth as she pondered that question. Everything had happened. Everything had changed. But how could she explain that to Meredith? How could she tell her poised, calm friend that she had been swept away by passion?

She couldn't. Instead, she focused on the case. That was the only area Meredith could truly assist her with at any rate.

"Do you remember how I asked you to look into Henry Bowerly's past?"

Meredith nodded.

"Well, I am beginning to believe that someone within the War Department itself may be involved in the attacks on the spies." She sighed. "And based on a few things Henry said, I wonder if he could be the one."

Meredith got to her feet and paced to the fireplace. "Have you brought this up to Lucas?"

Ana shivered as she thought of his face the night before. How angry and frustrated he'd been. How he'd shut her out, shut her down.

"Yes. He refuses to give my theory any consideration. He got angry, he turned away from me." To her horror, her voice broke and she darted a glance at Meredith to find her friend staring at her. Damn it. Of course she wouldn't miss a thing.

But instead of pointing out her emotionality, Meredith said, "Well, this is troubling, indeed. Although I suppose I understand why Lucas wouldn't want to believe his friend capable of wrongdoing. Did you speak to Charlie?"

Ana nodded. "I met with him very briefly before I

came here. I asked him to obtain some information about Cliffield's finances. If he has encountered any trouble, it could be a motive for turning on his own men."

Meredith nodded. "So with that background information being collected, all you're worried about is Lucas. His feelings on the subject."

"No!" Ana struggled to her feet. "I'm not worried about Lucas. Annoyed by him, yes. Frustrated. But not worried."

Meredith's eyebrows went up. "Please. I've known you a long time, Ana. Don't try to pull the wool over my eyes. I can see through you."

Ana winced.

Her friend took a step closer and her expression softened. "What happened, Ana? What has your face so pale and makes you shake when you hear Lucas Tyler's name? Was there more kissing?"

The heat of a blush rushed to Ana's face, tingling around her hairline. Meredith stopped moving and the level of her voice notched up.

"Was there more than kissing?"

Ana could hardly draw breath. She tried to calm herself, but Meredith's words only inspired more of those memories that had been assaulting her all night and all day. Every time they were powerful, every time they were sinfully detailed. They mocked her by forcing her to recall her own pleasure, her own surrender.

"Ana?" Meredith asked, reaching for her hands.

She shut her eyes. "Things got . . . out of hand between us last night."

Meredith sucked in a breath and her fingers tightened. "Out of hand? What do you mean?"

Tears pricked behind Ana's eyelids. She fought them, but they squeezed past her shut lids and slid down her cheeks. "We—I—"

"Did he force himself on you?" Meredith's voice was sharp.

Immediately, Ana's eyes flew open. "No! No, he gave me every opportunity to refuse him. And I didn't, Meredith. I never said no. I never wanted him to stop."

Her friend's face relaxed as she drew Ana into a hug. Then she slipped her arm around her shoulders and guided her toward a settee by the fire. Meredith rubbed a comforting hand over her back as Ana swiped away sudden tears.

"You did nothing wrong," Meredith assured her quietly.

Ana barked out a laugh. "Nothing wrong? I made love to my partner. A man who hardly even likes me. I probably hurt my case. And I did the one thing I swore I'd never do. Forgot my husband."

Meredith sighed. "As you have said before, Emily and I didn't love our first husbands, so I know we don't fully understand your continued attachment to Gilbert. However, I do know that when he died, you didn't join him in the grave."

And jolted. That was what Lucas had said, too.

"He has been gone a long time. There is nothing wrong with allowing yourself pleasure." Meredith hesitated. "There was pleasure, wasn't there?"

Ana blushed. "Yes, there was certainly that. More pleasure than I knew was possible."

Meredith smiled.

"Don't look at me like that!" Ana protested as she covered her face. "Don't you understand what that means? Not only did I betray my husband by letting another man into my body, but I betrayed him by . . . by *liking* it more! It shouldn't be that way. I loved Gilbert. I loved him with all my heart and my soul. Making love to him should have been better because we had our feelings to bind us."

"And those feelings are a powerful thing," Meredith said with a nod of her head. "They will always live in your heart. But that doesn't mean that you cannot or will not feel stirrings for someone else. That your body won't react to someone else. That you might not even develop a new kind of love for someone else."

"I don't love Lucas Tyler!" Ana pushed out of the settee.

Meredith looked at her. "I never said you did."

"Well, I don't." Ana fisted her hands at her sides. "I don't love him. So why does my body still *ache*, Meredith? Why do I want his touch even though I know it was a mistake to give in to those desires?"

Her friend shook her head. "What happens between a man and a woman to spark that fire of longing is a mystery, Ana. Desire isn't something you choose. It simply . . . is."

She sighed. "Yes. It is."

Meredith shrugged. "So what will you do now? Give up the case?"

"No!" Ana shook her head. "I've come too far to give up. I owe it to Emily to uncover the truth."

"Then you will have to find a way to ignore the desire you feel for Lucas." Meredith smiled again. "Or surrender to the power of it, because you'll be forced to work by his side."

Ana groaned. "Yes. We're attending the ball at General Mathison's home tonight. Our first true appearance since our 'engagement.' In fact, I should ready myself."

Meredith slipped an arm through hers and walked her to the foyer. As she pressed a kiss to Ana's cheek, she whispered, "Lucas Tyler is a handsome man, Ana, and you are a *widow*, not a wife. Being with him, wanting him . . . it isn't wrong."

Ana shivered as she gave Meredith a quick hug of good-bye and stepped outside. But as she got into her carriage, her friend's words echoed in her head. And as wrong as she knew them to be, she couldn't deny the thrill that rocked through her at the idea that she could continue an affair with Lucas while their case was ongoing. That she could repeat the pleasure of the night before without guilt or recrimination. But that wasn't true. It couldn't be. The reaction she'd had to Lucas was too powerful, too dangerous.

Her heart belonged to someone else, but she had realized Lucas could easily snatch it away if she allowed him a chance.

So she would come to him with cool businesslike detachment. It was the only way.

Chapter 15

Lucas read the report in front of him a third time and still had no idea what it said. Damn it, why couldn't he get last night out of his head? He needed to work, he needed to sleep, he needed to forget, but his mind revolted and instead bombarded him with images of Ana.

Ana as her dress drooped around her waist. Ana with her head thrown back, gasping when he touched her. Ana at the height of passion, fingernails digging into his back as she moaned out release and her body tensed and tremored around him.

He shifted as unwanted blood rushed to incredibly uncomfortable places. Damn it, damn it, damn it!

It was *sex*, for pity's sake. He'd had plenty of it, last

night was no different. It felt different, but it wasn't. It couldn't be. He refused to let it be.

"What is wrong with you?"

He started at Henry's voice. He'd all but forgotten his friend's presence.

"What? Nothing is wrong with me," he insisted with the wave of a hand. "Why would you think there was?"

Henry arched an eyebrow as he set aside the paper-work they had been reviewing. "You're behaving very strangely today. You have been ever since my arrival."

Lucas dipped his head to avoid his best friend's eyes. How the hell was he supposed to explain himself? He couldn't exactly come out with the information that he'd made love to a partner he never wanted, that it had been the most earth-shattering night in his recollection, and oh, by the way, she thought Henry was a vile traitor.

And how was your evening?

"Did something happen after you left your mother's home last night?" Henry asked, his brow wrinkling with concern.

"It was a nice gathering, wasn't it?" Lucas asked as he began to scribble nonsense on a paper in front of him. Nothing like avoidance to fill the time.

"Yes," his friend said slowly, drawing the word out. "Your family is always a pleasure and it was . . . enlightening to see Lady Whittig on the case."

Enlightening. Yes, it had been that. Now Lucas knew

much more about her than he had before. Like what her real smile looked like. And what her skin tasted like. And how tight and hot she could cling to him when she shivered with release.

Damn it.

"She—She is a much more complicated individual than I believed," Lucas admitted. That much was true.

Henry's eyebrow arched higher. "Really? Do tell me. Because as lovely as she is and as easily as she took on the role of your fiancée with your family last night, I still cannot imagine she's much use in the field. She's been so sheltered."

Lucas tensed as he was overcome by a strange, but powerful urge to defend Ana against the very accusations he'd once made against her.

"Actually, she has some interesting theories about the case," he snapped and immediately wished he could take the words back. The last thing he wanted to do was trouble Henry with Ana's ridiculous allegations.

Henry adjusted in his chair using his powerful upper arms. "How fascinating. What is Lady Whittig's theory? Tell me she isn't still stuck on the idea that the attacks are related beyond the fact that all are spies."

Lucas stiffened. Henry had been dismissing that theory for over a week. Now a thin sliver of doubt entered his mind. Why did his friend want to steer him away from the concept?

He shook his head. No. This was just Ana's foolish theory bouncing around in his mind. Creating doubt in a friend who he knew could not be involved. Henry had nearly been killed, for God's sake. There was no way he could be some kind of mastermind selling the secret identities of War Department spies.

"I'm not certain that idea is as ridiculous as you seem to believe," he said, trying to keep his tone and demeanor unreadable. A difficult task with a person who had known him all his life.

Henry's eyes widened. "You must be in jest. You really think the attacks are linked? By what, by whom?"

"I'm not certain." Lucas shrugged. "But Ana introduced an interesting idea last night. That the attacks are being orchestrated from inside the War Department."

Henry straightened up, his fists gripping the armrests of his wheelchair. His face lost all color, and his lips thinned with outrage and horror and anger. Lucas turned away from the emotion on his friend's face. He understood it all, and also understood that Henry must feel those reactions all the more keenly due to the bullet that had changed his life forever.

"Anastasia Whittig does not know us, Lucas. She doesn't know us," he said, deceptively soft. "How can she make such an ugly, disgusting accusation without knowing the men who work so hard to protect this country?"

Lucas nodded. "I know how you feel—"

Henry cocked his head. "Do you?"

"No." Lucas met his friend's eyes. "Not completely, of course. But when I think of all those men, working and dying for King and Country, I hate to think that any of them could be a traitor. That is the lowest a man can be, to barter others for profit or whatever the twisted motive is that drives him. But when I let myself move past the anger and the disbelief, I saw a kernel of truth in what she said."

"*A kernel of truth?*" Henry spat out. His fisted hands tightened until his knuckles were bright, bloodless white. "I don't understand you, Lucas! How you can believe that woman?"

"That woman," Lucas said softly, fighting to maintain calm despite the fact that he was starting to resent Henry's tone, "is no fool."

Henry stared at him. "Are you letting your mind lead you, Lucas? Or something else?"

"What?" Lucas's mouth dropped open in shock.

"I don't judge you for wanting her. She has a certain air about her that is undoubtedly pleasing, but I've never known you to let desire blind you. I hope you're not doing that now!"

Lucas bit his lip and slowly counted to ten. He would *not* react to that barb. He would not give in to his natural inclination, which was to defend himself.

"You know me better than that, don't you, Henry?"

Henry gave a noncommittal shrug before he began to roll his chair backward and turn it toward the door. "I don't know what to believe after hearing this nonsense. But I know you must ready yourself to meet Lady Whittig and go to General Mathison's soirée tonight. I think it's best if I leave you to it." He looked at Lucas over his shoulder as he opened the door. "I truly hope you reconsider where your loyalties lie, my friend. I'd hate to see you throw away your friendships over a piece of skirt."

Before Lucas could respond, Henry rolled away and left him alone. Lucas threw himself back into his chair with a groan. Henry's anger troubled him, as did his charge that Lucas was being lead by desire, not truth. Considering the fact that he hadn't been able to stop thinking about sinking into Ana's body since the night before, he feared that barb might be right.

But what was even more troubling than that was the fact that he hadn't actually told Henry the whole truth. He had withheld Ana's assertion that *Henry* could be the one behind the attacks.

And as much as he wanted to tell himself that he'd kept that fact a secret just to protect his friend from being torn apart by the idea, there was more to it.

Ana had succeeded in creating doubt. And the more he realized that, the bigger the doubt grew. Doubt in his best friend. Doubt in himself.

And he had absolutely no idea what to do about it.

Ana drew in a few deep, calming breaths. She needed to be focused, composed before she opened the parlor door. Lucas was there waiting on the other side and the last thing she desired was for him to see how torn apart she'd been all day.

She could have no reaction when she saw him. Give away no information that he could twist and use against her.

With a final breath, she went into the room. Lucas was sitting in a chair facing the doorway, and as she entered, he rose to his feet in a slow, cold unfolding that made her all the more aware of the strength in his body.

It also made all her good intentions of keeping emotion from her face fly out the parlor window. She couldn't help but draw in a harsh breath at the sight of him. The last time she'd seen him, he'd been wearing far less.

The thought brought a fresh wash of need through her. The desire was as demanding and overwhelming as it had been the night before. Perhaps more intense, in fact, because now she knew what it would be like to surrender to his demands. To give and take pleasure in his arms.

Wanting that made her feel desperate and achy. And from the stern, cool expression on his face, he felt nothing of the same. Which meant he had the upper hand.

Again.

"Good evening," she said.

He nodded once before he returned to his seat. She sighed. So he was still angry at her.

"Since we have a little time before we're expected at the General's, would you like a drink?"

"God, yes," he muttered.

She sighed. It was going to be a long evening if this is how he intended to behave. No, it was better this way. If he no longer pursued her, if he only showed her chilly courtesy, it would be easier to concentrate on their case. After all, she didn't want to be caught up in desire or emotion or any other troubling feelings he caused.

She just wanted to discover who was behind the attack on Emily. She didn't want Lucas.

She splashed a bit of sherry in two tumblers and turned to offer him one. His fingers brushed hers as he took the glass and her knees actually went weak for a brief, powerful moment.

So, she wanted him. But want and need were two different concepts. She just had to control the desire. Push it deep down inside herself and forget it was there.

That seemed impossible right now as she met his stare, but she could do it. She had to.

"Have you thought about last night?" she asked and immediately wished she could take the question back. So much for controlling the wanting.

Lucas's eyes widened and a little smile tilted one side of his mouth, hinting briefly at the existence of one dimple. "All night, I assure you."

She scowled. He was taunting her. And her traitorous body was responding to it.

"I meant, did you consider my theory?" She wanted ice to drip from every word, but instead her voice trembled. Blast!

His smile fell, and he took a long sip of his drink. "Yes, I thought about that. But my response hasn't changed. I agree with you that there is a possibility someone inside the War Department could be involved in the attacks. But I refuse to believe Henry could be the one. There is just too much evidence to the contrary."

She sighed. "Because he was shot?"

Lucas flinched before he nodded once.

"That would be the most convenient cover, wouldn't it?" she pressed, with the full knowledge that she was treading in dangerous waters. Lucas's glare confirmed that fact. "His injury would naturally take suspicion off of him."

The glare sparked with anger, and Lucas got to his feet and slammed his drink down.

"Are you implying he wasn't really hurt?" He didn't wait for her reply. "Because I was there. I felt his blood, I heard his pain. He *was* injured that night, Anastasia."

"I don't disagree with that fact." She made her tone softer to counteract his anger. "I'm only saying that his injury shouldn't automatically remove him from suspicion."

Lucas froze, his face twisting as he tried to find an argument. But there was none. Her heart went out to him. Despite his protests, his denials, he was a good spy. She could see he had been analyzing the evidence she presented the night before, turning it over in his head.

And it tore him up inside. Her anger toward him and his callous dismissals melted a fraction.

She reached for him, but just as he had before, he pulled away.

"It's time to go, Ana," he snapped as he walked past her to the door.

She let a long sigh escape her lips as she followed him out. Her heart stung even though she fought the feeling. It shouldn't matter how far Lucas pushed her away.

But it did. And she could no longer deny that fact.

The carriage rocked as it pulled around a corner. Ana shifted slightly, drawing Lucas's attention away from the window and toward her. Not that he hadn't been utterly aware of her the entire ride.

It was impossible not to be aware of her. He could smell that erotic combination of gardenia and jasmine even from across the carriage seat. And though the light in the carriage was dim, there was enough to see the lines of Ana's face.

Enough to be entirely captivated by every shift in

her expression, every hitch of her breath. She was holding tension in every part of her body and had been since they left her home less than a quarter of an hour before, leaving him to imagine all the wicked ways he could relieve that anxiety.

But there was so much between them at present. Their argument earlier had proven that. There was the little matter that she suspected his best friend of vile treason.

Oh, and the fact that despite how angry and frustrated he was, he still wanted to peel her gown off and take her right there on the carriage seat. But he didn't. Mostly because her claim that the night before had been a "mistake" still rang in his ears.

It was a mistake he wanted to repeat again and again, all her harsh denials be damned.

Ana's gaze moved to his, and he realized he was staring at her. Their eyes locked, and a long moment passed between them in the painful silence of the carriage. He couldn't tell what thoughts were in her head. Her skills at hiding her emotions were improving. That should have been a satisfaction to him . . . her openness could get her killed.

But instead he wished he could get a peek at what she thought when she stared at him with such focused intent.

Before he could ask . . . or worse, act on the wicked fantasies that played on the edges of his sanity, the carriage pulled to a stop. Her eyes still didn't leave his, and he couldn't seem to bring himself to look away.

Instead, he reached out and caught the door latch, holding it shut so that when the footman stepped up and began to pull it open, he was inhibited and immediately stopped trying to enter.

Ana's eyes widened and her breath caught. "Lucas . . ."

His eyes shut, and he held back a curse at the sound of her breathing his name out like a prayer. The *wanting* had never been so powerful with any other woman before. Just hearing her voice was enough to get him ready. How the hell had this happened with her, of all the women in the world?

With difficulty, he cleared his swimming head.

"I hope you will be able to work tonight." His voice sounded rough with desire.

Her eyes narrowed, and a flash of bright, emotional fury lit up and made them sparkle with a life she often hid behind the shield of her spectacles or widow's weeds. It was a pleasure to see her awakening, despite the fact that her anger was directed toward him.

"I am not the one with a problem," she ground out. "If you believe we won't be able to work together because of a—a—" She hesitated and he knew she was thinking about the night before. Pink tinged her cheeks before she continued. "Because we had a disagreement, then you are the one who should reconsider your abilities."

She pushed his hand away from the carriage door and turned the handle.

"Because I know what my duty is."

Then she took the footman's waiting hand and stepped outside into the night.

Chapter 16

If he wouldn't look at her, she certainly didn't have to look at him. Ana folded her arms and pointedly looked away from where Lucas was standing at the edge of the ballroom talking to a gentleman she didn't recognize. It was childish reaction and one she wasn't proud of, but right now her emotions seemed to be leading her behavior.

Growling out her dissatisfaction with herself, she returned her focus to the ballroom. It was quite a crush tonight. General Mathison was a highly decorated soldier who had come home to great acclaim and married a well-born lady. He was the current toast of the *ton*, which meant every important person wanted to align themselves with him.

Including Lord Sansbury, who was currently dancing with a young lady. Ana rolled her eyes. Despite the fact that she didn't particularly like Sansbury after he outed the secret of her first kiss with Lucas, she had lingering doubts about his involvement in this case. Looking at him with his vapid smile, she doubted he was mastermind material, though she could be wrong. After all, she'd thought the spy they'd watched in the park was a fool, too.

And Lucas was insistent, plus the information Henry kept providing to them boosted the case against Sansbury. Which only served to make Ana all the more suspicious of Henry. It seemed mightily convenient that he kept decoding information that pointed straight to the loose-lipped dandy. Especially since she had not been allowed to view the encoded evidence herself.

Her head spun. She looked away from their suspect to find herself locking eyes with Lucas's mother. Lady Dannington waved, and she lifted her own hand in greeting. She just hoped she would not be trapped into conversation with the woman a second time. She'd talked with her for over half an hour upon their arrival and every moment was torture. Not because she didn't care for her ladyship's company. On the contrary, she already felt a strong kinship toward the woman. But because Ana knew Lucas's mother was heading for a disappointment. When this case was over, when this "engagement" was quietly ended . . . his entire family would be hurt.

She hated that.

Lady Dannington's smile suddenly broadened and Ana looked instinctively to her right to see Lucas crossing the room toward her in long, purposeful steps. To anyone else's eyes, he certainly looked like a man off for a moment with the woman he loved. Everything about him screamed that he was staking a claim. Her heart leapt at the sight, despite the fact that this was all part of some formula he had been repeating all night.

They would dance. He'd hold her close and smile at her as he looked into her eyes. Then he would walk away and not spare her a glance for three or four dances. He spent exactly enough time with her to ensure the world believed their farce, no more.

It was becoming so frustrating that she fought the urge to turn on her heel and publicly refuse him.

"Ready?" he asked with a smile that didn't even come close to lighting up his gray eyes.

She took his arm with a sigh. "My, you are a romantic, aren't you?"

He took a position in the line of dancers across from her. At least this was a country dance, so she wouldn't have to press against him as she had when the waltz played.

"My lady," he purred as they moved together and touched hands. "Is it romance you desire from me?"

She bit her lip as they moved apart. She turned around the gentleman beside her, moved as she was supposed to do, but her mind was anywhere but in the steps she was performing. Insolent man.

They came back together and Lucas was smirking. She glared at him briefly before she forced her face into a more polite and warm expression. "Of course not."

His grin tilted up. "And what is it you *do* desire?"

As they parted a second time, Ana sighed. He did delight in tormenting her, that was clear. The worst part was that his questions were exactly the same as the ones she'd been asking herself since they made love. How could she have let things go so far?

And why, as their fingers brushed a third time while they moved down the line, did her body ache to do it all again?

She refused to meet his gaze, instead looking into the crowd behind him. She found Lord Sansbury in a group of gentlemen, but he didn't appear to be paying much attention to the buzzing soirée. In fact, he continually looked to the grandfather clock near the terrace doors.

Her brow furrowed. There was something very strange in his demeanor. Like he was nervous. She didn't think she'd ever seen him like that before.

"Look at Sansbury when you make the next turn," she whispered. "He is by the middle terrace door on the south side of the ballroom."

The teasing, testing light in Lucas's stare dissipated, and his face hardened. The rogue was gone, the spy was back. The shift was so subtle, she never should have seen it, but she was so damned aware of Lucas's every affectation that she couldn't avoid noticing the switch.

He glanced at the door as he made an elaborate turn, and his eyes narrowed. She followed his gaze as she moved back into place in line. Sansbury was moving toward the terrace. He cast a quick glance over his shoulder before he exited. Her heart began to race.

Lucas met her stare, his mouth in a thin line. "We'll follow when the music ends."

She nodded, quickly counting off the beats. The orchestra was playing a popular song and it had two movements left. The time that passed during those movements could be crucial. They needed to get out of the ballroom.

Now.

She drew in a sharp breath as she stepped out. The moment she set her slipper down, she wrenched her ankle to the side and went down with a gasp.

Immediately, the other women in the line rushed for her as Lucas went down on one knee.

"Are you all right, my dear?" one woman said as Lucas slipped a hand under her elbow. He met her eyes and she saw his fleeting smile.

"Yes," she said with a pretend wince. "Oh, how silly. I've twisted my ankle that is all."

Lucas tilted his head with the perfect amount of concern. "Let me help you, darling."

She slipped her arm through his and leaned against him, painfully aware of his body heat through his woolen coat.

"If I walk a bit, it might help," she said. "Will you take me for a turn about the garden?"

He nodded as the crowd began to pull back. "Of course."

"I'm very sorry," she called out as the dancers reformed their lines, and the orchestra picked up the song where they had left off. The crowd murmured as they passed through, but her smiles and assurances that she was quite all right seemed to soothe them. She even overheard a group of ladies whispering about Lucas's attentiveness.

Perfect.

He pushed the terrace doors open, and they moved out into the cooler night air. Quickly, she scanned the area, but Sansbury was not to be found.

"The garden," Lucas said, but they moved slowly. They were still close enough to the house that she exaggerated a limp just in case. But as they moved down the terrace stairs and began to weave their way down the garden pathways, she let the limp fade.

"That was quick thinking," Lucas said as they hurried along the trail that was lit by fancy, Oriental lanterns inspired by the Far East where the General had been stationed. "You saved us some time."

She shrugged, though his compliment warmed her. "We needed to follow."

"Look," Lucas's voice dropped to a sharp whisper as he pulled her down slightly and pointed ahead of them. Sansbury was moving away from the path at a fast pace, heading toward a small gazebo in the distance.

They followed, staying low behind the line of shrubs. When they reached the area behind the little building, Lucas dropped down even lower and began to make his way through the bushes, darting left and right until he found a spot less than ten feet from the enclosure. Ana drew in a harsh breath, prayed she wouldn't be seen in her light-colored gown, and started to move, following the path he'd taken until she reached his side.

She crouched beside him, positioning her gown in the hopes she could keep it clean for their return to the ballroom.

They were far enough away from the main house that the buzz of the ball did not reach her ears, but close enough that there were still a few decorative lanterns to brighten the area slightly. She peeked over the brush line to see Sansbury pacing the gazebo, checking his pocket watch from time to time.

Lucas leaned back and the heat of his breath suddenly touched her cheek, bringing her to the stark realization of their position. Crouched down behind the shrubbery, she was pressed against his side, his leg was rubbing hers every time he moved, and she could smell the spicy hint of his shaving soap.

"He's waiting for someone."

She nodded, though it took some effort. Now that she was aware of their proximity, it was all she could think about. God, he was warm. His arm shifted against hers, and she felt the muscles flex beneath his coat. Her thoughts began to trail away to dangerous places.

Dark and dangerous places.

Sudden movement from the corner of her eye blessedly distracted her from those thoughts. "There," she whispered, close to Lucas's ear.

Whoever had joined him, the person hadn't come from the party. The man slipped through the heavy shadows away from the house and stepped into the gazebo.

"Blast, I can't hear them clearly," Lucas breathed, craning his neck as if he would hear better if he leaned the right way.

Ana nodded. She heard the murmur of voices, but couldn't make out any clear words or recognize who was speaking. Still, the tone of the occasional murmur didn't seem cordial. It was harsh, short. Angry.

If only she could determine the identity of the man who had joined Sansbury, but there were no lanterns in the gazebo and the lights that illuminated the garden paths were dim at best. They didn't cut through more than a foot or so around them. All she could see were the hulking shadows of masculine shoulders.

"I can move closer," she whispered, preparing to crawl toward the gazebo.

"No!" Lucas grabbed her arm and yanked her back,

pulling her into his chest hard enough that the air left her lungs. "They're looking this way," he murmured as he flattened down, pinning her half under his body.

Ana shivered. Not from fear, not from cold as she knew she would later try to convince herself. Her tremors were absolutely caused by Lucas. His chest warmed hers, his arms around her as he lifted his head in the ready in case the two men stumbled upon them. In the dim lantern light, she saw the cords of muscles in his neck strain.

"Lucas," she whispered, shifting beneath his weight and wishing her body wasn't reacting so strongly.

"Shhh. Damn it, they're leaving. Hold still, Sansbury is coming this way."

She bit her lip as she waited. Sure enough, the sound of footsteps approached on the other side of the brush, then faded as Sansbury strolled back to the house.

"Let me up," she ordered, a little louder now that their suspects had departed.

Lucas looked down at her and he started, as if he hadn't fully realized their position, her on her back, him half on top of her on the grass.

He let her go instantly and sat up, pulling her to a seated position as they went.

"I beg your pardon, my lady. I was more worried about not being detected than your delicate sensibilities," he drawled.

She pursed her lips, intent on ignoring the taunt. "Should we follow?"

He shook his head. "No. Sansbury promised dances to several of the debutantes. There's no point in rushing behind him to watch him woo them." His eyes met hers. "So, does that help to clear your mind?"

"What do you mean?"

"Clearly, Sansbury was doing *something* tonight." He motioned toward the house where the other man had gone.

Her brow furrowed. "Yes. Clearly, he was. But how does that change anything?"

"You don't think that lends credence to Henry's assertions that Sansbury is involved in this plot?" His stare snared hers. "You don't think it clears my friend's name?"

She shook her head. "No! And I know you realize that fully. Why are you being so bullheaded? Is it because you're angry with me about last night?"

He snorted out a laugh. "You're the one who is angry about last night, Ana, not me. You're afraid of what happened between us. Afraid of letting go of the past. And you are using a dead man to keep life away, to keep any experiences beyond the ones you control away."

Her lips parted in outrage. "You aren't starting that again, are you? I have no intention of listening to your ridiculousness one moment longer."

She started to get up, but his hand snaked out and clamped onto her forearm like a vise. With a tug, she fell back, landing on top of his chest. His arms came around her and she was trapped.

"I didn't want to make love, Lucas," she whispered, unable to meet his eyes when she was lying.

He barked out a laugh. "Is that what you're telling yourself now? Then why didn't you say no?" His grip was suddenly gentler. His hands moved down her back, stroking her spine. "All the times I offered you a way out last night, why didn't you take any of them?"

His hands were still moving until finally he cupped her rear end and lifted, rubbing her against him. She stifled a moan. God, he was already hard as steel, pressed against her belly.

"Why aren't you saying no to me now?"

He leaned up and brushed his lips against hers.

Ana tried for just a moment to block her reaction, but her body's wants were far more powerful, and they swept away all the protests her mind had formulated, leaving only sensation behind.

"Say no, Ana," he whispered, just before he speared his tongue between her lips and swirled it around her own.

Desire spiked in her blood and her clenched fists relaxed, flattening against his broad chest as she met his tongue with a few fierce swipes of her own. He tasted so good. He felt so good.

God help her, she wanted him. Now. Here. Fast.

Her legs parted, like someone else controlled them, and she straddled his waist. His hands fumbled with her gown and the fabric fell forward to bunch around her waist. And then all she could feel was his mouth as he leaned up and wrapped his lips around her nipple.

She let out a low, hungry moan that echoed in the still, cool air. He swirled his tongue around the thrust of flesh before he pulled back.

"Was that 'oh' or 'no'?"

She glared down at him. Bastard.

He reached up and pulled her chemise down until the very edge of the top scraped across her breasts. She arched into the rough sensation.

"I wouldn't want for there to be confusion tomorrow," he pressed, not moving any further. "So if you want me to continue, I'm going to have to hear you say it this time."

She whimpered, her mind warring with her body. The silky fabric stroked back and forth over her skin and her hips bucked reflexively against his pelvis. The motion only increased the burning ache between her thighs.

"Damn you," she rasped. "You know I want this."

"You want me."

He stared at her, his gaze glittering even in the dim light. Her breath was short, she could feel her pulse pounding, hear her blood rushing.

"I want you."

He pulled the chemise down and his lips surged to catch hers. Suddenly he was sitting and she was straddling his lap, her dress caught between them as a last barrier between herself and surrender.

But not enough of a barrier that she couldn't feel the hard jut of his erection. But this time it wasn't pressed against her belly. It was pressed against the juncture of her thighs, pressing, insistent against the building ache.

She couldn't help herself. She rocked against him, feeling the stroke through her clothes and biting her lip as the tingling increased instead of dissipated.

Lucas smashed his mouth against hers, rough and demanding, sucking her tongue, rubbing her breasts against the rough wool of his coat. And she felt a sudden thrill as she realized that he was just as out of control as she was. He, too, was spiraling into madness.

And only she could bring him sanity.

He cupped her backside with one hand, rocking her against him as he hitched her skirt up with the other in jerky movements. The fabric seemed to go on forever, billowing at her waist, around their legs as he got closer and closer to the heated core of her desire.

And then she felt the stir of a breeze and shivered. He let out a low groan into her mouth before he brushed his thumb over her cleft.

Sparks seemed to flow from his touch, lighting her on fire as he rubbed a slow circle around the bud of pleasure there. She broke away from the kiss, her neck arching as the throb of pleasure intensified.

He brought his lips to her throat as he circled faster, harder, demanding with his touch, purposeful as he reached for her release. Her hips were rolling wildly, and she tightened her thighs around his hips.

Her vision blurred, and she forgot to breathe as he pressed down one final time. Then she cried out, a sharp sound he muffled with his lips as the bubble of desire burst and pleasure overwhelmed her.

Her sheath clenched, tremored and then she tensed. Lucas shifted as he tugged at the waist of his trousers. Suddenly the head of his erection nudged her slick opening. He started to move forward, but she was faster. Adjusting her position, she surged against him.

He slipped inside of her to the hilt, and the tremors of release that had been rocketing inside her doubled in their intensity. Her body milked at him as she thrust her hips.

Lucas shut his eyes at the pleasure of her body wrapped around him like warm, wet silk. Ana was wild, now, her bare arms wrapped around his shoulders, her hips lifting, circling. With each thrust, she bore down harder on him. Like an untamed thing inside of her had been awakened.

He looked at her. Even in the dim light, he could see pure pleasure on her taut features. She didn't care about the past. She didn't care about the consequences. She was alive in the moment.

And she wanted him.

He bucked up, lifting her with every thrust. Her grip on his shoulders tightened as she panted out low moans. Her fingernails scraped against his coat, her pelvis swirled as she reached for another release.

He cupped her neck and pulled her mouth to his and

she found what she craved. Her back stiffened, her body trembled and her sheath clenched so tightly that he nearly blacked out from the pleasure. He groaned against her lips as his seed flowed into her.

He wrapped his arms around her, pulling her close as his breathing began to slow, return to normal. Hers still came in pants, but to his surprise, she didn't pull away. Instead, she let her cheek droop down to rest on his shoulder as she clung to him.

It felt almost as good as being inside her. It felt right, holding her, smoothing his fingers along her back, feeling her heart slam against her chest.

He could have stayed like that forever.

Except he heard the voices. Female voices, two of them. And they were coming down the path toward them.

Chapter 17

Lucas cursed. How stupid was he to lose track of everything but lust in the middle of a garden, for God's sake?

"Ana, people are coming," he whispered.

Her head wrenched up and she began to shake.

"No, oh no!"

She was off his lap like a bullet, pulling at her dress as she peered over her shoulders toward the footsteps and voices that were coming closer by the second.

Lucas refastened his trousers, then reached for her. She flinched back and his heart sank. It seemed every time he made some headway with her, she found a reason not to trust him.

"Let me button you," he explained, pulling the

253

shoulder of her gown up. She swallowed, her lip trembling, but didn't argue as she turned her back to him. He fumbled with the little circles of mother-of-pearl, fastening as fast as he could even though he could tell he wasn't going to be fast enough. The voices were right on top of them now.

And blast. One of them was his mother.

Ana was shaking so hard that he could hardly button her gown at all. Guilt rushed through him. He had put her in this position by forcing her to admit to wanting him. Forcing her to say she wanted more. *He* should have been the one to stop the encounter, to let her go.

But damn, she'd felt so good. Making her throw caution to the wind was one of the most powerful experiences in his life.

One he couldn't regret even as two women came around the bend on the garden path and walked right up on top of them.

It was his mother and one of the women in the line of dancers who had expressed her concern when Ana twisted her ankle. Lady Westfield, he thought it was.

"Oh my!" His mother turned her face and Lady Westfield's eyes went wide as saucers.

Ana jumped to her feet and Lucas joined her. She was holding her hands up to her chest like she could shield herself from what had been done, from what the two women had already seen.

"I was—we were—" Her breath came in pants. "It . . ."

She trailed off as she looked down at her twisted, grass-stained gown. "Oh."

Lucas took her hand. She didn't pull away, in fact, she squeezed his fingers like he was the only thing keeping her upright. Slowly, he maneuvered her behind the barrier of his body.

His mother stared at him, eyes wide and mouth hanging open. Then her stare darted to Lady Westfield. Both women were pale.

"Ladies," he began, not that he had a ready explanation for anything. He struggled to find one, but Ana's disheveled appearance said it all.

"They are marrying by the end of the week," his mother blurted out.

The other woman folded her arms as a ghost of a smile tilted one corner of her lips. "I would hope so. Er, pardon me."

Lady Westfield shot one final glance around him at Ana, then went toward the house. The moment she was gone, his mother's eyes narrowed.

"Lucas!"

He winced at the tone of her voice, the expression in her eyes. What a situation he'd gotten himself into this time. And there was only one place it would lead.

"A special license, Lucas." His mother pointed toward the house. She was using her very best "motherly" tone as she marched Ana and Lucas forward. Ana had yet to lift her gaze and her cheeks darkened with every word. "You will procure a special license tomorrow. You will marry before a week has past."

Ana's eyes shot up, wild. His heart sank further. This engagement had never been meant to end in an actual marriage. And now the truth of that matter was sinking in.

The position they had put themselves in was not one he could avoid. They would have to marry now. A real marriage. For real reasons that had nothing to do with a case.

"Not in the house, Mother," he muttered as she started up the terrace steps.

"What?" She spun back on him.

He motioned with one hand toward Ana's gown. In the brighter lights that the house provided, the grass stains on her damp dress shone clear, practically telegraphing what they had done.

His mother nodded. "Very well."

Lucas led this time, taking them around to the front of the home and through a gate that lead to the drive. He found his carriage in a few moments.

"Wait here," his mother said with a glare for him. "I'll join you momentarily."

As he handed Ana into his carriage, he sighed. "Why do I feel like I'm nine years old all over again?"

She didn't smile. In fact, she hardly reacted at all except to stare at him, her face so pale that it scared him a little.

"She doesn't mean it." Ana shook her head. "She doesn't mean we'll be married."

Lucas shut his eyes as pain flashed through him. She looked sick to her stomach with the thought that this false engagement would soon be powerfully and irrevocably real. He wasn't sure what to think of that idea, himself. His mind was spinning too wildly.

Ana's reputation would be ruined if Lady Westfield talked. And even if his mother was correct and the other woman wouldn't speak about what she'd seen, it was a risk he wasn't willing to take.

"It is one thing for a widow to have a private, discreet affair," he said softly. "It is quite another to be found half naked in a garden."

He saw the light of acknowledgment in her eyes. Now that the shock was wearing off, they both knew marriage was unavoidable.

"I can't marry you, Lucas," she whispered, making one last, lame attempt at an argument.

He looked at her, still disheveled from his fingers, his mouth, his body. It was a powerful thing to recall her little moans of release, to remember the way her arms had wrapped so tightly around his shoulders as she found her pleasure.

It was even more powerful to realize that because of their actions, he would have her in his bed every night for the rest of his life. The thought wasn't so very unpleasant to him.

But it was to her. Because she still thought herself in love with a dead man. Someone he couldn't even make an attempt to compete with.

"We have no choice, Anastasia," he said with a shrug. "Not anymore."

Ana fought the childish urge to slouch back against the carriage seat and wail. Going into hysterics would not change the current situation. It wouldn't make her feel better, at least not for long.

What was happening . . . it was her fault. Lucas had given her choices. He'd offered to stop, both last night and this evening in the garden. Instead, she had let her body lead her to ruin.

Now she would suffer the consequences. Because if she refused, not only would her reputation be shattered, but the Sisters of the Heart Society for Widows and Orphans would be too. No one would give their funds to such a woman.

Not to mention the real work she and Meredith and Ana did would be compromised. Invitations would cease. The case she was currently investigating would be destroyed . . .

What a price to pay for passion. She stole a glimpse at Lucas and found him watching her. His face revealed nothing of his own reaction to this turn of events. He was still stoic, still calm. How she wished she could see his heart. Did he hate her for this? Was he sorry?

Did he even care?

And what about tomorrow? The day after? The

year after? Would he grow to resent her? Bore of her? Somehow that thought troubled her most.

The door to Lucas's carriage opened and Lady Dannington stepped inside. Ana turned away, too humiliated to face her after what she had witnessed. Dear Lord, what she must think of all this!

The carriage began to move.

"Anastasia."

She looked up, surprised that Lady Dannington was addressing her by her given name, and so kindly. "Yes, my lady?"

"Lavinia," she corrected with a soft smile. "I believe we have crossed any barrier that might have prevented you from calling me Lavinia."

Ana shook her head in disbelief. "I never intended—"

Lavinia raised a hand. "Of course you didn't." She shot her son a dirty look. "That is the way of passion, I suppose. Sometimes you have no intention, only consequence. Ah well. A rushed marriage would not have been of my choosing, but it is only hurrying what the entire family was already looking forward to greatly." She reached out and covered Ana's hands with her own. "I believe Lady Westfield to be discreet. This does not have to be a scandal. A quick marriage will put a halt to any talk that does crop up. Society already seems to be enthralled with the romance between you two. They'll forgive, even if there are a few whispers."

Ana could hardly breathe. The weight of this situation

was coming down upon her fully. It was crushing and overwhelming to think that within a few days she would have no choice but to exchange vows of love and forever with a second man.

Yet behind the fears and guilt that wracked her, she couldn't ignore another reaction. A dark, delicious thrill that she wanted to squash, but it was persistent. She looked at Lucas. He was still watching her. Just as he had while she shivered with pleasure. Just as she sometimes found him doing when they spoke, when they worked side by side.

What had he said to her in the park a few days earlier? That he would only marry for passion? Somehow she doubted a marriage to her, forced or no, would be any different.

The carriage came to a stop, and Ana looked outside to find they had come to the home she and Emily shared. Lucas shifted as the footman opened the door. Lavinia squeezed her hands.

"We will discuss this more tomorrow evening. You'll come to our home for supper."

Ana found herself nodding, powerless in her numb state. The servants helped her down and Lucas followed, catching her hand to put it in the crook of her arm before he took her to the door.

"I'm sorry, Ana," he whispered, still holding her hand for a moment.

She shook her head. "You offered me a way out . . . more than once. You told me to say no." Tears stung her eyes. "This is no more your fault than mine. We can discuss it tomorrow."

He nodded as her door opened. She slipped inside and peeked around the curtain beside the door. Lucas stood staring at the closed door for a moment, then headed back to the carriage, shaking his head.

As she let the curtain drop, Ana pressed her forehead against the wall beside the door. Tears she had been holding back began to slide down her cheeks in an unstoppable waterfall.

What in the world had she done?

Ana paced to Emily's window, then back to the fireplace, ringing her hands in front of her with every step. She felt Emily and Meredith's sympathetic expressions, but they couldn't help her. Not anymore.

"Won't you sit down and have a cup of tea?" Meredith asked, motioning to a seat beside her. "Please. You hardly slept at all last night, and I know you refused breakfast this morning."

"How do you know that?" Ana asked, wrinkling her brow.

Emily smiled, but it was distant, a little sad. "We aren't the only spies in this house, you know."

Ana managed a smile. House servants must have been the original spies.

She took the seat Meredith offered, but refused to touch the cup of tea that was poured for her.

"I want to ask you something," Meredith said,

exchanging a brief glance with Emily. "And you may not like it. What will you do now?"

Ana started, sitting up bone straight. "What do you mean?"

Except she knew exactly what her friend was asking. It was the same question she'd repeated over and over to herself since last night.

Emily met her stare with an even one of her own. "Do you plan to make this marriage real or will you continue to keep Tyler at a distance?"

Trust Emily to be so blunt. Ana leaned forward and put her elbows on the table. She rested her head in her hands as a mass of emotions raged in her. Fear, sadness, lingering pain from the losses of the past . . . but also desire. Anticipation of the future. There were so many things in her heart, so many new sensations, she wasn't certain what to do or feel or say.

"I just don't know," she whispered.

"Lady Whittig, there is a guest waiting for you in the parlor," Benson's voice intruded from the doorway before either of her friends could provide council.

She rubbed her fingertips over her eyes, wishing she could block out the world as easily as she could block out the light. "Let me guess. It's Mr. Tyler."

"No, madam. It is the Dowager Lady Whittig."

The world Ana had been wishing to block out suddenly came into stark relief, sharpening and brightening to a painful degree. Her ears rang and her heart throbbed as she staggered to her feet.

"T-Tell her I will join her momentarily. And be sure she has whatever she desires while she waits."

Benson bowed away. When he was gone, Ana covered her mouth and turned to her two friends. Both of them looked as pale as she felt. "I did not know my mother-in-law was in Town," she whispered, but her voice sounded far away, like she'd slipped beneath the surface of the water.

Meredith got to her feet. "Would you like me to come with you?"

Ana pondered that for a moment. It would be so easy to hide behind Meredith, but she couldn't. "No. I owe Francesca a private audience." She shivered as she moved to the door. "She's heard of this engagement, I'm sure. And if she desires to let me know how angry and hurt she is . . . well, I owe her that, as well."

The walk down the hallway was the longest one of her recollection. With every step she was bombarded by memories of Gilbert and of his family. Francesca had been nothing but kind to her, like a second mother. She dreaded the moment where she lost that welcoming embrace or kind smile.

But there was no avoiding it. She had made this particular bed. She had surrendered to her body's desires, even let her emotions become involved. Now she would suffer every one of the consequences.

Opening the parlor door, she put on a smile that she did not feel. Francesca got to her feet as the door opened. For a long moment, the two just looked at each other.

Gilbert had inherited his mother's bright blue eyes. It always shocked her to see them, but never more so than today. It was like having her husband look at her, his stare full of questions and worries . . . perhaps even judgments. Then she shook her head and the moment was gone.

Her mother-in-law was a slight woman, very pretty, and was aging well. Yet in her face there was a lingering sadness. Muted by the passage of time, but lingering. She'd never gotten over the loss of her son. She never would.

"Francesca," Ana said, forcing herself to come forward with hand outstretched. "I'm sorry it's been so many months since I last saw you."

To her surprise, the other woman's face lit up like a crystal chandelier, and she stepped toward Ana, drawing her into an embrace no less warm and welcoming than ever before.

"My darling, congratulations."

Ana stood in shock. Congratulations? Had she heard Francesca correctly?

"I'm so sorry," she whispered as she let her embrace tighten. "I should have written, but everything has happened so quickly and I—" She hesitated. She owed this woman the truth. Or at least as much of it as she could give. "I was afraid of how you would feel."

Francesca drew back. She looked confused and concerned by that statement. "Afraid? Do you mean you thought I would be angry that you have found love a second time?"

Ana flinched. That was the rumor she and Lucas had perpetrated. A great love formed in secret and then developed for society to see. But hearing those words out loud still surprised her. Shocked her. Stirred her in ways she stuffed back down deep into her soul. She did *not* love Lucas. Desire, yes. To her own detriment, overwhelming desire.

"I'm sorry, so sorry," she whispered.

"Oh, Anastasia," Francesca took her hand and led her to the settee. They sat together. "My sweet girl, I could not be angry with you. You loved my son. I know you did. And he loved you. That was cut short." She hesitated and Ana saw the sparkle of tears in her eyes. "Far too short. But Gilbert never would have wished for you to mourn him for the rest of your life."

"But I promised—" Ana began.

"You kept whatever promises were made." Francesca shook her head. "Please don't tell me that you've hesitated in the fear that you would betray Gilbert."

Ana dipped her gaze away. She had been doing that. For years she had locked herself away, preserving her life in the exact way it had been when Gilbert died. Only Lucas had forced her out of that mold she created for herself. Only Lucas had awakened the person she forgot lived inside her, a person she had never let free before.

Francesca cupped her chin. "Darling, you are still so

young. Keep a piece of Gilbert in your heart, but you must love and live again. You mustn't hold back in the fear of what he would think. He loved you. He would want your happiness. He would want you to have a happy home and make a family, not be his grieving widow forever."

The words sunk in, pushing past the shroud of grief Ana had surrounded herself with since the day Gilbert died. Would he wish this for her? Feelings for a new man? A life with Lucas? Perhaps even children and a future?

Wouldn't she have wanted that for him if the tables were turned?

"When is the marriage to take place?" Francesca asked.

Ana started. There was no avoiding this. "In a few days. We're marrying by special license."

Francesca looked at her in shock for a moment, but then the corners of her lips tilted into a knowing smile. "I know Lady Dannington in passing. You will be very happy in that family." She got to her feet. "I only arrived in Town today and there is much for me to do. I wanted to see you, though."

Ana clamored to her feet. "Will I . . . see you again?"

Francesca tilted her head. "Of course! You will always be my daughter in my heart. I hope to see you often, and meet this new husband of yours. Now, I must go. But I'll speak to you after your wedding."

Ana walked her to the front door, numbed by shock.

There, Francesca turned and embraced her again. This time it was tight, like she was saying good-bye to Gilbert one last time. And Ana realized that perhaps she was. The next time they saw each other, she would be another man's wife.

"Be happy, Anastasia." Francesca kissed her cheek and then she was gone.

Ana closed the door and turned to lean back against it. Her mind was spinning. She'd expected a lot of things from her meeting with Gilbert's mother, but not this. Not this permission to live again. Not this *order* to love. Not this feeling that Gilbert himself had blessed her union and told her it was time to let go.

She covered her mouth. Let go. Was that truly possible? To give up the life she had forced upon herself for so many years and perhaps find a new one?

There was only one way to find out. And she needed Lucas's help to do it. She could only hope he would assist her, and that she would find a way to reconcile the feelings of her past with her inevitable future.

Chapter 18

Lucas stepped on the overhanging branch of the large beech tree. He looked down. The trick of it was to get to the window ledge without slipping. The rosebushes that would break his fall did not look particularly pleasant. He could only imagine picking thorns out of his ass for a week.

Still the window was partly open, so he pushed off and leapt for the ledge. He landed perfectly, catching the edge of the window for balance before he swung it open and stepped inside.

Anastasia turned from the fire at his grand entrance. She looked less than impressed, though very beautiful. After enduring her in widow's weeds for so long, he didn't think he'd ever tire of seeing her in color.

Like tonight, in rich green that made her brown eyes dark and alluring.

"You're late."

He shut the window and latched it before he turned back to her, arms folded. "Good evening to you, too. Thank you, I managed to get inside just fine. No, I'm not injured in any way. Yes, I would love a drink if you have anything."

Her lips pursed at his sarcastic tone, but she moved toward a table in her sitting room where a decanter of scotch was waiting. He doubted that was her drink of choice, which meant she had asked for it for his pleasure. As she handed him a tumbler and he took a sip, he smiled. Perfect.

It was a little suspicious.

"Well, my lady, you beckoned and I have come as you asked. Though I don't know why you required me to risk my neck coming through your window." He took another sip of his drink before he set it down and looked around. So this was Ana's chamber. The sitting room they were in was pretty and feminine, understated in its elegance. And then he noticed the pile of scribbled notes. The empty beaker.

Some things were absolutely Ana. He couldn't help but smile.

"The last thing I wish for is more gossip," she said with a sigh. "But I needed to talk to you tonight, so I thought sneaking in was the lowest risk."

He nodded, but he was paying more attention to the

way her lips moved than to her words. He hadn't seen her since the night before when they'd been caught in such a delicate, delicious position.

They certainly hadn't had much time to discuss these suddenly impending . . . and very *real* nuptials that were being planned. He sighed. Today he'd made arrangements for the special license. His mother was busily throwing together the rest.

Ana just stood staring at him. Was it possible for her to be *less* interested in their wedding? In a marriage to him at all?

The pain that accompanied her reaction was swift and powerful, jolting through his body like a knife stuck through his heart. With violence, he shoved that reaction away, buried it deep. It was the last thing he wanted.

"Why did you need to see me tonight?"

How he wished he could squelch that insistent part of him that wanted to stake a claim on Ana. Not on her body, but on that part of her heart and her soul that she was always withholding. The part that clung to her late husband like he was a lifeline on a sinking ship.

She'd rather love a dead man than give herself to him.

"The estate where my husband is buried is half a day's journey from here," she said, breaking their eye contact as she fiddled with the hem of her sleeve. "And I want very much to go there tomorrow. Would you take me?"

"You—You want *me* to take you there?" he repeated in shock. This was the last thing he had expected.

She nodded slowly.

"Why?"

Her gaze snagged his, and her hands clenched at her sides. "I—Do you want the honest answer?"

At the moment, he wasn't sure, but he nodded. "Always."

She swallowed hard. "Going there is difficult for me, and this time will be even more so. But when I'm with you I am"—a dark blush suddenly swept across her cheeks—"more brave. I would like your support, though I know it is a strange request."

Lucas stared, unsure whether to be warmed by the fact that she wanted him by her side, or horrified that she was asking him to chaperone her trip back in time. But when she looked at him like that, so open and trusting, and told him that he made her brave . . . how could he refuse?

He managed to smile. "If that is what you want, I'll take you there."

Her face relaxed with relief, and she stepped toward him. Her fingers trembled as she reached out and briefly touched his hand. Her skin was so soft, so warm against his own. But the moment was all too brief. She almost immediately pulled away.

"Thank you."

"Is there anything else you want?"

He tilted his head to chase her gaze, looking for any

sign of her heart and mind. She looked at him for a long, silent moment. It seemed an eternity stretched out as she opened her mouth, readied herself to speak. He found himself leaning forward in anticipation and hope . . . hope for something, though he didn't know what for certain.

But then she shook her head. "No. That's all I needed."

He pursed his lips. Of course. "Very well. I will come around to fetch you tomorrow morning just after dawn."

He pushed the window behind him open again and stepped onto the ledge and the cool night air. He sighed as he looked at the tree and thought of the long voyage down to the bottom and a cold, empty bed at home. Casting a final glance over his shoulder, he looked at Ana. She was watching him as he went, the emotion in her eyes hooded and her face unreadable.

She was getting to be a better and better spy. He just wished she wouldn't use those talents against him.

"Until tomorrow," he murmured before he made his hop and began to pick his way down the tree.

Lucas slammed the door behind him and stalked toward his office without even bothering to greet the stunned servants who peered into the hallway at his entrance. He raked a hand through his hair and found a little twig tangled. With a growl, he tossed it aside and the reminder of how it had gotten there.

He strode to his office and slammed the door behind him. The bluster began to bleed out of him and he leaned his forehead against the door as his night with Ana sunk in.

"Lucas?"

He stiffened at the sound of Henry's voice from behind him. Until recently, his friend had been a source of relief to him. With Henry, he could talk openly. His best friend knew he was a spy, knew his assignments, so he could share things with him he couldn't share with anyone else.

But now, thanks to Ana's accusations, having Henry in the house caused more anxiety than comfort. He found himself checking his every word, watching Henry's reaction as he searched for the truth.

Slowly, he straightened and turned to look at his friend. There was real concern in Henry's eyes. Genuine friendship. Yet Lucas still wondered about him.

"Good evening," he ground out between clenched teeth. "Have you been here long?"

Henry shrugged as he set the book in his lap aside. "For about an hour. I came straight away after I heard something very troubling."

Lucas cocked his head. "About the investigation?"

"No." Henry's eyes narrowed. "About you. And that woman."

With a sigh, Lucas sat down at his desk. "That woman. You mean Anastasia?"

"Of course I mean Anastasia." Henry rolled his

chair forward. "Please, please tell me that the rumors I heard this evening were not true. Please tell me that you aren't actually *marrying* her!"

Lucas shut his eyes. His mind was spinning out of control. Was Henry angry because Ana had accused people inside the War Department of being responsible for the attacks on the spies? Was he worried about Lucas's well being, not wanting him to be forced into a marriage Henry knew he didn't desire?

Or was there something more? Was Henry frustrated and trying to hide the truth about his own dealings, as Ana kept saying?

Lucas wanted to throw something, break something, anything to make all the theories stop swirling around in his mind. Anything to stop the tormenting images of Ana leaning up to accept his kiss. Ana letting the strap of her chemise droop over her shoulder.

Ana telling him she wanted to go see Gilbert's grave.

He slammed a palm down on the desk top. "What would you have me do? I am a gentleman, am I not?"

Henry seemed surprised by the harsh, loud tone of his voice. "Of course you are, but—"

"But nothing! She is a lady. Conducting a private affair with a widow is one thing, but it's quite another to be caught in a garden with half her clothing undone."

And it was a beautiful thing, as well, though he shoved that thought aside.

Henry's eyes widened. "Is that what happened?"

Lucas rubbed his temples. "Yes, unfortunately.

Caught by my mother and Lady Westfield, last night at the General's soirée."

"In the garden?" Henry repeated slowly.

"Yes." He looked up. His friend was pale, but then his expression changed.

"I appreciate your trying to do the right thing, but this is a mistake. You don't want to marry this woman. The engagement was for the sole purpose of the investigation. If you do this, you'll have to live with that mistake for the rest of your life." Henry held up his hands, silently pleading.

"It's not a mistake." The anger Lucas had felt all night was beginning to grow, stoked by Henry's harsh words. It was like he had to . . . to defend Ana somehow. "This is just the way it has to be."

"But you'll be shackled to a woman who is so unlike yourself. She isn't bold; she's hardly interesting. And she wants to turn you against your friends."

Lucas's nostrils flared and hot blood rushed to his face. He found himself analyzing each and every word Henry was saying. And he hated himself for it.

"Actually, I find her very interesting," he growled. "And bold in unexpected ways. As for turning me against my friends, that is unfair. Ana is trying to expose the truth, just as I am. She's simply more willing to consider the full range of possibilities. I may not always like what she says, but I cannot help but take it seriously."

Henry had been sitting forward, pulled away from

the seat cushion of his chair, but at that comment, he flopped back in surprise. "No. I cannot believe you feel that. She's a siren, that's what she is. She's dragging you into dangerous waters, Lucas. And if that bi—"

Lucas was on his feet before Henry could finish. He took a step toward his friend before he even realized he'd done it. Any other man he already would have had against the wall by the scruff of his neck.

Lucas clenched his fists behind his back as he tried to find some level of calm. "I will marry Anastasia in three days, Henry. She will be a part of my life, my family's life. So there is no point to continuing this conversation. It does neither of us any good to argue over what is destined to be."

Henry's lips thinned. "Perhaps you're right. There is no point in talking about this anymore." He wheeled to the door, but hesitated. "I would hate to see you come to harm or pain because you aligned yourself with this woman, Lucas. You know I would never want to see you hurt."

Then he was gone. Lucas sat down at his desk again and stared at the mound of paperwork before him with unseeing eyes.

What was Henry referring to? Was he saying marrying Ana could hurt him personally? That pursuing her theories could put his position in the War Department in jeopardy?

Or was it a threat?

Chapter 19

A na glanced up from her lap as the carriage they were traveling in eased around a curve in the wide road. Lucas was sitting across from her, reading through some paperwork with a seemingly focused intent. And if he had turned one of the sheets in his lap in the last half hour, she would have believed he was truly engrossed. Only he hadn't. He was just as uncomfortable as she, herself was. Probably more so, considering the odd circumstances.

"Lucas?"

He looked up in surprise. They hadn't spoken in over an hour. Not since the driver had informed them that they were nearly at their destination.

"Yes?"

She cleared her throat. What did she want to say? She had no idea. All she knew was that she didn't want this heavy silence between them. She wanted the casual conversation they sometimes shared. The teasing.

She just wanted things to be normal again.

"Where did you go when you used to run away from home?" His brow wrinkled in surprise and she hastened to explain. "At supper with your family, they mentioned you used to disappear. You claimed you didn't recall where you went, but I don't believe that. I could tell by your face that it was important to you."

He drew back as he closed the file in his hand and set it on the seat beside him, but he didn't answer immediately.

"I never knew you paid such close attention to my expressions, Anastasia."

Heat rushed to her face and she wanted to turn away from his gaze, but she fought to hold her ground. She wanted to know more about him, this man who would be her husband in such a short time. Something more than that he was a master spy or that he made her tremble with desires she had long tried to deny. She wanted to know him as a man.

"You shouldn't pretend you aren't utterly aware of how handsome you are," she said with a wobbly smile. "But you don't have to share your past with me if it is too personal."

He laughed softly. "Oh, I think we moved beyond

claims that anything is too personal when we sealed our fate in the General's garden. I am happy to tell you of my past, but at a price."

Ana stiffened. A price. She could only imagine what kinds of demands Lucas would make of her. Sensual ones. Ones she couldn't imagine granting considering the purpose of their journey today.

"I can't . . . Lucas, we shouldn't . . ."

His smile fell. "I only meant information. A question for a question. After all, I know as little about you as you do about me."

"What do you mean?" Ana gasped. "You know my history completely!"

He shook his head. "There is so much more to you than the fact that you were once another man's wife. You had a life before you married Whittig. You had a life after his passing. That is what I want to know. Is that fair?"

She examined his face closely, considering what he was asking of her. Finally, she nodded.

"Good. You began our game by asking where I went." He hesitated and his gaze moved to the passing countryside. "I am the youngest boy of an important family, as you know. But you may not understand the feeling of having no place that a man in my position goes through. My eldest brother's duties in life were well defined. He was to be the Earl. And Martin was the spare, so he had duties of his own. But I was not likely to inherit any title. And in many ways that left me at a loss for what to do. As a child, I felt my lack of place keenly. So I ran away. Searching for . . ." He drifted off. "I don't know what I was searching for. But I found it when Henry told me he had joined the ranks of His Majesty's spies."

She flinched. "Henry helped you make your way in the War Department?"

His nodded slowly, and she could see from his frown that he was troubled. Thinking of their investigation and her accusations against his friend. "I told you, we have been the best of friends for as long as I could remember."

Silence returned to the carriage for a long moment and Ana shifted. She was responsible for Lucas's doubt in a man he cared for. God help her if her intuition was wrong. God help them both if it was right.

He shook off whatever thoughts were working through his mind and smiled at her. "And now it is my turn for a question."

Tension stiffened Ana's shoulders as she waited for his query. Of course it would be about Gilbert.

"You have older brothers and sisters, yet you never speak of them. You talk about the grief of losing your parents and your husband, but you never talk of the rest of your family." He leaned closer. "Why?"

She shrugged, surprised that this was the topic he'd chosen to pursue. "My siblings were all much older than I was. Fifteen years or more. I was an unexpected addition to the family. And, I think, unwelcome for some of them. We were never close my entire life. They resented how my parents doted on me, I suppose. When my mother and father died, it cut off whatever contact I had with the rest of my family. I only hear from them once a year, if that. They are more like distant acquaintances than family. That is why Emily and Meredith are so important to me."

His eyes narrowed, and she could see him digesting what she had said. Suddenly he reached out and covered her hand with his. "You life has not been easy."

Starting, Ana let her gaze come even with his. "No, I suppose not."

"When we first met, I said you were sheltered," he continued.

She flinched as she recalled that afternoon that seemed so long ago. "Yes."

He let his fingers move up to stroke her cheek. "I was wrong, Anastasia. You are the strongest woman I have ever known."

Her lips parted in surprise at that statement. She stared at Lucas and was rocked by the way he looked at her with such . . . tenderness. Understanding. And most of all, respect. No one had ever given her those things. Not like this. Not like him.

"Lucas," she breathed, but before she could continue, the carriage slowed and then stopped.

He pulled his hand away and she nearly grabbed for it, grabbed for him, to keep him close. "We are here," he said softly.

She turned to look outside. Sure enough, the high stone walls of the Whittig estate rose up before her, taking her back in time.

"I have not been here since . . ." She trailed off.

His brow furrowed. "Why?"

She was startled by the question. She hadn't realized she'd even made the statement out loud. And she wasn't sure she even knew the answer he sought.

He shrugged at her hesitation and his dark eyes moved away. "I apologize. My question is out of turn, isn't it?"

She tilted her head. The withdrawal of the question was almost as troubling as the asking, and she felt an overwhelming need to breech the gap between them.

"This home is an old family estate," she explained, waiting for pain to grip her heart as it always did when she thought about the past. But it didn't. A tingle was there, yes, but it was dull. Muted. "Gilbert loved it here. He liked being so close to town, but still in the countryside. That is why he is buried here, because he enjoyed it so much."

Lucas nodded wordlessly.

"That is why I have found it very difficult to come here. In fact, I've only been back a few times since his death."

She hesitated as the footman opened the door. Her words seemed to fall away as her mind spun with images and memories of this house and the man she had lived in it with. But like her pain, her memories were not as sharp as they once were. They no longer brought tears to her eyes. They no longer made her shake with the power of the emotions they evoked.

She found herself casting a glance at Lucas without even realizing she'd done it. When she looked at him, the emotions were strong. She wasn't sure what they were . . . but they were powerful.

He moved to the carriage door and stepped down, then turned to help her out. She looked up at the house just as the front door opened and the housekeeper, Mrs. Gray, came bustling out.

"Lady Whittig, we didn't know you would be coming." The housekeeper wrung her hands. "We would have prepared—"

"I won't be staying, Mrs. Gray," she interrupted. "I—I just needed to do something. May I present Mr. Lucas Tyler, my—he's my—"

Lucas's face tensed. "I am Lady Whittig's fiancé."

Ana flinched as the housekeeper's gaze slipped over to Lucas, then snapped back to her. She couldn't tell if she was being judged or not by the woman who had once lovingly served her and her late husband.

"A—A pleasure to make your acquaintance, Mr. Tyler," Mrs. Gray said. "Won't you come in and have a bit of tea?"

Ana took Lucas's arm and followed the woman into the house. Clearly the rest of Gilbert's family avoided the home he'd loved as much as she did. As she entered the sunny foyer, she noticed some of the furniture was covered with sheets and most of the doors, which had been thrown open in welcome when she was mistress here, were shut.

"I'm sorry about the state of the place, ma'am," Mrs. Gray said as she bustled ahead. "We weren't expecting anyone for another few weeks."

She tilted her head. "Another few weeks?"

"Yes. The new Lord Whittig will be arriving then." She stopped as she opened the door to a parlor. Her eyes were wide. "Didn't you know?"

Ana shook her head. Of course she knew Gilbert's younger brother had taken on the title. In fact, he had married a year ago, and he and his bride had recently welcomed a son. But she hadn't realized the new Lord Whittig and his family would take up residence here. She shut her eyes. This house would be full of laughter again. The squeals of children. It would no longer be a house of mourning and memory.

She waited for that to sting. But instead it gave her a small feeling of . . . joy.

"I'll fetch the tea," Mrs. Gray said. As she passed by, the housekeeper reached out and briefly squeezed Ana's arm.

Lucas took a seat and looked at her. Emotions hidden, as always. But so quiet. So serious. She wasn't sure what to think.

"She seems very kind," he said, motioning to the woman's retreating back.

"She always was." Ana let out a sigh. There was no

putting if off any longer. She needed to do what she'd come here to do. Waiting for tea wouldn't make it any easier. In fact, the longer she waited, the more nervous she became about her duty.

"Will you tell her I'll have my tea when I return?" she asked. "I want to do something. I *need* to do something first."

He got to his feet slowly. His eyes were filled with understanding. And a little frustration, too. But he didn't express either. "Of course. Shall I go with you?"

She halted, staring up at him. She'd brought him here for that purpose, to hold her hand, to hold her up if need be. But now she felt strong. Perhaps because he said she was. And she realized that she needed to face this final demon, this final moment in this house, alone.

"No. I think I must do this by myself."

His gaze turned hooded, his emotions buried in an instant. "As you wish."

She turned her back, drew in a deep breath, and left the room. She'd come all this way only to find that the house, that the family, had begun to move on, finally.

And now she had to do the one thing that would allow her to do the same.

Would it be wrong to ask for whiskey instead of tea? Would it be wrong to get stone drunk and ask rude questions about Saint Gilbert?

Lucas sighed. He supposed it would be. And it

wouldn't change anything. He would still be in the other man's house, following the other man's servant, waiting for a woman who very well might always consider herself another man's wife.

Even when she was his.

He clenched a fist as Mrs. Gray led him around a corner into long, wide hallway that brought the east and west parts of the house together.

"This is the family gallery," she explained. "All the portraits are here."

"Hmm." He stared at the faces, bored out of his mind. Where was Ana? Upstairs lying in her old bed? Sobbing hysterically as she walked the halls through the family quarters? Or was she at Gilbert Whittig's grave?

"And here are the most recent Lord and Lady Whittig," the housekeeper continued, stopping before a portrait that had been hung at eye level.

Thoughts bled out of Lucas's mind as he stared at the painting. It was Ana, a younger Ana. Softer eyes. More naïvety and innocence. There wasn't a sense of loss about her, but also less sensuality in her stare.

She was sitting in a chair, a pretty blue gown arranged in perfect folds around her. And on her shoulder was a man's hand. He looked up and found himself staring face to face with the person for whom he had come to nurse a powerful hatred in the last few weeks.

He'd never seen an image of Gilbert. Ana hadn't spoken much of him beyond her assertions that she had loved and would love him forever. This face was not the one he'd expected for his enemy. He was almost as young as Ana. With bright blue eyes and ruddy cheeks. There was a lot of hope and light in that stare.

"How did Whittig die?" he asked.

The housekeeper halted, her face pale as she turned back. He met her gaze evenly. It was an impertinent question, but he needed to know. Some part of him had to know.

"It was a hunting accident." She looked away. "He lingered for nearly a week, with her ladyship fighting to keep him on this earth."

He shut his eyes. No wonder Ana was so protective of Emily, why she constantly fretted over her condition. Like her husband, Ana's best friend had been shot. She'd seen life bleed away before, she'd tried her best to keep that life with her . . . only to fail.

"He was very young," he said, tilting his head a bit more.

"Aye, very young." The housekeeper swiped a sudden tear. "Too young."

A silence filled the hallway and finally Lucas stepped away, unable to look at the portrait anymore. Unable to look at the younger Ana's hopeful expression when he knew that just a few years later her life would be ripped out from under her.

The housekeeper began to walk again. She kept her eyes forward as she said, "Lady Whittig seems happy now, Mr. Tyler. And that is what we all would wish for her."

"Happy?" he barked out a laugh. "You thought she looked happy today?"

The woman paused and turned to stare at him. "Sir, she's only been here three times since he died. And every time, she's been sick with grief. Today I saw her joy." Color flooded the housekeeper's cheeks. "Now I'm just rambling on. Come, I'll fetch you some tea."

He held up a hand. "No, thank you." He could barely speak as he fought a sudden ache in his chest. "I think I'd like to take a walk around the grounds if you don't mind."

The woman nodded. "Of course. Don't hesitate to ask any servant if you require assistance."

He nodded as he made for the door. The cool air hit him like a wall and he realized how stifled he'd been inside, surrounded by another man's life.

But Mrs. Gray said Ana was happy, after all this. Happy. He just didn't see it. There were always walls she erected. He'd thought her emotions were clear on her face the first day he met her, but since then he'd come to realize just how complicated she was. How much she concealed. How much he wanted to know that was buried beneath the surface.

He wanted to know everything. And he wanted her to be what the housekeeper had claimed. He wanted the joy and hope that he'd seen in that portrait.

But *he* wanted to be the man who put it in her eyes. His feelings had changed somewhere in the weeks they'd worked together. What had at first been mere lust and fascination had altered, shifted to something deeper. Something more.

And yet she was still in love with someone else. Someone he couldn't compete with and couldn't even hate now that he'd seen his portrait.

"Damn it."

He paced along the lawn, moving away from the house toward some hills a few hundred yards away. He just needed to move, to run from the ache that was starting to build inside him. Why was this happening? It made no sense.

He crested the first hill and looked up. What he saw brought him to a shocked halt. Through a little grove of six or seven trees, he saw the outline of a low fence that surrounded a tiny graveyard. And just as he suspected, Ana was there. She was looking down at a headstone that had to mark Gilbert Whittig's grave.

He found himself moving forward, even though he didn't want to hear. Didn't want to see.

"I will never forget," she said, reaching down to let her fingertips trail along the top of the stone.

Lucas screwed his eyes shut. More of the pain he'd felt the night before, the pain he'd been feeling all day, rushed back. But this time it was even more powerful than before. Those words were the most hateful he'd ever heard. Here, practically on the eve of her wedding day, Ana was . . . what was she doing? It sounded like pledging her continuing devotion to a dead man. Nausea churned in Lucas's stomach at the thought.

Ana turned and jumped as she saw him standing not ten feet away.

"Lucas!" she cried. "How long have you been there?"

He was ashamed to have been caught, especially with his emotions so raw and twisted. "Not long. May I escort you back to the house?"

She took a last glance at the headstone, then nodded. As she slipped her arm through his, he, too looked back. Was there any overcoming such a powerful love?

He wasn't sure. All he knew was that he was willing to try.

Ana looked at her shaking hands, then back up in her reflection in the mirror. Lord, she was pale. Then the light caught on the band of gold around her finger.

She was married again. A wife again.

As if reading her thoughts, Lucas appeared behind her in the reflection, his gaze focused on hers in the mirror. She stiffened as he reached for her, his warm hands cupping her shoulders before he turned her.

His warmth surrounded her, his masculine scent weakened her and then he bent his head and brushed his lips against hers. The touch was soft, gentle, but heat was behind it all. A heat she could not deny anymore . . . and truth be told, she didn't *want* to deny it.

She had said her good-byes to Gilbert. She had accepted the future she'd never considered for herself. And she was willing to be a wife in more than just name to Lucas.

If he wanted that. Despite the flash of desire in his stare as he pulled away, she wasn't sure what he wanted. He was too difficult to read. Would it always be that way? A wall between them? A knowledge that this marriage wasn't one either of them had chosen? Would there only be desire, perhaps even respect, but nothing deeper?

And why did it matter? Did she really want more?

"Are you ready to face them?" Lucas asked, offering her an arm.

She laughed. *Them* was a small collection of friends and family who had gathered below to celebrate this union.

"I've certainly gotten my fair share of practice when it comes to my acting abilities on this case," she said as she took the arm he offered.

His smile faltered as he led her down the stairs into the foyer. "Yes."

She tilted her head at the sudden shift in his posture, the way the lines of his face drew down. But before she could ask him about any of it, he moved them into the parlor. Suddenly, they were surrounded by friends, being kissed by family. With a warmth building in her, Ana looked at the wide smiles every one of her new in-laws flashed.

She belonged with them now. Unlike the remnants

of her own broken family. She searched the room and wasn't surprised not to see any of her older siblings. It was so late in the Season, they were all back at their country homes. Too busy with their own families to see her married.

With a sigh, she shoved the past aside. Whatever had brought her here, this was where she belonged.

"Congratulations!" Meredith was suddenly at her side and she was wrapped in a bone crunching hug that she returned without hesitation.

When she pulled back, she saw her friend's eyes misted with tears.

"Don't forget, Mr. Tyler, that this woman is my best friend," Meredith continued as she shook Lucas's hand. Ana was sure she saw him wince in pain for a brief moment before he pulled away.

"I don't think I could forget, my lady," he said with a laugh as he subtly shook his fingers and offered them to Tristan. "Lord Carmichael."

Tristan shook his hand with a solemn smile before he kissed Ana's cheek. "Should we go to Emily? I can tell by her face that she's going mad confined to that chair."

As they moved toward her, Ana looked across the room at Emily, who was seated in the most comfortable chair in the house. Though she was pale and her face occasionally twisted with pain, she looked so much better. For that, at least, Ana could be grateful.

"Thank you for coming over," Emily said as they

reached her. "I was beginning to fear Lady Greenwich was planning to come by and regale me with more home remedies for my 'ailment.'"

"That story is working then?" Ana asked.

"Yes, everyone believes I was struck by a fever and am slowly recovering." Emily batted her eyelashes. "Do I look the part of the demure convalescent?"

Lucas choked out a laugh. "I cannot picture you reclining prettily while you are waited on, no."

Emily shot him a brief smile, though Ana could see her friend sizing him up. And she felt the same analysis when Emily's bright blue eyes moved to her.

"Henry!" Lucas called out, waving as his friend was wheeled into the room.

Both Meredith and Emily looked at Ana before each woman craned her neck to see the other man.

Henry's servant maneuvered him through the crowd toward their small party. Ana couldn't help but notice the stares of the other guests, but Henry didn't flinch or even seem to notice their expressions. His gaze was too focused on Lucas.

She looked at her new husband. Though Lucas had a friendly smile, there was something in his eyes that said he was troubled. And something stiff and strangely formal about the way he shook Henry's hand when his friend reached them. A little hope flared in her chest. Was he beginning to believe her?

She watched as Lucas introduced his friend to their group and also watched the way her friends interacted with the man she suspected of so much evil. Consummate professionals that they were, neither her friends, nor Tristan, betrayed their inner thoughts or suspicions about Henry.

"Lady Allington," he said, sparing a quick glance for Emily. "I'm glad to see you recovering well."

Emily arched a brow. "Thank you, Lord Cliffield. I appreciate that."

His gaze darted away from her and hit on Ana. For a moment, she thought she saw his eyes narrow, but then his expression became kinder. "Congratulations, Anastasia."

Lucas stiffened at her side and his smile grew tighter as she answered, "Thank you. I'm so glad you could come."

He nodded. "I do have a bit of business to discuss with Lucas, though. May we talk for a moment in private?"

Lucas hesitated, but then nodded. "Yes, of course."

With a brief look for her, he excused himself.

Tristan smiled. "Clearly you all need drinks. I shall return."

Meredith smiled as he made his way into the crowd and Emily laughed. "He has good instincts, I will give him that."

Ana smiled, too, but the expression was forced. She was too busy thinking about the way Lucas looked when Henry came in. And worrying as she remembered that flash of panic in Henry's eyes when she questioned him about his position in the War Department. If her fears about Cliffield were correct, Lucas could be in grave danger. Being best friends with a traitor couldn't be a good position.

"What did you think of Henry?" Ana asked, dropping her voice to a whisper.

"Something seemed off between him and Lucas," Meredith said as she rose up on her tiptoes to watch the two men leave. "A stiffness. Is that usual?"

Ana shook her head. "No."

"I spoke to Charlie before Tristan and I left for your wedding." Meredith folded her arms.

Ana smiled sadly. How she wished he could have been there, but there would be no way to explain his presence when he was not a member of Society's upper echelon. To keep their relationship a secret, he had stayed away.

"He says he has a stack of paperwork about Henry and his activities to review with you."

She nodded, her heart skipping more quickly at the news. "Good. I'll make my way to his office tomorrow and review what he's found."

"Will you bring Lucas with you?" Meredith asked. Emily leaned forward to hear her answer.

"No." Ana sighed as she thought of his reaction to her accusation the last time. "Until I have solid proof, I won't bring the subject up with him again. I don't know whether to hope to God I'm right about the man or hope to God I'm wrong. Either way, Lucas will be hurt."

Emily drew back a little and exchanged a brief, but meaningful look with Meredith. Ana held back a curse.

"You're worried about Lucas's feelings?"

Ana folded her arms. "Of course I am, he is my husband."

Emily snorted. "Not out of choice."

"Emily!" Meredith interrupted.

But Ana shook her head. "You're right, Emily. This marriage is not one either of us foresaw actually coming to fruition. But it doesn't change the fact that it has happened. It also doesn't change the fact that I wouldn't willingly harm Lucas for all the secrets of all the villains in England. And if Henry turns out to be as wicked as we suspect, that will break his heart. If he doesn't—" She cut herself off with a wince.

"If he doesn't?" Meredith asked, her voice more gentle than Emily's.

"Then I will have damaged their friendship irrevocably. I saw the hesitation in Lucas's eyes when Henry approached. He will never forgive himself for that if our accusations are proven unfounded."

"Hesitation?" Emily repeated. "I never saw such a thing."

Meredith shook her head. "Nor did I."

Ana stopped as the full ramifications of her friends' statements sunk in. Lucas's emotions were as stoic to them as they always had been, but Ana knew what she'd seen.

Which meant that she knew Lucas. She could see the subtle nuances in his expression that gave away his heart. Like a good wife would.

Meredith touched her arm. "I worry about you in this marriage. I worry about the fears and guilt you discussed with me before."

Ana bit her lip. "I don't know what the future will bring for me. But I went to Gilbert's grave and I . . ." She hesitated. "I said good-bye to him. I can't live in the past. Perhaps it's time to allow the future. And that future is, for better or for worse, with Lucas now."

For a moment, neither of her friends had readable expressions. But then both of them seemed to relax, as if they had been waiting a long time for that statement. And when Ana thought about it, she realized they probably had.

Lucas had said it to her many times. She lived holding up Gilbert as a shield, using her grief as an excuse to hide. To fear. To keep life and the world at an arm's distance.

And now she didn't feel the weight of keeping up that facade. For the first time in a long time, she looked forward to living. And she looked forward to seeing what a marriage with Lucas would bring.

Chapter 20

~~~
           ❦
~~~

Lucas opened the door to his bedchamber and motioned for Ana to enter. For a moment, she couldn't make her legs move. She'd been in his home . . . no, *their* home . . . before, but never upstairs. Never in his private quarters.

She sucked in a breath and forced herself to walk inside. The room wasn't anything like she'd pictured it, and she *had* pictured it in detail in her darkest fantasies. Somehow she'd thought it would be mysterious and sinful and everything Lucas embodied.

Instead, it was filled with light from candles and the glowing fire. Friendly. Open. Exactly the kind of room she would have wanted if she had closed her eyes and envisioned a chamber of her own. And then she saw the bed.

Big and soft and just beckoning to be laid in, slept in . . . a place to make love all afternoon, all night.

She turned her face, the heat of a blush warming her cheeks as Lucas shut the door behind them. She didn't look at him, but she couldn't escape him so easily. Her thoughts reminded her that this home was the first place they'd made love. Angry and passionate love.

Now it would be different. Now she was Lucas's wife. And she no longer had the guilt of Gilbert's presence hanging over her, making her curse every touch as much as she welcomed it.

She lifted her gaze to Lucas. What was he thinking? What did he want from this reluctant union?

"There is a sitting room here," he said, his voice gruff as he motioned to a door beside the bed. "And through that is the other bedchamber, your chamber."

She nodded, but made no move to go through the door. "Do you want me to sleep there?"

She held her breath as his eyes moved to meet hers. The stare was blatant. There was no misreading it. She would not be sleeping in the other room tonight unless that was her demand.

"No. I want you here. With me," he admitted. "But I realize you may not desire that. And I would not force you—"

She smiled as she stepped toward him and reached

up to cover his lips with two fingers. "Look into my eyes, Lucas. What do I desire?"

His expression shifted, as did his posture. The hard edge in his eyes softened, the stiffness of his shoulders relaxed. Slowly, he darted out his tongue and stroked across her fingers. Immediately, her knees went weak.

He lifted her fingers away from his lips and pressed another kiss against her wrist, up her forearm, to the crease of her elbow. Her sleeve was in the way then, so he put her hand on his shoulder instead and glided an arm around her waist to pull her closer.

She sighed as her breasts brushed his chest. Heat and need burned at her, but he would relieve the desire. And this time there would be no fear of interruption. They had all night and a big, comfortable bed to explore their every wish.

She did want to explore, too. In the past, she'd allowed herself to be swept away. But tonight, she wanted to see Lucas's body, to take her time and touch him, learn how to bring him pleasure.

Her fingers trembled as she hooked them against his unbuttoned jacket and slowly worked the heavy fabric off his shoulders. It hit the floor with a loud crumple and all the intense body heat that had been caught within the folds of fabric curled out to wrap around her.

She flattened her palms against the broad expanse of his chest and reveled in the low, feral growl Lucas made when she smoothed her palms down.

"Ana . . ."

With a smile, she whispered, "Just let me touch you, Lucas. I—I've been too afraid to properly do it in the past."

His expression softened again, and her chest ached at the sight. "You aren't afraid now?"

She shook her head. "No. For the first time in a long while, I'm not afraid."

He swallowed hard enough that she saw his Adam's apple work, then his embrace loosened. He let his arms drop to his sides, and she knew he was giving her what she had asked for. Access. Freedom.

The idea made her giddy with power, yet she still felt lost. What did she know about pleasing a man? She only knew what things Lucas did that made her gasp, which touch made her quiver.

Her lips tilted into a smile. That was all she needed. She'd use her own body as a guide.

Drawing a deep breath, she went to work on his shirt. He shed it to join the pile on the floor. Her heart raced as she stepped back to look at him. It had been a while since she saw him bared like this, but her memory had not been faulty when it recalled him as beautiful, perfect. He was those things and more. He was hers.

She leaned closer, letting the tips of her fingers slide against his skin. He hissed out a breath, but he didn't move. Didn't wrap his arms around her, though his fingers fisted at his sides. It was clear he was fighting his instincts in order to give her the power and pleasure she craved. Ana's heart soared as she lifted her lips and pressed them against the ridge of his collarbone.

Lucas tried to think about anything except the brush of Ana's lips against his skin. Anything to stay in control. Anything at all. It wasn't working, of course. Her touch was too intoxicating not to filter into his wildly racing mind, not to dull his reaction to everything except for her. She *was* everything.

And she was focused on him. Only him. Her lips drifted in soft caresses across the chest, sweeping back and forth as she inched lower. Lucas shut his eyes and fought to keep a groan from escaping his lips.

Another battle lost.

He had been with women who were more experienced than Ana, but none of them had ever made him feel like he did when she darted her tongue out to swirl it over his skin. No one had ever made his body so hard. Certainly, no one had ever involved his heart in seduction.

Ana did. Ana always had. Without trying, she brought him to his knees. And if she pulled away, he would be on those very knees begging.

But she didn't. Instead, she wrapped her soft lips around the flat disk of his nipple and sucked ever so gently. Pleasure crashed through him, and his good intentions were lost. He let out a cry as his fingers found their way into Ana's hair, sending pins scattering while her locks tangled around his hands and wrists.

She glanced up at him without breaking contact. He expected her to be timid, as she had been the first time they touched. Pull away. Apologize. Instead, she winked.

Lucas's mouth came open in shock, and his erection, which had already been straining, swelled even harder at her uncharacteristic boldness. There *was* a wicked temptress under those spectacles. He'd always sensed it and suddenly she was there, gliding her mouth across his chest to repeat the same explosively pleasurable caress on his opposite nipple.

"Little minx," he growled as he clenched his fingers against her scalp and tilted her face up. Ana arched a brow in challenge and it was just too much. He bent his head and pressed his lips against hers.

Her arms came around his neck and she lifted up on her tiptoes to meet the fire of his kiss with equal passion and need. He slipped his hands from her hair and the heavy length of it fell around her back as he stroked his fingers down her spine. She shivered, but didn't break the kiss. Not until he cupped her backside and lifted her off the floor against him.

"Lucas," she moaned, clinging to him tighter. Her leg hooked around his back as he moved toward the bed. Now it would be *their* bed, and he had the rest of his life to explore every inch of this woman's body and introduce her to all the pleasures he could think of.

That was an overwhelmingly erotic thought.

He set her down and instantly went to work removing her gown. He hardly even looked at his fingers as he unfastened buttons and clicked hooks free. All he could do was watch her face, feel the brush of her fingers as she stroked her hands up and down his bare sides.

As the last of her clothing fell away, Ana sighed with pleasure. There was something undeniably erotic about the way the fire warmed her naked skin, the way Lucas's heat warmed it even more. The way her bare breasts were just tantalizing inches from Lucas's chest.

He lifted her onto the mattress and joined her at her side. For a long moment, he didn't touch her, just leaned on one elbow and looked down at her. There was such tenderness, such warmth, to his expression that tears tickled her eyes at the sight.

"I want to please you," she whispered. For the first time she was able to say such a thing without blushing.

He smiled. "You please me enormously. More than any woman I've ever known. I wonder how you know how to do that."

Now the heat she had been able to stifle came to her cheeks. "I think of all you do that pleases me and do the same."

The warmth and gentleness that had been in his

eyes flicked away, replaced by hot, possessive desire she had seen many a time before. Her body reacted to the sight of it, nipples hardening and wet heat flooding her thighs.

"Do unto me as I do unto you, eh?" he asked as he finally placed the flat of his palm against her bare belly.

She gave a mute nod, too caught up in sensation to form coherent words.

"Then let me give you a wider education."

He sent her a heated stare before he rolled over to wrap his body around her. For an all too brief moment, she felt the swell of his erection through the fabric of his trousers, but then he was sliding down, down, down. He mimicked the things she had done with her mouth earlier, stroking her skin with his lips as he edged at a painfully slow pace to her nipples. When his breath steamed hot against the peaks, she arched up with a wail of pleasure.

He chuckled against her skin as he suckled there, plucking the sensitive flesh until she thought she would burst from the pleasure that shot through every nerve in her body and settled, heavy and wet, between her trembling legs.

Lucas wasn't done yet, though. He continued his journey down her body, tasting every inch of her skin, nipping her with gentle teeth, arousing her to a feverish level that had her tossing her head back and forth against the soft pillows.

His tongue slipped over her hip as he parted her legs with one hand. Ana's eyes flew open as she realized what he was about to do. She could scarce believe it, but then it happened. He pressed his mouth against the apex of her thighs.

Steamy heat burned at the sensitive outer lips of her core, and she let out a cry of pleasure and surprise. Lucas pressed a gentle hand against her belly to hold her steady while he opened her with the fingers of his opposite hand. His mouth returned, tongue teasing the slick opening, moving aside folds of sensitive flesh until he stroked the hooded button of pleasure at the top of her entrance.

Ana shivered with the feeling, gripping the pillows, the sheets in an attempt to gain purchase over the powerful sensations her new husband was creating with his skillful tongue. Her hips lifted of their own accord, pushing his hand up even as he exerted force to hold her still. Yet his mouth played on. He suckled, he stroked, he thrust into her. With each action, her body tipped closer to madness, the edge of coming undone. She seemed utterly out of control of her body now as she trembled and bucked under his gentle touch.

When he swirled his tongue one final time, she couldn't hold back any longer. Every fiber of her being exploded into a colorful kaleidoscope of pleasure. She trembled as wave after wave washed over her, washed her away. She lost her breath, lost her voice as she screamed, and yet he went on and on, continuing his torment until her last shudder of pleasure ended.

It took her a blurry moment to realize he was getting up. She opened her eyes wide, blinking as she tried to focus past her still shaking body.

"Lucas?" she murmured breathlessly.

He smiled as he shoved his trousers and boots away with impatient fingers. "I'm not finished yet," he reassured her as he rejoined her on the bed.

He pulled her over on her side so they lay face to face. His erection, now gloriously bared to her hungry eyes, pressed hot against her belly, twitching every time she drew a panting breath.

"You want to please me?" he whispered.

"Yes," she groaned as she clenched her fingers into a shaking fist against his bare hip. "Yes."

"Seeing you find release like you just did gives me more pleasure than you can imagine," he murmured as he caught her by the waist, dragging her on top of him as he rolled to his back.

"Lucas?"

"Straddle me," he ordered.

Normally, she would have considered this just another of his overbearing demands. But there was a slight tremble to his voice, a flash of pleading in his eyes. He needed this. Wanted this. And as unsure as she was, she was more than willing to give him what he desired.

She spread her legs, and gasped as the length of him

stroked her wet cleft. He shut his eyes with a harsh curse and the cords of muscle in his neck flexed.

"Yes, like that. Now just ease me inside and—"

He didn't get a chance to finish his direction. She repositioned herself and took his length into her in one smooth movement. They both moaned in unison at the feel of him stretching her body, filling her completely.

She moved and gasped at how full she felt in this position. How much control she had over the power and speed of her pleasure. And judging from the way Lucas moaned whenever she did so much as flex, the speed of his release, as well. With a wicked grin, she began to move in slow, rolling motions. But as Lucas's fingers tightened against her backside, as he pulled her forward to latch onto her nipple with his mouth, the control she'd been so pleased with faded. It was replaced by a wild drive to release, both hers and his. Her hips moved uncontrollably as the pressure built with blinding speed and finally she threw back her head and cried out, only to hear Lucas's moans join hers as he spilled his essence deep into her clenching body.

With a last groan, she collapsed onto his sweaty chest, shivering from the power of their joining. They lay like that for a long time, clutched in each other's arms.

After her heart rate returned to normal, Ana began to brush her hand back and forth along Lucas's hip.

She loved the feel of his skin, the bulge of muscles beneath, the slick slide of lusty sweat.

"Lucas?" she murmured.

"Hmm?" His response was sleepy, satiated, and it filled her with a giddy power.

"What you did with your mouth—" She lifted her head and watched his eyes come open with interest.

"Yes?"

"That would be something that would please you, too?"

From the way one corner of his mouth lifted and a dimple flashed, she knew the answer.

"Oh yes," he said with a chuckle that edged on a groan. "Most definitely."

She bit her lip as she began to inch her way down the length of his body.

"Teach me."

Lucas lifted his head from his pillow as the sound of knuckles rapping against the door sounded a second time. He looked over. Ana was still asleep, her tangled locks spread across the pillows. The sheets were pulled down around her waist, baring the soft curves of her breasts.

He suppressed a groan at his body's renewed craving for her and slung his legs over the side of the bed. He reached out to pull the sheet up for modesty, though when he brushed his knuckles against her nipples and they hardened instantly, he almost ignored the knocking and dove back in beside her to wake her up in the most pleasant fashion.

Instead, he forced some fraction of control. Pulling a robe on as he crossed to the door, he yanked it open.

"What is it?"

He could tell how fierce his expression was by the way the color drained away from the young footman's cheeks.

"I—I'm sorry, Mr. Tyler, but an urgent message just arrived for you." He held out an envelope with trembling fingers.

Lucas stepped into the hallway and pulled the door nearly shut behind him as he took the letter. The footman stepped back to give him privacy while he read.

The seal was that of his superior from the War Department. He broke it and withdrew a short note written on heavy, expensive paper.

Sansbury dead at home. Come immediately.

Lucas let loose a curse that made even the previously pale servant turn red up to his ears. He pushed the door open and looked inside at his wife. Ana had rolled over on her stomach, her arm across his side of the bed. She remained asleep.

"Is the messenger still outside?" he asked, folding the note to burn it later.

The footman nodded. "He was instructed to wait for your reply, sir."

"Tell him I will be on my way shortly. And have my valet meet me in her ladyship's chamber." He returned to the bedroom and looked at Ana again.

He should wake her. This was a huge break in their investigation, and she would want to be part of it. In fact, he was certain she would insist.

But then he thought of all her theories. Of the questions he was beginning to have about Henry, himself. No. If his best friend was about to be implicated in the deepest, most desperate treason, he wanted to be the one who uncovered the information.

And if Henry's name could be cleared, he wanted to be the person who did that, as well. He would let Ana sleep and face her wrath later.

Gathering a few things from the armoire, Lucas slipped past his wife into the sitting room and into the adjoining bed chamber to ready himself.

Chapter 21

Lucas had seen death before, but violent death like this was never something easily stomached. He exchanged a glance with the man from the Watch who was investigating the crime, and they both grimaced.

"It was a personal attack," Lucas murmured.

The Watch guard scribbled in his notebook. "Why do you think that, sir?"

Lucas looked down at Sansbury's body. It was disfigured now, the skin smashed, bone sticking through in the arms and through a tear in the trouser leg. His face was twisted in a mask of horror and fear, though his eyes—or the eye that wasn't swollen shut—were empty of all emotion or life.

Lucas shook his head. "There wasn't any reason to beat him so severely. A few of these strikes to the head would have incapacitated him. But the killer kept hitting. He was trying to cause pain." He motioned to a few of the uglier marks. "To punish."

The guard wrote furiously, and Lucas cast him a quick glance, knowing the man would likely take credit for Lucas's comments in his report. Not that it mattered. His Majesty's spies would solve this case, not the Watch. They were fine for breaking up a drunken rout, but not this kind of horror.

The man caught his eye and had the decency to blush before he left the room. Lucas crouched down beside Sansbury's twisted frame and tilted his head, looking for any clues before he moved the dead man. He didn't want to miss anything.

"Mr. Tyler is there, sir."

He turned at the mention of his name. Charles Isley was standing in the parlor door with the guard, face pinched as he took in the bloody scene around him.

"Thank you."

Isley took a few steps inside, carefully dodging overturned furniture and blood splatter. "Good morning, Tyler," he said. "Ugly mess, eh?"

Lucas got to his feet and nodded. "Ugly, indeed."

As ugly as the guilt that suddenly slashed through him. Isley's appearance only served to remind him of how he'd snuck out of his bedroom an hour before, leaving Ana blissfully ignorant of this very big development in their foundering case. She would be justifiably angry when she found out, and probably hurt, especially after she had opened up to him the night before. Gave him so much of herself while they made love. After she found out about this, he would definitely lose ground with her.

"Where is Ana?" Isley asked as he peered around.

Lucas flinched. There was no avoiding the subject now. "She—"

Before he could make some lame excuse, the Watch guard returned to the room with a round, older woman behind him. When she looked around, her knees buckled. Lucas rushed forward, catching her just before she hit the floor. He glared at the young man.

"Dear God, have you no decency! Don't bring the woman in here."

The guard flinched. "I—I'm sorry, sir. This is the housekeeper, Mrs. Farnsworth. She found the body."

Isley shot Lucas a glance. Lucas nodded, guiding the woman into another room with the other two men at his heels. He helped her into a chair while Isley poured her a glass of sherry from Sansbury's sideboard. The man probably would have begrudged her that kindness in life, but his opinion was no longer an issue.

"Mrs. Farnsworth," Charlie began as he handed the glass to the woman. "Can you tell us what you remember?"

The housekeeper sipped the liquor slowly, her hands

trembling. "Yesterday afternoon, his lordship demanded his servants take leave of the house."

Lucas's eyebrows shot up. "All of you?"

She nodded in a few jerks. "Yes. Everyone and for the entire night."

"Was that a common occurrence?" Lucas asked.

A blush darkened the woman's lined cheeks. "Y-Yes, sir. Lord Sansbury did a lot of . . . evening entertaining. He didn't want servants underfoot when he had his . . . his female companions here. He did things with them that were—"

Charlie held up a hand. "We understand, madam. You needn't elaborate if it troubles you."

The housekeeper nodded with relief. "Thank you. I assumed that was what he was doing last night. This morning when I came back from my sister's, the house was very quiet. I thought nothing of it, I believed his lordship to still be abed. He doesn't—*didn't* like to be disturbed after one of his nights. Then I went into the parlor to light the fires and—"

She broke off and her skin turned a sickly green. "I found him."

Lucas nodded slowly. "And is there anything missing from the house?"

"Nothing I've found so far, sir." She drew in a few harsh breaths. "The other servants are looking. I'll inform you if they find anything."

"Thank you," Charlie said with a warm smile for the woman. "You may go now."

As the woman stumbled away, the Watch guard's face lightened. "So it's a whore we're looking for."

Lucas got to his feet, smoothing a hand over his face. "No. I doubt many women could do such damage to a grown man of Sansbury's strength. And most lightskirts would have taken the valuables in the room. There are many expensive items that were left behind completely untouched. I don't think Sansbury was expecting a woman last night. But he *was* expecting someone."

Charlie nodded in agreement. "Have you searched the body?"

Lucas shook his head. "No. Not yet. I was about to do so when you arrived."

Isley looked at the guard. "Continue interviewing the servants."

The young man seemed disappointed not to be involved in the grisly work ahead, but he went away as ordered. Lucas went back into the bloody parlor with Isley at his heels.

"I'll search the body if you want to look in that desk on the west wall," Lucas suggested.

Charlie met his eyes and Lucas could see he hadn't forgotten the subject of Ana's absence, just set it aside for the moment. There was mistrust in the other man's round face and annoyance at the idea that one of his spies had been left out of the investigation.

But as Lucas looked around him, he was happy she wasn't there. She shouldn't have to see such carnage.

Such brutality. Truth be told, he didn't want to see her beautiful face surrounded by the ugliness, either. Didn't want her tainted by the blood and turmoil.

"Very well," Charlie finally answered. "I'll look at the desk."

As the other man crossed the room, Lucas hunched down. Sansbury was laying on his back, arms raised in front of him in a failed attempt to shield himself from the attack that took his life. One hand was clenched into a fist, but the other was mangled. Lucas reached out and touched the rigid fingers. They were all broken, torn backward.

He tilted his head. Hidden amongst the blood in Sansbury's palm was a little piece of paper. A corner from a larger piece. Gingerly, he removed the slip and turned it over. There was nothing on the paper, but it was a heavy sheet. Expensive.

"He was clenching a paper. Someone broke his hand to get to it," he called out.

Charlie joined Lucas. "Let me see."

He took the piece gingerly to examine it. Lucas thought he saw some look of recognition in Charlie's face, but then it was gone. He pursed his lips. If the other man knew something, he wasn't going to tell him, likely as punishment for leaving Ana out of the scene.

He probably deserved that.

"Did you find anything?" Lucas asked, giving Charlie a look of challenge.

The other man's face remained stoic. "There's nothing

new to be found, I don't think. Except that Sansbury isn't the man behind these attacks after all."

As Charlie returned to the desk and his search, Lucas sighed. Yes, that much was becoming clear. He couldn't believe that Sansbury's brutal murder didn't relate in some way to the deaths of the spies in the field. And if he'd been murdered for what he knew, that meant someone else knew more. Someone else had secrets to keep of their own.

The only solace he could take was that Henry couldn't be responsible for this attack. In his wheelchair, there was no way he could brutally murder someone in this fashion.

He straightened up. He couldn't believe he was even thinking such a thing. Taking the time to eliminate Henry from a crime he wouldn't have even considered him a suspect in just one month before.

And he could only pray he was right in eliminating his friend from guilt.

"Sansbury is dead?" Ana repeated, sitting down in a chair across from Charlie with a thud. "When? Where? How?"

Charlie's forehead wrinkled. "Blast that Lucas Tyler! I knew he kept you in the dark."

"What do you mean?" she whispered, even though she knew exactly what her superior meant. Her chest tightened. When she'd awoken alone, with only a note from Lucas, she'd been too flushed with the night's pleasures to question where he had gone. What a fool she was!

Here she'd been fantasizing about his touch all while he'd left her out of the case. Her face burned with embarrassment.

"Lucas was on the scene this morning, along with members of the Watch. He avoided all my questions about your whereabouts." Charlie rubbed his eyes. "He did not inform you of anything?"

"No, I have not seen him this morning. When he left Sansbury's residence, he didn't return home." She folded her arms. "Please fill me in."

Charlie nodded. "Sansbury was found dead this morning."

"How?" she pressed, leaning forward. The anger was still burning inside of her, but she set it aside to do her work.

"He was bludgeoned to death some time during the night." Charlie grimaced. "Ugly business."

She nodded, though some part of her was suddenly glad she hadn't gone with Lucas. She'd seen the dead before, but it was never something she relished.

"Tell me everything."

She listened in horror as Charlie steepled his fingers and quietly recounted the brutality of the murder. And the fact that Sansbury had been expecting whoever took his life.

"So he probably knew the man."

She thought of the shadowy figure she'd seen with

Sansbury the night of the General's soiree. Neither she nor Lucas had been able to make out his face in the dark. Though she'd heard snippets of angry words, she hadn't been able to place the person's voice, either.

"Is this connected to the attacks on the spies, do you think?"

Charlie shrugged. "We aren't sure, but it fits. As you know, there has been a cloud of suspicion around Sansbury for weeks. Nothing in the house was stolen except for a piece of paper the man was holding in his hand during the attack. Tyler found it in the man's broken fingers."

Ana winced. "Do you have it?"

"No." Charlie barked out a humorless laugh. "He insisted on keeping it as evidence. But I found something else. Something I kept from him as deftly as he kept all this information from you."

She cocked her head. "You did?"

"Yes. While your new husband was searching the body, I found this in Sansbury's desk drawer. It was jammed into a book." He pulled out a piece of paper that was covered in scattered numbers. "It is written on the same kind of paper as the scrap found in Sansbury's dead hand."

She snatched it up. "These numbers could be code."

He nodded. "I thought perhaps Sansbury invited his killer there to blackmail him with whatever was written on the note in his hand."

She smiled. "Do you think he might have written

it out twice, once encoded, just in case he needed it for leverage later? Do you have the book this sheet was in?"

Charlie nodded as he opened a thick file and withdrew a heavy tome. "I took it as evidence, as well. Why?"

Ana looked at the book. It was a thick volume about animal husbandry. Her suspicions pricked.

"Perhaps Sansbury wanted us to find this." She held it up. "It's certainly not the sort of reading a man of Society would normally have in his desk at his fashionable London home. I think this is a book code."

"Book code?"

"The numbers coincide with page numbers, line numbers, and letter numbers in a book." She clutched the volume against her chest. "Probably the one he hid the note in. Charlie, I could kiss you!"

The other man smiled, his red cheeks reddening even more. "But you won't. You'll go home and decode this letter." His smile fell. "Now, would you like to see the evidence I've uncovered that involves Henry Bowerly?"

The joy Ana felt over the potential power of the evidence in her hand bled away at Charlie's reminder of why she had been summoned here initially.

"Yes," she said softly as she put the encoded letter and the book in her reticule. "What did you find?"

Charlie motioned to a mountain of paperwork on the table behind her. Together, they walked over to it.

"It was not easy to obtain, I assure you. The War Department isn't keen on our organization."

"I can imagine," she said, staring at the pile.

"And since Cliffield does internal work for them, getting access without it being common knowledge was even more difficult. But I called in a few favors and I can only hope my contacts will be discreet."

Ana nodded. She had the feeling Lucas had not yet told Henry her assertions when it came to his potential involvement. She could only imagine Cliffield's reaction when he heard she suspected him of treason.

Especially if she was correct. That could be a terribly dangerous prospect. If the man was capable of murder and maiming his fellow spies, people he claimed to like and respect, what would he do to her? What would he do to Lucas?

And how had he orchestrated it all from his wheelchair? That was another lingering question she had yet to find an answer to.

"I've yet to sift through most of it," Charlie admitted as she thumbed through a few pieces. "But I did find some troubling things in the pages I did review."

"Which ones?" she asked.

He picked up a slim pile and handed it over. She skimmed the lines and found they were internal reports from Henry's superiors. Each was dated before Henry's attack a year before.

"It seems the Marquis of Cliffield was investigated at least twice just before his injuries," Charlie said. "Once he was reprimanded for mishandling evidence that was 'lost' on a case. And once for taking a large sum of money in another case. But he was cleared of that."

Ana found the file he was talking about and read over the lines. "This has a notation at the end about seeking another internal investigation."

Charlie leaned over her shoulder and looked. "As I said, I only gave these things a cursory look. But . . ." He hesitated and flipped through the papers on the table. "I do have the file that notation refers to here."

She took the new file and flipped it open. As she read the record, her eyes widened. "After Henry was cleared, another spy was arrested for the theft." Her heart was pounding so loudly she could hardly hear her own voice. "But before he could come to trial, he was found dead. *Bludgeoned* to death in his prison cell."

Charlie took a stumbling step back and the two locked gazes. "That bodes poorly."

"Yes." She set the file down. "Oh, Charlie. Why in the world would a man like this turn to the darkness of being a traitor? He has rank, he has money . . ."

"Well, he had money." Charlie sorted through the pages until he came upon what he was looking for. "These financial records indicate his estate has had a few problems in the past two years. Some poor investments. Perhaps money was part of the motive after all."

She nodded, but the idea didn't fully fit. "It seems like such a sacrifice, such a risk, for something so small."

"Perhaps." Charlie's face twisted and Ana saw the pain, the wear of years around his eyes in a way she hadn't before. "But men have done worse for far less."

"May I take these papers with me?" she asked, gathering the piles. "Perhaps I'll find more clues if I review them more closely."

He nodded. "Of course." He handed her a large satchel, which she put the papers into, her mind buzzing with possibility. As he walked her to the door, he smiled. "And I hope you plan to take Lucas Tyler to task for leaving you out of the investigation."

Her eyes narrowed. "Oh don't worry, Charlie. My new husband will definitely hear from me on that score." She gave him a wave as she moved into the foyer. "Good afternoon. I'll send word the moment I've decoded this or if I find anything else that helps us sort out this madness."

With Charlie's good-byes ringing in her ears, Ana headed down the walkway to her waiting carriage on the street. She was still a few feet away when from around the opposite side strode Lucas. Judging from the fire in his eyes and the harsh set to his jaw, he was as displeased with her as she was with him.

"Where have you been?" he snapped as he opened Charlie's gate and walked toward her.

Her mouth dropped open. He had the gall to question *her* whereabouts when she knew full well that he'd hidden his own location just hours before?

"I might ask you the same thing," she said, folding

her arms. The big satchel full of evidence bounced against her hip and she shifted under its weight.

Lucas's eyes narrowed as he reached out and slipped the bag from her arm, opened the carriage door and put it inside. But when he motioned for her to follow, she shook her head.

"I know where you were, Lucas. I know about Sansbury."

His gaze darted around, but there was no indication anyone else was around, let alone paying attention to their argument.

"Mind your voice."

Her eyes narrowed. "Mind my voice? You actually have the gall to tell me what to do when you hid a suspect's murder from me?"

He reached for her, but she pulled her arm from his grasp. "I planned to tell you this evening," he explained, his harsh whisper grating across her already frazzled nerves. "I needed to see myself."

"Why?" she snapped. "Why did you leave me out of this crucial element?"

"Because I—" he began, his frustration clear in both his expression and his tone.

Before he could finish, though, there was an explosion of gunpowder behind them and the fence in front of Ana splintered as a bullet struck it from above.

Lucas didn't think, he didn't stop, he simply lunged forward, covering Ana with his body and rolling toward a row of nearby bushes. When they were under enough cover, he looked at where the bullet had stuck.

Just inches from where she had been standing. His heart doubled its time with the horror of that fact.

She shifted beneath him. "Let me up," she whispered.

"No. Not yet. That shot was no accident."

She met his eyes and one eyebrow arched. "I never said it was, but I can't breathe."

He shifted and she moved, leaning up to join him in looking above. Suddenly, she tugged his shirtsleeve.

"There!"

High above, on top of Charlie's town home was a man. The dark scarf wrapped around his face whipped in the breeze as he turned to run along the roof away from them.

Immediately Lucas was on his feet, running along the perimeter of the house until he saw a ladder that had been propped up in the alleyway. Probably by the person who intended to shoot Ana. He was halfway up the rungs, going two at a time when he felt the ladder shift below him.

He continued to climb as he shouted down, "No! Stay there. Let me follow!"

The shaking below didn't stop. If anything it increased. Of course she wouldn't listen.

"You cannot keep me from this, Lucas. I'm coming with you," she shouted.

He clenched his teeth and kept climbing, vaulting

onto the rooftop in a smooth motion. If there were more time, he would gladly stop and argue with her, but the man who had shot at her was already at the edge of Charles Isley's roof. He made a leap and landed like a cat on the next building. He didn't miss a step before he was running again.

Lucas swore, tossing a glance behind him to see if Ana was struggling to get on the roof. He was surprised to find she was right behind him.

"What are you waiting for?" she said as she started to run. "Come on!"

Lucas pursed his lips and followed, but he was faster and soon passed her. He watched as the man they were chasing vaulted over the next rooftop. Damn it, they might not catch him now.

The edge of the roof was fast approaching. Lucas knew he could clear it, but with Ana in tow . . . With another curse, he stopped at the edge.

But to his shock, Ana kept running. Her face twisted and with a grunt, she leapt.

His heart nearly stopped as he watched her fly through the air, hovering over the empty space between the buildings. He tensed as she started her descent, expecting to watch her plummet to the cobblestones below. But instead, she landed on the next roof, dropping down with bent knees to reduce the jarring effects of the landing.

For a moment, she remained that way, her back to him and he jolted. Was she hurt? But then she turned and she had the widest, brightest smile he'd ever seen.

"I cleared it," she said, her voice registering shock. Then she shook it off and was all business again. "Can't you?"

His eyes narrowed. Cocky little minx. He took a few steps back and ran, jumping right at the edge of the roof. But the moment he started to fly through the air, he realized he wouldn't clear the gap. And judging from Ana's horrified expression, she knew it, too.

Chapter 22

Lucas hit the edge of the building with enough force that the wind was knocked out of his lungs. He clawed at the rooftop for purchase as he slid backward toward the alleyway below. If he couldn't get a grip, he was going to fall two floors. He would probably break his legs, if not worse. Horror gripped Ana, but she couldn't stand by and just watch him struggle. Instead, she lunged and caught his arm as her heart rocketed to her throat.

"Pull yourself up," she said, straining to talk as she fell back on her backside and braced her feet on the roof's edge. Lucas was so much heavier than she was and her arms tensed to bear his weight. "Come on, Lucas. You aren't going to fall. I won't let you."

He looked up at her, his eyes wide with surprise at her statement, but he didn't argue. At least not yet. She felt his muscles contract as he pulled, then his leg lifted over the roof edge and he was up. She fell back now that his weight wasn't pulling her toward the edge and he landed half on top of her.

She laid there for a moment as the entire scenario played through her mind. The facts were slowly sinking in. *She* had jumped across the building. *She* had cleared the gap.

And Lucas, who had proven himself to be a talented spy again and again, *hadn't*.

She stifled a little giggle. Lucas lifted his head and stared at her.

"Are you hysterical?" he asked, getting to his feet and brushing off his dusty trousers.

She couldn't help it, another laugh escaped her throat. She smacked her hand over her lips at the dark look he shot her. Clearly, he didn't find the situation all that amazing.

He offered her a hand, yanking her to her feet. He looked over her shoulder and let out a long string of curses, each saltier than the last. The last one actually made her blush.

"He's gone," he spat, then turned away and kicked at a few pebbles on the rooftop viciously, sending them flying into the alley below.

Her high emotion fled. "If he's growing bolder, we'll

catch him." She reached out and touched his arm. "We almost did today."

He spun around and caught her arms, pulling her against his chest. His eyes were stormy, but he seemed unable to speak. Finally, he let her go and looked around for a way down from the roof they were on.

She stared at him. "Lucas?"

He glared at her over his shoulder. "Just come with me."

He motioned to a drainage pipe along the side of the house they stood on. She watched as he swung around onto the pipe and motioned for her to get on his back. She opened her mouth to protest, but his sharp glare stopped her.

With a ginger step, she wrapped her arms around his broad shoulders and clung tight while he eased his way down inch by inch. She could feel his tension in every muscle until they had their feet on solid ground.

"Lucas?" she repeated, trying to catch his gaze.

"Not now," he growled as he snatched her hand and marched out of the alleyway. As they reached the street and started heading back to the carriage, she saw Charlie standing on the walkway in front of his house.

He stared at the hole in his fence and their disheveled appearance. "What the hell happened?" he asked as he moved toward them.

Lucas spun on him and his gaze hesitated on the bullet hole. His face twisted into a look as fierce as any Ana had ever seen. Her stomach flipped. He looked like a warrior. Her protector.

"She was *shot* at, Isley, what do you think?"

Charlie's eyes widened, but before he could reply, Lucas threw open the carriage door and placed a hand on the small of her back. She stepped in at his insistence, and he followed, slamming the door behind them and pounding on the wall.

The carriage rocked into motion and Ana watched him. This was definitely not the man she was used to. No smile. Not even a hint of one. And his eyes were so intense, so expressive in their fierce emotion that she couldn't help but stare.

Her pulse was raging, and not from leftover adrenaline or excitement of the chase. Not from lingering pride that she had vaulted over the gap in the buildings when Lucas could not.

This excitement was housed lower in her belly. An ache she recognized and was shocked could happen with just one glance from Lucas. She *wanted* him. Despite his clear upset and anger and frustration.

"Lucas," she began, fighting the want and trying to maintain some distance.

He held up a hand. "He almost killed you, Ana. If his bullet had hit a few inches to the left, he would have found his mark."

She shivered. "Of course I realize that, but—"

"But nothing." He moved over to her side of the carriage and suddenly his hands were on her. His fingers smoothed across her arms, her back. "Do you know what that felt like, Ana? Do you know the thoughts that ran through my head when that bullet rushed past you?"

His face was so close to hers, his eyes just inches from her own. In them she saw everything. His fear. His desire. His anger . . . but at himself for feeling what he felt. All those things were hers and hers alone. Her heart melted.

"Lucas," she whispered, cupping his cheeks. "I wasn't hit. I wasn't harmed."

"By the grace of God, that is true." He put his arms around her and pulled her closer, into his lap. "But I need to feel that you're whole."

She realized his hands were shaking as he cupped her neck and drew her lips down on his. His whole body was shaking, though his kiss was as strong and powerful as ever. She clenched her fists against his shoulders, holding him against her with all her might, letting him feel that she was unharmed. Letting him feel how powerfully his fear touched her. It made apparent the fact that he cared for her in some way and that knowledge rocked her to her very core.

Lucas sucked in a breath as he broke the kiss and looked up into Ana's beautiful face. She smiled, soft. Not like the magnificent blaze that lit her face when she cleared the rooftop and finally realized just how strong she really was. This was something else. Something comforting.

And it was just for him. Just as the way she leaned down and gently brushed her lips back and forth against his was just for him. It was comfort. It was pleasure.

It touched him to his very soul and a powerful realization struck him like a lightning bolt. He loved her.

There it was. The truth revealed to him by fear. No. Not fear. Terror. Watching that bullet tear a hole in the fence, a hole that was meant to be ripped through his wife, was terrifying. He wanted to hold her like this forever. Keep her safe.

Instead he pushed away all his reactions and the internal arguments against the fact that he loved her and surrendered to the comfort she offered. The peace that flowed over him as she threaded her fingers through his hair. And the desire that pumped into his system when she shifted on his lap to straddle him.

He pulled her mouth down and kissed her again, this time without gentleness. He just wanted to feel her and taste her . . . *own* her. Love her. Every time he allowed that thought to enter his mind, it seemed more right. More true.

He embraced that feeling. Let it fill him up in places he hadn't realized were empty.

Ana's hands were moving now, her breath harsh as she placed a hand between their bodies and rubbed his erection to full hardness. He groaned at how easily she could unman him, make him forget everything except how much he wanted to bury himself inside her warm and welcoming heat.

He shoved at her dress, pulling at layers of fabric while she fumbled with the buttons that kept her from touching him. His erection sprung free, and she stroked him from base to head, once, twice.

His head lolled back, his hands loosening their hold on her as blinding pleasure rushed through him. His hips lifted, filling her hand as he sucked in his breath. She smiled, this time sly and with full knowledge of the power she had over him.

"I am whole, Lucas," she whispered, her warm breath brushing against his ear. She pressed a hot kiss against his neck. "And I'm yours."

He caught that promise with his mouth and kissed her so hard and hot that his head spun. His fingers found her gown again and he lifted it, finally removing the barrier between his bare skin and her waiting body. She lifted up, positioning herself above him and then began a slow descent, wrapping her wet heat around him with painful slowness.

He couldn't wait for her torture, lifting his hips until he surged into her fully in one hard stroke. Ana wailed out pleasure, her body contracting as it welcomed him, gushed heated desire over him. She clung to his shoulders, riding him with jerky movements.

Lucas dug his fingers into her hips, controlling the rolling movements, guiding her to move slower, to smooth her strokes. Her eyes fluttered shut and he looked up into her face. Her pleasure was reflected in every twitch of her muscles, every sigh that escaped her parted lips.

"Let go," he whispered through clenched teeth. "Let go, Ana. Give yourself to me."

Her eyes opened, revealing the warm depths of brown heaven. In them he saw emotions. Tangled. Hopeful. But not fully surrendered yet.

"Yes," she moaned just before her spine stiffened and she arched against him with a few hard thrusts. Her body clenched at his, stroking him with the tremors of her pleasure. Whatever control he had been exercising spun out of his reach. His blood moved, his body shivered, and he clutched her against him, growling out her name as he poured everything he was deep into her womb.

Ana's breath came short as she gently dropped her forehead to rest against his. They sat like that for a long moment until their ragged breathing finally slowed, matched. Then she pressed a soft kiss against his temple and lifted away from him. When their bodies separated, Lucas stifled a groan of displeasure. He felt so empty when she wasn't near.

That niggling reminder that he loved her buzzed in his ear, but he pushed it aside. Nothing had changed between them just because he realized his heart. As he watched Ana slip to the opposite side of the carriage and fix herself, he knew that to be true.

Today's events proved that they were still battling for position in this case. She still suspected Henry of wrongdoing.

And beyond that, he had seen her at her late husband's grave. Even now, during this powerful and emotionally charged encounter, she hadn't been ready to give her heart completely. She was much more open with her body since their marriage, yes, and that gave him wild and powerful hope that one day she could offer more.

But until they solved this case, Lucas couldn't take the time to woo her properly. To win that heart that she kept buried. He could only please her body and hope it was enough to keep her bound to him until he could do more.

But when this was over, he would have her as his wife in every way. He *would* win her love.

As the coach slowed, he quickly refastened his trousers and smoothed his wrinkled clothes. Their eyes met, and Ana smiled, but the ever-constant wariness was there in her stare.

"We have much to talk about," he said, forcing himself back in investigative mode. "I think we each have a lot to say about what happened today."

She nodded slowly. "Yes, we do."

The carriage stopped and in less than a minute, the footman opened the door. Lucas sighed. "Then we will go inside, have some tea, and do just that."

* * *

Something had changed. Ana looked at Lucas across the room, sitting by the fire, a cup of tea in his hand. There was something different between them now.

On their wedding night, she had given her body to him fully. But today, in that intense, emotional coupling in the carriage, she felt him give himself. Something much deeper than merely his body.

Something that terrified her. Thrilled her. And the thrill was starting to outweigh the fear.

"We can look at each other all afternoon," Lucas said before he took a sip of tea. "Which I am not opposed to. Or we can discuss the subject that is hanging in the air between us. This case. And our differences of opinion regarding it."

She shoved her emotional response aside. There would be time to analyze that later. At least, she hoped there would be. She, of all people, knew how fragile life could be, and even more so when so much danger surrounded her and Lucas at every turn.

With a shiver at that thought, she struggled to find her anger again. The disappointment and hurt she'd felt when she heard he went to the scene of Sansbury's murder without her.

It returned without any difficulty.

"Why didn't you wake me before you left this morning?" she asked, folding her arms. "Did you think I wouldn't find out that Sansbury was dead or that you had gone to the scene of the crime without me?"

His face changed, twisted with guilt, but also memory. "I had to go alone, Ana."

"But why? Did you think I couldn't handle the horror? Did you think I wasn't strong enough?" She held her breath as she awaited his reply.

He set his cup away. "Your strength had nothing to do with it. It had to do with mine. I had to go alone, I had to see—"

He broke off and his mouth twisted with anguish. She'd never seen his pain reflected so clearly before.

"See what?" she whispered as she crossed the room to him.

He got to his feet and paced away. "I had to see if there was evidence implicated Henry."

"And was there?"

He shook his head. "No. But I doubted him. By searching for evidence there, I proved that I have lost faith in him."

She winced. God, what he would feel when he heard what she had found out. She loathed telling him, breaking his trust in Henry further. Instead, she put it off a bit longer.

"Lucas, we are partners. Whether you like it or not, Sansbury's murder was as much my business as it was yours. You should have taken me."

He stared at her for a moment, his gaze unreadable. Then he nodded. "You are right, of course. I apologize, Ana. It was wrong of me."

She staggered back a step. He was admitting his wrongdoing? He was telling her he wouldn't shut her out again? Had the world shifted on its axis in the night and she didn't know?

Then he arched a brow. "And would you admit that you should not have gone to Isley's home today alone?"

"I go to Charlie's home regularly, and he visits me," she argued.

"But were you discussing the weather, my dear?" Lucas set his tea cup down. "Or perhaps it was this case."

She ducked her head as his question sunk in. It was really a statement more than a query. A reminder that while she was up in arms about being shut out, she had done the exact same thing. Going to Charlie, working through the papers that were still in the little bag beside the door, doing those things without giving Lucas the choice of joining her was no better.

And just like her, he deserved to know the truth. No matter how much it pained him.

"We *were* talking about this case," she admitted as blood rushed hot to her cheeks. "I was wrong to go there without you. And I've been wrong to investigate Henry behind your back."

Lucas stood stiff, his face a mask of unreadable emotion. No. It wasn't unreadable. It was pain. It was anger. It was disbelief . . . but that disbelief was starting to waver, revealing fear. Fear that she was right.

"Did *you* uncover new evidence?" Lucas asked.

She nodded slowly. "I did. And I would like to share

it with you now if you'll hear it." She reached out and touched his hand and was relieved when he didn't yank back. "Lucas, it's time we put our differences aside and really work together."

He nodded. "Show me what you've found Ana. No matter what, I want to know."

Chapter 23

Lucas stared at the evidence Ana had collected against his best friend. A man he considered as much a brother as Peter or Martin or his sisters' husbands. There was so much. It was so damning.

And Lucas hadn't known about any of it until that moment. Oh, there had been whisperings of internal investigations against spies. He and Henry had even discussed them, wondering who it was who had been accused of stealing from a case, of tampering with evidence.

And all along it had been his friend. Henry had lied to him over and over about his whereabouts and his associations.

Lucas set the last report aside and rubbed his eyes.

His first instinct was to deny these things. He wanted to push them away and pretend he didn't now know that his friend had so many dark secrets. But he couldn't. Those were his emotions talking.

He couldn't ignore the truth. Perhaps Henry wasn't involved in the attacks on the spies. After all, he had been attacked, as well. That was the missing piece of this puzzle. But his friend had kept things from him. He'd lied.

And that didn't bode well.

He hated the doubt, the questions, but he had to look deeper now. Because he couldn't ignore Ana's evidence or her instincts.

Getting to his feet, Lucas looked around the room. They had relocated to Ana's chamber, the one attached to his by a lone sitting room. In just a day, she had already begun to transform it into a new laboratory. A new place for her to break codes and invent things.

Which meant she was making it a home for herself. And that warmed him. Despite everything, that pleasant emotion could wiggle its way through the despair.

"I'm so sorry, Lucas." She stood up from the chair where she had been quietly watching him read over the proof she had gathered. "I swear to you, I would rather bleed than cause you such pain and doubt. But I cannot ignore what I've found."

He nodded, reaching out to cup her cheek. Just touching her gave him a little relief. "Nor can I, Ana."

Her face softened. She'd been ready for him to argue, to deny her abilities, yet again. But he couldn't do that anymore.

"I need to go to the War Department," he said, shocked by how his voice rasped with emotion. "I need to speak to some of our superiors about these charges against Henry. And I need to access some files from his office there."

She immediately turned toward her armoire. "I'll come with you."

"No!" Lucas said the word much louder than he had intended. She winced as she spun back to face him, pain and disbelief reflected on her face.

"Lucas, we promised to work together, we promised—"

He caught her hands, gave them a brief squeeze, then let her go. "I know. But if you come with me, we'll lose time with explanations. Some of these men won't speak in front of you when they realize who and what you are. And if Henry is there . . ." He sighed. "If Henry is there and all that you believe about him is true, it will rouse his suspicions. I need you to stay here and work on that coded letter Isley uncovered. Please, Ana."

She looked up into his face and he saw she understood. She felt his pain and recognized his desire to prove all these accusations wrong. And she also saw that he was beginning to realize they might not be disproved.

Her fingers brushed his cheek, tracing the lines

around his mouth gently. Then she lifted up on her tiptoes and drew him down for a gentle kiss. One that gave him the strength that had been sucked from his body when he read about the checkered past Henry never shared with him.

"I will do that," she promised as she stepped away. "And I'll also pray that I'm wrong, Lucas. Because I don't want to see you come to even more pain."

He nodded, numb. "I know."

Then he moved to the chamber door and away, feeling her eyes on him with every step. As he went downstairs and got into his waiting carriage, he too prayed that every accusation, every rumor about Henry was unfounded. Otherwise, he had been best friends with a stranger all these years.

A stranger capable of devious deception . . . and worse.

Ana held back a gasp as her eyes strayed to yet another graphic illustration of the intricacies of mating animals. She had to give it to Sansbury, he'd chosen an interesting subject matter in which to hide his correspondence. Anyone who found it would be more distracted by the illustrations than interested in the sheet of numbers inside.

She was beginning to understand the cadence of the code. Just by looking at it, she could see where sentences ended and began, as well as which numbers were page numbers in the book and which were line and letter numbers. Now that she had the system down, it was just the tedious business of sorting out which number corresponded to which letter and transcribing them onto a new sheet.

Her fingers flew over the page, writing letter after letter, pausing for sentence breaks, flipping to the next page in the husbandry book. Finally, the last letter had been decoded and she faced the task of breaking hundreds of letters into a series of sentences.

Slowly, she sorted out the work until finally she had a complete, neat message sitting before her. Drawing in a breath, she began to read from beginning to end.

And her heart sank into the pit of her stomach, even as the thrill of clicking the last piece of the puzzle into place roared through her.

She had been right all along. Henry *was* involved in the plot against the War Department spies. In fact, he was the mastermind. And Sansbury had been ready to blackmail him. This letter, which had clearly been a bargaining chip Sansbury planned to use, detailed evidence of all kinds that would put Henry in Newgate for the rest of his life, if not have him hanging from the gallows for his part in the plots.

Her hands shook as she got to her feet and backed away from the damning evidence. Nausea hit her in a wave, tears stung at her eyes. Never had she been so unhappy to have her theories proven as she was at that moment. All she could think about was Lucas. Her husband would be destroyed by this.

"Ma'am?"

She jumped at the sound of one of her maids at the door. Ana turned to give a false smile at the woman. She was so used to the servants in Emily's home, who had been trained not to disturb her when she was at work.

"What is it, Harriet?"

"This was just delivered for you, Mrs. Tyler. From Mr. Tyler."

Ana rushed across the room and took the note from Lucas. As soon as she excused the girl, she broke the seal on the envelope and quickly read its contents. He had uncovered something at the War Department that he needed to share with her in person and gave an address for her to meet him.

She shook as she put the letter on the table beside the damning evidence against Henry. Dear God, how much deeper did this conspiracy go that Lucas couldn't write down his suspicions? That he wanted to meet her somewhere outside of their home?

There was only one way to find out. She got her wrap and rushed downstairs. And hoped she could find a way to comfort Lucas when he learned the truth about a man he loved as much as his own brothers.

Lucas hardly acknowledged his butler as the servant opened the door for him. His mind was spinning and his heart was breaking. He needed Ana. Needed to see her and feel her.

He needed to tell her she was right and apologize for his denials before they went to confront Henry. He owed her that.

"Is my wife still working upstairs?"

He pictured Ana huddled over that encoded letter, her spectacles balanced on the end of her nose. He hardly needed to see the letter now. Dear God, the evidence. Things he never knew existed. Lies Henry had told. It was too much.

He'd seen Henry's solicitor and after some prodding, bribing, and a small bit of threatening, he'd discovered his best friend was drowning in debts and involved in a hundred questionable schemes to make money. Worse, he'd started to have an increased flow of capital about a year ago. The first large deposit had been made into his accounts just a few days after the first attack. The one that nearly took his friend's life. Every time another spy was killed or injured, Henry's bank account increased.

Lucas wanted to vomit.

The butler cocked his head. "No, my lord. Is she not with you?"

"Of course not." Lucas looked at the servant. "Why would she be with me?"

"We understood that she was going to meet you as you asked her to do in your message, sir."

Blood roared to Lucas's ears, and it took all his self-control not to grab his butler by the lapels and shake.

"What message?"

"The one you sent nearly an hour ago."

The servants stared at him like he was crazy and Lucas was beginning to feel like he was. It certainly felt like a mad, out-of-control fear in his belly.

He spun on his heel and rocketed up the stairs, praying that Ana had left the supposed message behind. Or at least some clue as to where she had gone.

Because it hadn't been to him.

He burst into her room. Paperwork was in piles everywhere. He raked a hand through his hair as he swore. Damn it, he might never find a note here if it did exist.

He rushed to the nearest table and began flipping through piles, finally sweeping the entire mess onto the floor in frustration. The next pile was the same, odd notes and formulas, encoded bits, things he didn't even understand. All in Ana's neat, even handwriting.

And then he saw the book and the encoded letter sitting on her escritoire. He hurried over and found, sitting on top, a note that was in his hand. On his personal stationery. In an envelope that had been sealed with his mark.

But he had done none of it. He poured over the letter as horror froze colder and colder around his heart. The note fluttered from his trembling fingers, landing on top of the encoded one. He picked it up, only to discover the paper beneath wasn't the encoded work from Sansbury's home at all. Ana had solved the riddle while he was gone.

He read over her notes.

Oh, God. Henry.

The building had been abandoned long ago, that much was clear. Ana shivered as she stepped inside through a back entrance Lucas had instructed her to use. The neighborhood was one of the worst in London, and she knew her carriage would attract too much interest. She'd sent it away, but now she longed for the protection the vehicle and Lucas's driver gave. Her only consolation was that soon she would be with him and feel safe again.

Until then, however, she dipped her hand into her reticule and pulled out the perfume bottle she had been carrying with her for weeks. She had worked so hard to get the correct blend of diluted kerosene and pepper extract, but hadn't tested it yet. It was meant to blind. To incapacitate without killing.

She didn't want to have to test it in the field, but she pumped the dispenser a few times to prime the spray mechanism. Then she put it back in her reticule carefully.

"Lucas?" she called out into the dusty, dim hallway. This had clearly been a shop of some kind at one point, but a fire had ravaged a portion of it, collapsing the roof on the east end. But on the west, one room had survived. As she peered around, she saw a dim, sickly light coming from beneath the door.

Pushing on the aging wood, she stepped inside.

"Lucas?"

There was a man standing in the shadows beside a low fire, and he tossed on a log to raise the light before he turned. But it wasn't Lucas who awaited her. It wasn't safety that she had discovered. It was something else entirely.

"Henry," she gasped, stumbling back. "Henry, you're standing!"

He smiled as he raised a pistol and pointed it straight at her heart.

Chapter 24

"**H**enry," she repeated, still too shocked to fully comprehend everything that was happening. All she knew for certain was that Henry Bowerly was coming toward her, a gun pointed at her.

And he was walking. *Walking* without any aid.

"Thank you so much for joining me, Anastasia," he said as he reached for her.

She shook off her astonishment and turned to bolt from the room, but Henry was faster. He grabbed her shoulder and yanked viciously, pulling her back inside before he kicked the door shut and threw her across the room. She hit the floor and her reticule skittered away as the air was knocked from her lungs.

She flipped over on her back, trying to remain calm.

Trying to recall all her training, all the times she'd practiced the art of physical defense with Emily in her cellar work room.

Fighting a man who was probably five stone or more heavier than she, not to mention actually willing to kill her, was an entirely different experience.

"Henry—" She pushed herself to a seated position on the floor and scooted backward toward her bag. "What are you doing here?"

He advanced on her in long, sure steps. The gun never wavered. From the look in his eyes, it was clear that he'd lured her here with one intention and one alone. He was going to kill her. Judging from the smile on his face, he was going to enjoy it.

"Don't play me for a fool," he said as he stepped between her and her bag. She spun around, ready to use her feet and hands as weapons if she had to. "I have already fallen prey to your act of innocence and meekness before. I won't again."

She shook her head. "Act of innocence?"

He nodded. "When Lucas was ordered to work with a Lady Spy, I never thought she would be a threat. But Lady Allington was clearly too intelligent for her own good. I thought if I got rid of her, that would end this foolishness. But they assigned you, instead. Who knew you would end up being more of a threat than anyone else?"

Ana flinched. "You. You *did* orchestrate the attack on Emily."

He smiled. "No. I attacked her myself. Wiley little thing managed to slip into the shadows, even after I put a bullet through her." He shrugged. "But it served its purpose."

Rage boiled up inside of Ana. She'd never felt something so powerful, so overwhelming, before. "How could you? How could you do any of this? These men you attacked, they were your comrades. Some were your friends! And Lucas—" She broke off as she considered all the ramifications. "My God. He loves you like family."

At that, Henry's face twisted. The pistol shook in his hand and she cowered back in the fear he would depress the trigger. "I know that. Why do you think I've worked so hard to keep him from the truth?"

She wanted to scream, but didn't. Calm was her only weapon. Unless she could distract him enough to attack physically or get to her reticule and use her special "perfume," there was no escape in sight. And riling him would do no good. Her only recourse was to keep him talking as long as she could.

"What do you mean?"

He smiled. Thin. Unpleasant. "How do you think I was shot that night?"

She thought of all she knew about Henry's attack. Lucas had been so emotional, so guilt-ridden about his wheelchair-bound friend and how he hadn't been able to save him. She'd focused on his emotions. On his vulnerability.

But now she recalled another detail.

"Lucas wasn't meant to be there," she whispered.

Henry nodded. "It was supposed to be another man. Another spy. I never liked the bastard, it was a pleasure to use my connections to bring him down. But at the last moment, Lucas arrived in his stead. I couldn't signal the shooter. I couldn't stop the attack. So I pushed him out of the way."

Nausea built in her stomach again, churning to her throat where the sharp taste of bile choked her. "And let him believe that you had been hurt even worse."

"I was already suspected after my prior investigation." Henry smiled. "Oh yes, I know you've been looking into my past, my lady."

"But why pretend to be confined to a wheelchair?" she asked, trembling at the twisted nature of the man before her.

"Once I was hurt, the War Department turned its eye from me. They saw me as a cripple, so they saw me as no threat. And they gave me more power than ever when I made my triumphant and miraculous return to the offices."

She lifted a hand to cover her mouth. "They put you in charge of the cases. The spies."

Henry's handsome face broke into a wide smile. It would have been likable and friendly if she hadn't known the true nature of its owner.

"I hope you know—" Henry took a step closer and raised the gun to her head. "That this is not a personal problem I have with you. I actually like you, Anastasia. But you are interfering with my business. And if Lucas begins to believe your accusations, you'll be interfering with my friendship and ability to protect him."

Ana shook her head, though she was surprised she could make the action when she was trembling so hard. "Killing me won't prevent that. Lucas already knows. He has already looked at the evidence I've collected and is following up on it even as we speak."

Henry shut his eyes for a moment, too brief for her to push past him or risk an attack. Then he looked at her and his face had twisted.

"You bitch," he growled. "Don't you know what you've done?"

"Please." Tears pricked her eyes. "Please, don't make things worse for yourself by hurting me."

"If Lucas truly does have knowledge of what I've been doing, then everything I've done to keep him safe, to keep him away from death will be for nothing." Henry backhanded her so suddenly that she wasn't prepared for the strike, and her head snapped back with the force of the blow. Stars exploded before her eyes as she fell back against the dirty floor, her cheek throbbing and her head spinning.

The fearful parts in her, the parts that had allowed her to hide for so many years after Gilbert's death, told her to just lie back and let Henry Bowerly take her life. That fighting wasn't worth the pain. That it would be over sooner if she just allowed him to do as he wished.

But the other part . . . a part she hadn't recognized until earlier that day on the roof . . . a part that she never would have found if not for Lucas and his searing touch and belief in her, screamed at her to sit up. To use her training. To fight to get home to the man she . . .

She loved.

The shock of that thought jolted Ana into a seated position and she held up her hands to defend against any more blows to come.

But before Henry could move again, before she could plan her next action, a voice boomed from the entryway and shook the very rafters.

And gave her a blossoming flower of hope and a burst of powerful, undeniable love.

"If you touch my wife again, I will blow your fucking head off."

Lucas staggered back at the sight before him. Ana, reeling from a vicious blow. And who was threatening his bride?

Henry. Henry, who was standing on his own two feet. Henry who was no longer the man Lucas had called friend most of his life. A Henry who was a stranger.

A stranger Lucas wanted to rip apart with his bare hands for daring to threaten Ana. For daring to betray everything Lucas had come to love, honor, and cherish.

His first instinct had nothing to do with training or investigation. He wanted to run in and sweep Ana out of danger. To make sure she was unharmed.

But the spy in him knew that would only guarantee death for them both. Especially when Henry's pistol didn't waver from its position against her skull. Even as he inched his way around her to face Lucas.

"Just step outside, Lucas," he said, in the same low, calm tone he had used many a time during their years as friends. As if Lucas was deep in his cups and wanting to cause trouble, and Henry was there to get him home in one piece.

God, it made him sick. And sicker still when he saw the fear in Ana's eyes and the welt already forming on her cheek as the light from the fire touched her face. But she met his gaze with a strength and calm he never would have guessed she possessed the first time he met her, when he dismissed her for a hysterical woman who would only get in his way.

Instead, she had shown him the way.

"Step outside," Henry continued. "And let me take care of this problem. Then you and I can talk rationally and decide what our next step will be."

Lucas moved forward, just one step. Easy and smooth, though it took all the willpower in his body and soul to do so.

"You expect me to walk away while you harm her?"

His harsh voice echoed in the empty shell of a room. Around the empty shell of his former friend.

"I realize it is difficult." Henry was still trying to soothe with his voice. "Because you have married her and you don't want to see her harmed. But you must realize that she will only get in my way. And it could be *our* way, Lucas. Together as it used to be when we were boys, causing havoc all over the countryside."

Lucas blinked, disbelieving what he was hearing. "You want to compare a few childhood pranks to the deepest treason there is?"

"You don't understand." Henry's hand shook slightly.

"Make me understand." Lucas kept his gun pointed at his friend as he moved forward a few more inches. He stole a glance at Ana and realized she was sliding her eyes back and forth between him and her discarded reticule on the floor. He edged in that direction. "Tell me why you're doing this."

"If you've listened to *her*"—Lucas motioned toward Ana with the pistol, and she sucked in her breath through her nose with a noisy gasp—"then you have probably looked into my finances."

Lucas nodded. "I know the debt you are facing, but greed, Henry? Could all this only be for greed?"

"You don't know." His friend's eyes grew vicious. "You have been and always will be golden, Lucas. You were always the strongest, the best, the brightest. Even when I introduced you to the world of spies, you quickly overtook me in talent and ability. I wanted more. So much more. I tried to get it and failed. This was only supposed to happen once. Just reveal Warfield to the enemy. I would garner a handsome reward and eliminate a man I hated all at once."

Lucas swallowed against a tidal wave of nausea. "But I showed up instead."

"Yes." Henry jerked out a nod. "And I was hit while trying to protect you. The War Department was ready to dismiss me, but the other side embraced me all the further. They offered me money. And I had power, Lucas. Once I started, I couldn't stop."

Ana met Lucas's eyes. He saw her fear lighting higher, but it was matched by pity. Tears trickled from the corners of her eyes, and he knew they were for him. For the friend he had lost long ago, but never known was gone until she opened his eyes.

He let his gaze hold hers.

"I don't want to have to kill you, Lucas."

Henry's statement shocked Lucas's attention back. "You would kill me?"

Henry nodded, but the movement was erratic. "I've tried to protect you all this time. I fed you false information, I tried to assign you to cases that would keep you clear of my involvements. When Anastasia was assigned to partner you, I believed that would be perfect. I encouraged your desire, knowing she would resist. I thought her inability and your want for her would keep you busy, keep you away until I could cover myself. But she interfered, Lucas. She put you in danger. Now I can't let her go."

He moved the pistol against her head again, and Ana's eyes squeezed shut for a brief moment. Lucas jumped forward before he checked himself. No. Remember the training. He was so close to the reticule now. Clearly there was something inside that Ana thought could aid her. If he could distract Henry long enough, she might be able to grab it and get free.

Henry leaned forward, his expression pleading. "But if you join me, we will be unstoppable. The money, the women, Lucas. The power. I would split it all with you."

Lucas shook his head as he slipped his boot toe beneath the little bag. "I could never join you, Henry," he whispered. "And I cannot let you harm the woman I love."

Henry's face twisted. "Love her?" He swung the pistol away from Ana and toward Lucas. "You're telling me you love her?"

Lucas locked eyes with his wife, despite the danger of the weapon now pointed at him. He smiled.

"I love Ana more than I have ever loved anything in my life. I would die for her. I would kill for her." He let his gaze move to the best friend he'd ever known. The worst enemy he'd ever had. "Even you, Henry."

Then he flipped the reticule toward Ana and fired a shot.

* * *

The world seemed to slow to a frustrating crawl as Ana watched her reticule circle toward her. The explosion of Lucas's gun rang through the air as she caught the bag and tore it open to pull out the perfume bottle.

Henry staggered back and Ana jumped to her feet as she saw he had been hit in the right shoulder. But somehow he managed to keep the gun in his hand.

"For her?" he bellowed as he raised the gun again. Lucas kept his ground, reloading his pistol.

Ana stared at him. How could he not run? How could he not take cover when Henry was armed?

Because of her. He wanted to protect her.

She turned on Henry, who was lifting his mangled arm to point his pistol at Lucas. Gripping the perfume bottle and praying the concoction she'd created would work, she charged him.

"Don't you dare!" she screamed as she sprayed a mist of the kerosene and pepper oil directly into Henry's eyes, then followed with the hardest punch she'd ever thrown.

He howled with surprise and pain, lifting his hands to cover his face. Ana staggered back as some of the mist back sprayed at her, filling her lungs with the pungent odor and making her eyes water.

Henry collapsed to his knees, swearing as he rubbed at his eyes. Ana coughed and backed away.

But he wasn't ready to quit. He swung the gun in the direction she had approached from.

"Bitch!" he screamed over and over as he waved the

gun in her direction. She tried to move, but her own vision was clouded by the backlash of her invention.

A gun fired a second time and Ana braced herself for the impact. But none came. Instead, Henry slumped forward, his weapon clattering away uselessly as he let out one final rattle of breath.

Chapter 25

"**Y**ou're certain this spray won't have a lasting effect?" Charlie asked as Dr. Wexler looked at Ana's eyes.

She shook her head. "I can't be sure, but the stinging has lessened since we rinsed my eyes. My lungs no longer hurt and my throat is raw, but it doesn't burn. I believe the spray did exactly its job. Blinding and incapacitating without maiming permanently."

She shot a glance in Lucas's direction. He was leaning against the wall in the hallway of the abandoned building. He had hardly spoken since he gathered her up into his arms and carried her away from the broken, bloody body that had once been his best friend.

Charlie and men from the War Department had

arrived, Lucas had answered their questions, but he had refused to leave her side. And refused to look at Henry's body, even when they carried him away, covered in a blanket.

"This is amazing, Ana," Charlie looked at the pretty perfume bottle. "Another invention that will assist us in our duties."

She smiled, but the expression was forced. Somehow Charlie's praise and even solving this case no longer meant everything to her.

Lucas did. And she needed to talk to him desperately. Needed to touch him. Without these people here. Without their prying eyes and questions.

The doctor put his things away. "You'll come to see me tomorrow, Anastasia," he ordered. "And I will check you for the next few days to insure you aren't permanently damaged."

She nodded absently, hardly hearing his orders. All she could do was stare at Lucas and watch him stare back, utterly unreadable, just as he had been when she first met him.

What had he said to her then? That she had to learn to break the rules.

"I'd like a little air. Could Lucas take me outside for a moment?"

Charlie nodded. "Of course. But we'll need to speak to you both further."

"Just for a moment."

Lucas straightened and wordlessly offered her an

arm. She took it, clutching at his heat and feeling his muscle contract beneath her hand.

"I'll bring her back in a few moments," he promised.

They stepped into the gathering dark. The moment the door closed behind them, Ana took his hand and hurried him toward their carriage, which had been swung up to the line of other vehicles for the officers and men inside.

"What are you doing?" Lucas asked, following behind her as she threw open the door. She pushed at him to go inside, whispered a few words to the driver and jumped in beside him.

He stared at her as the coach rolled forward. "What's going on here, Ana? They need further statements from us, there is paperwork—"

"Rules were meant to be broken," she interrupted. "I need to ask you something, Lucas. I need to know."

He dipped his chin as if he anticipated what her question was. "Go ahead."

"You told Henry that you loved me," she whispered, her voice cracking and not just from her raw throat. "Did you mean that, Lucas? Do you love me? Or was it just a tactic to distract him?"

When his gaze lifted to hers, she saw the answer even before he said it. And it awed her.

"I meant every word, Ana. I have loved you since . . . probably since the moment I saw you." He caught her hands and drew them to his chest. "I know you do not wish for love. But I think, given time, you could grow to love me. I feel that in every part of me. I feel it in your kiss. I won't ask you to love me now. But I hope that you will one day allow me into your heart, even in some small way. Even if you never give me as much of yourself as you shared with Gilbert."

Ana stared at him, this man who had just poured his heart out. Offered her everything without any thought that he would receive anything in return.

He loved her.

And her love for him, which had seemed so surprising when she realized it a few hours before, flamed up and overcame her.

"I loved Gilbert," she said softly, and her memories didn't overwhelm her. "He was the boy I loved from the time I was a little girl. And being his wife was every childhood dream I ever had come true."

Lucas swallowed hard and he nodded. "I know."

"Wait." She held up her hand. "I am no longer a child, Lucas. My dreams and my wishes and my fantasies are not the same as they were then. You helped me see that. Helped me see who I truly am. You are the *man* I love now. With all my heart. All my soul. Everything I have in me wants to belong to you. I *do* belong to you, Lucas."

His eyes went wide and she realized that for the first time since she met him, she had shocked him into silence.

But then he didn't need words. He caught her cheeks and drew her mouth to his, kissing her with a wild passion and pure joy that made her heart sing. She threw her arms around him, hugging him so tightly that she could feel his heart pounding against her own. The two were in perfect time.

He pulled back to grin down at her. "Where are you taking me?"

She reached up and pulled him closer again. "Emily, Meredith, and I bought this little home in Southwark. No one knows about it but us. And tonight it will be ours. No one can find us to file their reports. Or ask us questions."

"It sounds like heaven," Lucas laughed.

She lifted her lips to his.

"If you are there, it will be."

Avon Romances
the best in
exceptional authors and unforgettable novels!

AVON TRADE *Paperbacks*

978-0-06-089022-3
$13.95 ($17.50 Can.)

0-06-081588-4
$12.95 ($16.95 Can.)

0-06-087340-X
$12.95 ($16.95 Can.)

0-06-113388-4
$12.95 ($16.95 Can.)

0-06-083691-1
$12.95 ($16.95 Can.)